Fractured Hearts

A Fractured Rock Star Romance

L. M. DALGLEISH

To my husband and children, for their patience as I stumbled my way through writing and publishing my very first book.
Love you!

Chapter 1

The blinding lights faded to black, but the screaming only grew louder. Connor's heart pounded in his chest, and beads of sweat dripped down his face and body as he tried to catch his breath after the encore performance. The spotlights flashed back on, illuminating him and the three other members of Fractured. If possible, the screams grew louder, and he could hear the band's name being chanted by the mass of fans that filled the stands. Connor looked out over the seething crowd, seeing the ecstatic faces and reaching hands, cell phones held high to take that one last photo.

A hot blonde in the front row caught his eye and he smiled, giving her a wink. Her jaw dropped and the next thing he knew she'd pulled her top up, flashing an impressive pair of barely contained tits at him. His smile widened in appreciation. *Not bad*.

Giving a final salute to the crowd, he strode toward the stage exit with Tex, Noah, and Zac, while the stadium erupted in protest that the show was over. Tex jogged up next to him and slapped him on the back. "Great show!"

Connor smirked. "I don't know, I think the guitar solos were a little off—" That earned him a numbing punch in the arm from Tex, who proceeded to turn around and walk backward so he could flip Connor the bird. Connor returned the favor, and Tex grinned before catching up with Noah and Zac and slinging his tattooed arms around their necks.

Still smirking, Connor ran a hand through his dark hair. But with the screams of the crowd still ringing in his ears, his smile dropped. He blew out a deep breath and wondered, not for the first time, when being one of the world's biggest rock stars had stopped being something he wanted, and what the hell he was going to do about it.

He scrubbed both hands over his face.

Fuck.

***

Two hours later and he was kicking Tex, Zac, and Noah out of his hotel suite, the door swinging shut behind his bandmates as they headed back to their rooms. They had all gathered for a drink after that night's gig, foregoing heading out to a club, since they had an early start the next morning. Not to mention the US leg of their world tour was kicking off soon, which meant another long three months of concerts coming up.

Connor finished the last of his whiskey in one swallow, the smoky peat flavor of the single malt doing little to relax him. He'd have to kill some time before heading to bed because adrenaline from that night's performance still filled him with a restless energy that suggested he wouldn't be getting to sleep for a while.

Luckily for him, before the door had a chance to fully shut behind his friends, Drew, Fractured's manager, caught it and swung it back open. He strolled in without an invitation as usual.

"Hey, old man." He smirked at Connor. "Not heading out tonight? Is it past your bedtime, then?"

Connor pulled a cushion out from behind him where he sat on the leather couch and hurled it at Drew's grinning face. "Watch who you're calling old, you bastard," he grumbled, fighting a smile. The slight Irish lilt he'd retained since moving to the States at fourteen softened his words, even when he didn't want it to. "I'm twenty-eight and you're thirty-two, so I guess that makes you geriatric."

"I guess so. That's why I gave up the party lifestyle a long time ago." Drew put on a quavering old-man voice. "Not like you young whippersnappers!"

Connor laughed and got up to go to the bar to pour himself another whiskey, raising an empty glass and lifting a dark eyebrow at Drew in question.

"Nah, I'm good, mate." Drew sat down on the chair opposite where Connor had been sitting. "I've got something for you to look at."

Connor wandered back to the couch with his drink and settled his six-foot-two frame onto the seat. "What's this, then?" He used his half-full glass to indicate the large envelope Drew held.

Drew opened it and slid a stack of photos out into his hand. "Time to find yourself a photographer," he said, handing the stack to Connor, who groaned in response. He'd forgotten he'd signed up for this. The other three had cheerfully handed off responsibility for choosing someone to document the upcoming leg of the tour for an official photo book. But he'd decided in a fit of enthusiasm that he wanted the final say in how the book turned out.

He put his glass down on the coffee table and began looking through the glossy photos, which proved to be printouts from the portfolios of the industry's most respected music photographers. After a few minutes, they all seemed to blend into each other: bright lights, screaming fans, various famous musicians crashing out on tour buses between shows.

Disillusioned with the whole endeavor, he tossed the photos on the table, half of them sliding off the other side and landing on the floor. "No one's really standing out to me. Maybe you should just pick someone and get it over with."

Drew scrubbed his hand over his face. "Come on, Connor. I know this whole thing was the record label's idea, but you asked for creative control, so you need to put some effort into it. This guy will be with you for three months, so he has to fit well creatively and personally. It has to be someone you like, or can at least tolerate for that long, otherwise you'll end up scaring him off with that scowl of yours." He pointed at Connor. "Just like the one you've got on your face now. The label won't be happy if the photographer leaves halfway through the tour since they're investing a lot of money in promoting this book."

Connor grumbled to himself, but Drew was right. If he wanted the finished product to reflect his vision, he had to put the effort in. After all, the band was at the pinnacle of success, and the label had convinced them that a photo book of their latest sell-out stadium tour was the best way to celebrate.

If only he felt more like celebrating. Unfortunately, he'd

been struggling to feel enthusiastic about much of anything to do with the tour, let alone picking a photographer to take endless shots of the band onstage singing their greatest hits to hordes of screaming fans.

He glanced over at the scattered photos, then groaned and reached instead for the glossy magazine that was the only other thing on the table and began flipping through it. He'd look at the photos again later; hopefully his interest would return by then.

Pausing on a photo spread in the center of the magazine, his eyes narrowed. Now, this was interesting. It wasn't a music-related photograph, but rather a black-and-white streetscape. In the picture it was raining hard, the gloomy clouds low and oppressive. People walked through the scene, umbrellas held over their down-turned heads to protect them from the deluge. In the background, a young girl without an umbrella stood with her head thrown back in glee while sheets of silvery rain fell on her upturned face. Her arms were outstretched, and she was laughing. The expression of innocent joy on her face was so luminous, it shone through the dreariness of the rest of the scene and brought the entire thing to life.

Now that was more what he was looking for: a photo that actually made him feel an emotional connection.

He didn't just want this photo book to show the obvious bright lights and screaming fans. He wanted to really feel the passion their music inspired. Not just in the people that spent their hard-earned cash and crammed into stadiums to see them, but in everyone else that was involved in this crazy roller-coaster ride.

Because God knew, he hadn't been feeling much passion

for it himself lately. If he could find someone to capture those emotions on camera, it might help him rediscover that sense of connection and shared experience that playing live music always used to give him. He was a lucky bastard to have the life he did, a life he'd dreamed of since childhood, but lately he'd been struggling to regain the feeling of purpose he'd always had.

Maybe seeing his life through this person's lens, he'd start appreciating what he had again. The photo certainly spoke to him in a way none of the others had.

He stood and tossed the magazine on Drew's lap.

"I want this one," he said.

***

"She says she's not interested," Drew announced when he came back from making the call.

"Everyone's interested; this book's a career-maker." Connor frowned, unsure if he was more annoyed or impressed that the photographer had knocked them back. "What did she say exactly?"

"Well, first off, she didn't believe me when I told her I was calling on your behalf. Then, after I convinced her of that, she said she was very flattered, but she wasn't a concert photographer, and she felt someone else would be better suited to the job."

"And you just gave up?"

Drew gave a long-suffering sigh. "No, I told her you'd seen one of her photos and had loved it, and you specifically wanted her. She seemed to think that was funny, because she laughed, said something about rock stars being crazy, thanked me again for the offer, and hung up."

Drew sat back down across from him. "You know she's got a point, mate. You didn't even look at any of her other photos to check whether you like them. It doesn't matter now since she said no anyway, but maybe you could do a bit more research on the next random photographer that catches your eye."

Connor smirked and shook his head. "You're right. I should make sure I check out more of her work before I call her back. In fact, pass me my cell phone, I'll do it now. If I like it, I'm going to need you to give me her number."

Drew raised his eyebrows in surprise and then sighed in resignation as he handed his phone over. Connor knew Drew wouldn't bother arguing with him; once he had an idea in his head, he was hard to sway. And for some reason, this photographer had generated some much-needed enthusiasm in him. He felt genuinely engaged as he typed the photographer's name into the search engine on his phone and began scrolling through the results, a slight smile curving his lips. After a few minutes, he looked up, his eyes meeting Drew's. "I'll need that number now."

A short time later, he hung up with a smug grin.

"I take it she said yes, then?" Drew asked him, looking up from his cell phone where he was now browsing the photographer's portfolio.

"Yep, we need to arrange for her to fly down on Friday. Can you get the lawyers to draw up the contract now so if we hit it off, she can sign then and there?"

"I'll call Bob tomorrow and get it done. You know, I can see why you like her stuff," Drew commented as he scrolled through photo after photo. "She's got a very distinctive style.

It's all very... evocative."

Connor raised his eyebrows. That was high praise from their very down-to-earth manager. He studied the photo in the magazine again, something like anticipation flickering in his chest. "Let's hope she can evoke something in me," he murmured.

Chapter 2

Lexie hung up the phone and collapsed on the couch. She couldn't believe she'd just been talking to Connor Byrne, the lead singer of Fractured! Or that he'd somehow talked her into flying to LA this Friday to discuss the project in person.

She huffed out a breath in disbelief. She had no idea why they wanted her, and Connor had been cagey about his reasons on the phone. While it was more than flattering to be asked, concert photography wasn't her specialty. She couldn't imagine what they could say at the meeting that would convince her she was the right person for the job.

She opened the calendar app on her phone to double-check her availability. Due to a cancellation, she was between jobs at the moment. And since she liked—no, *needed*—to keep busy, a compelling project would be welcome right about now.

Still, maybe not something quite as compelling as three months on tour with a world-famous rock band. She had no doubt it would be an eye-opening experience, but she wasn't sure how she'd handle the whole sex, drugs, and rock 'n' roll thing. She was more used to taking her camera and escaping into the wilderness or losing herself in the bustling humanity of city streets.

This *was* a once-in-a-lifetime opportunity though, so it wouldn't hurt to hear Connor out. If the project didn't interest her, she had no problem saying no. It wasn't like she was desperate for work; she'd probably be able to pick up something else fairly easily if she decided she wasn't interested in Connor's proposal.

That reminded her, she hadn't been online since returning from her most recent job late last night. She needed to respond to any comments on her latest blog post—a tutorial on how to take good landscape photos—as well as check her email for any requests from potential clients.

First things first though, she jumped up and headed into the kitchen to make herself a cup of tea, finding a hair tie and pulling her long brown hair up into a messy bun while she waited for the water to boil. When her tea was done, she headed back to the living room with the steaming cup in hand, grabbing her laptop on the way.

Putting the tea on a coaster on the coffee table, she sat cross-legged on the couch and navigated to her blog. There were dozens of comments and questions about her landscape tutorial that she needed to respond to. Lexie smiled as she typed her replies. She loved communicating with people that shared her passion and liked to imagine that at least a few of them would go on to have a fulfilling career in photography too.

After finishing with the blog, she opened her email. There were several messages from potential clients, and she went through them, weeding out any that didn't appeal.

There was a short-term job for next week, local to where

she lived in San Francisco, and she replied immediately to accept it. There were a couple more job offers that were scheduled for various dates over the next few months. Since she didn't know what was going to happen with the Fractured job, she replied to those clients to let them know she'd get back to them next week.

A warm sense of satisfaction filled her as she finished going through her emails. Her hard work over the last few years was paying off now that she had a steady flow of work. Being able to turn her love of photography—dating back to when her parents gave her a camera for her thirteenth birthday—into a successful career hadn't been easy. She'd spent her teenage years wandering around the small Californian town she'd grown up in, taking photos of people and scenes that intrigued her. After winning a few amateur photography competitions, she'd managed to make a name for herself locally, and started booking small jobs. From there, she'd set up her website and blog, building her freelance photography business up from scratch. She was proud of what she'd managed to do on her own—

Her thoughts faltered.

It hadn't all been on her own. Damien, her childhood sweetheart and later her husband, had been with her at the start. He'd been her biggest supporter; always there for her. Until suddenly he wasn't. Stolen away by a senseless accident and leaving her alone.

Lexie blinked away the tears that prickled the back of her eyes. Three years on and the thought of losing Damien still brought her to tears on a regular basis.

Photography had been the distraction she needed in the ensuing years, and she'd thrown herself into it to escape the grief. Which probably explained why, at twenty-six, she'd done as well as she had.

Now she was well-established in her field, regularly doing work for a wide variety of clients, both national and international, which meant she got to do a fair bit of traveling. She loved being at home too, though. And when she wasn't working, she spent her free time with her small group of close friends. Despite what she'd lost, she'd managed to carve out a good life for herself. And if there was one gaping hole in that life, well, that's why she kept herself busy.

That brought her mind back to the offer of working with Fractured. Going on tour with a world-famous rock band would be a good distraction; something completely different from anything she'd ever done before.

She chewed her lip, debating the pros and cons of the idea. She didn't know much about Fractured, apart from having heard their biggest hits—they were played on the radio so much it was hard not to—but she didn't consider herself a fan and didn't know much about the band members themselves. While she had a vague recollection of seeing a magazine cover with four tall, good-looking men on it, she hadn't taken much notice at the time.

Her mind wandered back to the phone call with Connor. His lilting voice had been almost hypnotic, which probably explained why he'd been able to convince her to meet with him on Friday.

Giving in to curiosity about the man that had been so persuasive on the phone, she opened her browser, pulling up the first fan site she came to and navigating to Connor's profile page.

According to his bio, Connor had been born in Kilkenny, Ireland. Tragically, his mom had passed away when he was only eleven. Lexie swallowed the lump that came to her throat, knowing from personal experience how hard it was to lose someone you loved.

Apparently, a few years after his mother's death, and with no explanation given, Connor ended up living with his aunt in Ohio. At sixteen, after honing his musical talent, he and his three best friends started Fractured. By the time he turned eighteen, the band was playing gigs in bars and clubs across the state. It was at one of those that they were "discovered" and the rest, as they say, was music history.

Lexie clicked on the Gallery tab and scrolled through various photos of Connor, pausing at one that caught her eye. It was a photo of all four band members and seemed to have been taken at a club. The light was low, and several stunning, barely dressed women surrounded them. The three other band members were oblivious to the camera, but Connor had his head angled toward the photographer, his piercing green eyes staring down the lens. His dark brown, almost black, hair looked like he'd just raked his fingers through it, and his seductively curving lips were tipped up in what might have been a smile, if not for the slight narrowing of his eyes and the tension evident in his chiseled jaw.

Lexie blew out a breath. With his height and broad shoulders, there was no doubt the man had won the genetic lottery.

He used it to his advantage too, because in almost every photo, some model-like beauty hung off him—never the same one twice. The website she was on had posted an

13

interview where he'd been asked about having a girlfriend. Connor had replied that he didn't "do" relationships, and when the interviewer asked why, he'd shut the guy down with a terse "why the fuck would I need to?" Then promptly changed the topic.

Lexie's nose wrinkled. As charming as Connor had been on the phone, he seemed to be a typical rock star—high on his own sense of self-importance, fueled by the people that threw themselves at him because of his good looks and celebrity status. She couldn't imagine spending three months with a person like that. *Make that four people*, she corrected herself. The three others in the band would more than likely have inflated egos too. Well, that was just one more reason to say no to the job on Friday.

She scrolled through a few more photos, taking note of the ones where all the band members were together; wondering what it would be like spending three months with such imposing men.

All four of them were attractive, but in every photo, she found her eyes drawn to Connor. Apart from his dark good looks, it was the intensity of his gaze she found so fascinating. Idly she wondered what it would feel like to be the subject of that kind of intensity. A slight tremor passed through her at the thought, but she shook her head, dismissing the feeling. After all, there hadn't been a man in the world who had caused even a small spike in her heart rate in the last three years.

Before logging off, Lexie's eyes were once again drawn to Connor's photo. She studied his face as if she could somehow tell what kind of man he was through the pixels on the screen.

Well, she supposed she would find out on Friday when she met him in person. Taking a deep breath to ease a sudden bout of nerves, she shut her laptop and tried to think about something else.

It proved to be harder than she thought.

Chapter 3

Connor sat on the couch in Drew's office, waiting impatiently for his meeting with Lexie. The photographer's contract was printed and stacked on the coffee table in front of him.

He was on his own because the other three had decided they'd rather spend the day by the pool than an hour meeting with their potential tour photographer. He wasn't too annoyed by their lack of interest since he'd only got this involved because he'd been bored. But now he was committed, and he wanted the book to be something special. While he spent most of his spare time writing music for the band, it was satisfying to explore a different creative outlet.

A knock on the door distracted him from his thoughts, and Drew stuck his head through the gap. "She's here," he said, waggling his blond eyebrows and smiling. Now, what did that mean?

He figured it out soon enough when Drew ushered Lexie into the room.

Well, fuck.

He'd seen a small profile picture of her on her website, but it had in no way done her justice. He certainly didn't expect her to be so gorgeous. She had long, wavy dark chocolate-colored hair pulled back in a ponytail and stunning gray eyes. She was petite, but the professional-looking button-down shirt and jeans she was wearing couldn't hide her lush curves. Realizing he'd been staring at her longer than was polite, Connor stood and stuck out his hand for her to shake. "Nice to meet you, Lexie."

Since the top of her head barely reached his shoulders, she had to tip her head back to meet his eyes. Up close, he could see she had a smattering of freckles across the bridge of her nose, and soft, pink lips, which were currently turned up in a nervous smile. "Nice to meet you too Mr. Byrne."

"Connor's fine."

"Right. Nice to meet you, Connor," she said, still smiling but with a slight hint of color staining her cheeks.

Connor smiled to himself. Convincing her to sign on as tour photographer would be no problem now they were in the same room. Not too many women could say no to him once he turned on the charm.

He realized Lexie was still standing, so he ushered her to the couch with a hand on the small of her back. The heat of her skin through her thin shirt warmed his palm—a far too pleasant feeling considering how attractive she was—and he quickly dropped his hand. The last thing he needed was to start lusting after their potential photographer. No matter how sexy she was, she'd be off-limits if she signed the contract. He needed her talent for this project; he couldn't afford to screw it up by trying to screw her.

After seating himself on the couch opposite her, he said, "So Lexie, did you get a chance to read the contract Drew emailed you? I'm hoping we can sign the paperwork today and get started on making plans."

She nodded. "I did give it a read through, but honestly Mr. Byr... uh, Connor, I really don't think I'm the right person for the job. It sounds like you're looking for a professional tour photographer. There are some excellent ones out there that I'm sure would jump at the opportunity to work with the band. I focus more on landscape and street photography, so I don't understand why you approached me for this."

"You and me both, love," Drew mumbled from the corner of the room where he lounged behind his desk.

Connor narrowed his eyes at Drew before turning back to Lexie. "Look, I may be a crazy rock star." He smiled to himself when Lexie flushed bright red at the reminder of the comment she'd made to Drew on the phone. "But there is a good reason. I don't want this book to be the same old thing the record labels trot out when they think their cash cows have reached the height of their success. It's not like we need to make any more money."

Drew snorted from the corner and Connor rolled his eyes. "The truth of the matter is, the reason we agreed to do it and why I asked for creative control is that I want this to be something different. Something better."

Lexie leaned forward in her seat, eyes fixed on his and a slight crease of concentration between her eyebrows. Encouraged by her response, he continued. "I want to take the spotlight off us and shine it on the tour experiences that are usually overlooked. Of course, the band has to be a big part of it. The book needs to show what it's like for us to spend months on the road. But I also want the story to focus on the people that are actually responsible for making it all happen. The fans, the support crew, hell, even management." He smirked as he slanted a look at Drew.

Drew held both hands up in the air. "Hey, I'll try not to outshine you, but I can't promise anything."

Lexie laughed and shot Drew a smile that lit her eyes up, making them sparkle. Connor could hardly believe it when Drew blushed. Damn, even his cynical manager seemed to be affected by Lexie's natural beauty.

Feeling annoyed for some reason, he cleared his throat, and Lexie turned her attention back to him. "At the end of the day, our success is built on a partnership. The people on the other side of it are giving their all to support the vision and to help us realize it. So, that's one thing I want the book to show."

Lexie raised her eyebrows. "What else do you want it to show?"

Connor hesitated. He wasn't sure how much to say, particularly in front of Drew, but he needed her to agree to this job, for some reason he couldn't quite articulate.

He took a breath and continued in a lower voice. "The other thing I want to show is that we're not these larger-than-life figures. What most people see of us is a construct, what the label and the fans want us to be, not who we are, or at least not who we want to be. And that's understandable. Fans want to buy into the fantasy and be taken out of their own lives for a while. The problem is most people will only ever see that. We aren't human to them anymore; we're the embodiment of their desires, or someone who means nothing more than a lucrative record deal.

"I want this book to show the humanity behind the hype, the reality of who we are as people. I don't want it to be just another product selling the fantasy. I want the reality. The ups and downs, the good times and the bad. As well as the most important things, like the joy of making music with friends, getting to work with amazing talent every day, and being able to connect with people from all over the world. The things that get misplaced along the way but are the only things that make this entire circus act worthwhile. That's what the focus of this book should be—all the amazing shit that ends up getting lost in the shadows when the spotlight gets too bright."

Although he was looking at Lexie as he spoke, he didn't miss seeing Drew's head jerk toward him in surprise. He was even surprised at himself for revealing so much of his feelings to a stranger. He wasn't sure why he'd said all that, except that the way she looked at him—eyes wide and curious—made him want to be honest with her.

She was nodding thoughtfully, her expression serious, as if she got it. Now he just needed her to know why he wanted *her*. "With your photos, I feel like you're seeing everything hidden in the background, looking past the obvious and shining a light on what would otherwise be missed. That's what I want to see in this book, and that's why I chose you for this. Your photos were the first that made me feel a connection. That made me want to know the story behind them."

Feeling like he'd exposed too much of himself, he finished with a forced laugh. "But I'm not a photographer, so I'd like to hear what you think." He drummed his fingers on his thigh as he waited for her response.

Lexie was silent for a few seconds, her brow furrowed while she collected her thoughts. "Well, first of all, you're very persuasive since I was pretty much set on turning you down today. Going on tour with a bunch of rock stars was never on my bucket list. But now I'm not so sure. What you said reminds me of a quote by August Sander—he's a famous German photographer. He said, 'In photography, there are no shadows that cannot be illuminated.' It's a quote that's always stuck in my mind."

She glanced down at her hands for a second. When she looked back up, her eyes were clear and unguarded. As her gaze tangled with his, an emotion he couldn't name washed through him.

"I love the idea of what you want to do, the concept of trying to show what's happening in the shadows around the spotlight," she said.

Her focus seemed to turn inward then, and he imagined she was picturing in her mind how the photos might look. Her vibrant gray eyes went hazy, and her soft lips parted slightly as she thought.

An image of her naked in his bed with that same soft expression on her face popped into his head, shooting a bolt of lust straight to his cock. He shook his head to clear it. That was not what he needed right now. This had to stay professional; he needed to shut those thoughts down fast.

He leaned forward in his seat, the movement bringing Lexie's focus back to him. "So, does that mean you're interested in being a part of this, then?" He gave her his most charmingly seductive smile. The one that always worked to get what he wanted from women.

Rather than returning it, Lexie cocked her head to the side, her eyes clear and appraising. Connor had to restrain himself from shifting in his seat. He felt stripped naked, and not in an enjoyable way. Her expression seemed to say she could see straight through him, and the feeling was uncomfortable. He wasn't used to women making him feel that way.

As if she'd suddenly decided, Lexie gave a sharp nod and stated, "I'm in."

Then she aimed her brilliant smile in his direction, and Connor's heart thumped heavily in his chest. He had a bad feeling he might have bitten off more than he could chew.

Chapter 4

Drew escorted Lexie out of the office. Nervous energy thrummed through her veins when she thought about what she'd signed up for. Although she had to admit, part of her shakiness had to do with the man she'd just said goodbye to. The memory of his warm hand on her back as he'd walked her to the door still played on her mind. She had wondered before what it would feel like to be the subject of Connor's intense gaze, and now she knew. It had felt... good. A little too good.

The way his green eyes had lazily perused her from head to foot should have had her hackles up. Instead, an unexpected warmth had flooded through her. She hadn't been even remotely attracted to any man since her husband's death, no matter how good-looking he was. That she'd felt the stirrings of it then had thrown her off-balance for the rest of the meeting.

He'd also surprised her when he'd started talking about the project. The sincerity behind his words and the soft lilt of his Irish accent had drawn her in. She'd been able to picture how the photos would turn out, and that had made her want to be the one to bring the concept to life. Still, she couldn't quite believe she'd ended up agreeing to go on tour with them. Now she had three weeks to organize herself before it all kicked off.

Drew led her out to the car waiting to take her to the airport. She realized that while she'd been thinking about Connor, Drew had been filling her in on everything she needed to know before joining the tour. Luckily, he finished by saying he'd email her all the details, so she didn't feel too bad for tuning him out. After shaking his hand, she got into the car for the drive back to LAX.

Lexie spent the return trip thinking about what she needed to organize over the next few weeks. She didn't typically do event photography, but that didn't mean she had no experience. She'd done a couple of music festival shoots before and helped some friends with their band's promotional photos. Sitting on the plane on the way home, she pulled out her phone and made notes of the techniques she'd have to use and what equipment she needed.

Lexie realized she was nervously chewing on a nail as she thought. She was usually confident of her skills, but this project had her feeling all kinds of nervous. She forced herself to relax into the airplane seat. Now she'd signed on, there wasn't much she could do but trust her instincts, and hopefully not screw it up.

***

After she got home, Lexie made herself dinner and then curled up on the couch to call Piper, who was her best friend as well as Damien's sister. She'd known Piper since high school, the two of them had been friends even before Lexie and Damien started dating. Once they had become a couple, the three of them had often hung out together. Piper had even been her maid of honor.

While she waited for Piper to pick up, Lexie looked at a framed photo that stood on the mantel. It was a picture of her and Damien dancing at their wedding. They were standing close together, heads tilted toward each other. The light had caught the gold of Damien's hair and reflected in Lexie's eyes as she looked up at him, highlighting her happiness. Love radiated from their broad smiles, and Lexie had to close her eyes and turn her head away before the tears came.

Still, her sister-in-law's exuberant greeting when she answered made her smile. "Lexie, it's so good to hear your voice!"

"Hi, Piper, it's good to hear your voice too! I'm sorry for not calling more often, work has been so busy these last few months."

"No problem, honey. I know things have taken off for you, and I'm glad. You deserve it."

Piper's warm tone made Lexie smile. She could always rely on her friend to cheer her up. Even in the darkest days after Damien's death, Piper had been her rock. Her shoulder to cry on. And she'd returned the favor when Piper's own pain had become overwhelming.

Together they'd managed to get through the grief. Even though Piper had moved to Arizona a year ago, they kept in touch regularly, although Lexie wished she had more time to visit her friend.

"So, what's up?" Piper asked.

"Well, I've just signed a contract for a really big job."

"Ooh, intriguing! What have you got yourself into this

time?"

"I'm going to be the official tour photographer for Fractured!" She couldn't mask the mildly hysterical tone of her voice, as if even she didn't quite believe what she was saying. There was silence at the other end of the phone. "Piper, are you still there?"

"You are freaking kidding me, aren't you?" Piper's shriek was piercing, and Lexie held the phone away from her ear.

"Um, no, I'm not. Although I can't believe it's true either."

"That's incredible, Lexie! What an unbelievable opportunity! Oh, I'm so jealous—I love those guys! Do you need an assistant? Because I'm willing to help you out. Just as a favor to my favorite sister-in-law, you understand. I wouldn't do it for anyone else."

Lexie laughed. "I'm your only sister-in-law. And sorry, but it's a one-person job."

"So how did this even happen? It's not your typical line of work."

"Connor saw one of my photos in a magazine and liked it. He called me up, and I flew to LA this morning to meet him and the band's manager."

There was another lengthy pause and then Piper's voice came back sounding choked. "You met Connor Byrne this morning? Oh my God, he is so freaking hot! What was he like? Did he sing to you? No, of course he didn't sing to you, why would he sing to you? Did he sing to you? Lexie, why aren't you telling me? Come on, spill the beans already!"

Lexie couldn't help but laugh. "I would if you'd stop for a breath."

Piper snorted. "Sorry, but you can't drop these things on me and not expect me to explode. I've had a crush on that guy—all those guys actually—for years, and you casually mention you met one of them this morning. But seriously, what was he like in person?"

Lexie paused, not sure whether to mention her unexpected reaction to Connor. She chickened out, settling on a lackluster "He's quite charismatic."

There was a disbelieving silence. "I'm sorry, did you just describe Connor Byrne as 'quite charismatic'? Wow, talk about damning someone with faint praise. He's one of the hottest men in the world, has the voice of a god, not to mention an Irish accent that would make any woman swoon, and the best you can come up with to describe him is 'quite charismatic'? Now come on, you can't tell me he didn't make your lady parts tingle, even a bit. And you're going on tour with him! Think about the possibilities…" Piper let out a wistful sigh at the thought.

Lexie knew Piper was joking, but she still felt uncomfortable talking about another man with Damien's sister. "He's very good-looking, of course, and he seemed like a nice enough guy, for a rock star. I'm looking forward to working with him, but that's all—I'm not interested in him in any other way. I'm not ready for anything like that yet."

This time Piper's sigh was sad. "Lexie, God knows I know how much you loved my brother, but it's been over three years. You have to start moving on, sweetie. His death was a tragedy, but it was him that died in that car crash, not you. You can't let it stop you living your life."

A rush of hurt flooded through Lexie. "I haven't let it stop me! I've spent the last few years building my business. I'm traveling, seeing the world like Damien and I always planned to do."

"I know you have, Lexie. You've done amazing things, and you'll keep doing amazing things because that's the kind of person you are. But you're moving forward in every way but the most important. You're young and beautiful and one of the warmest and most loving people I know, but it's like you've put up a wall around your heart. I understand why, I do. It takes a special kind of bravery putting your heart out there after a loss like that. You've been brave in every other part of your life; you have to be brave with this too."

Lexie tried to protest, but Piper kept going. "Look, I'm not saying that you should fall in love with Connor Byrne. In fact, I'd seriously recommend against it, considering who he is. But there's nothing wrong with a bit of healthy sexual attraction, and if anyone should inspire that it's him. Or God, any of the other guys in that band, since they're all gorgeous. At the very least, Lexie, if you can admit to yourself that you're attracted to someone, then maybe that will be the first step toward falling in love again."

Lexie let Piper's words sink in. Her first instinct was to deny everything, but she made herself think about what her friend was saying.

Her relationship with Damien hadn't been perfect of course—no relationship was—but it had been everything she had wanted. They'd fit together so well, almost as if they'd been made for each other. He'd been gentle and sweet and easygoing, and they had been so in love with each other. She'd seen their lives together play out in her mind's eye a thousand times. All their dreams, the plans they'd made, thoughts of starting a family…

Even though Damien had been gone for three years,

admitting she was attracted to someone else seemed like the worst kind of betrayal. As if she was throwing away the future they'd once envisioned together.

She knew it was irrational—that future was gone for good. She just wasn't sure she was ready to confront the reality yet. And if she was honest with herself, she was scared to go through any more heartache. Putting her heart out there risked exposing her to more pain if things didn't work out. She wasn't sure if she was strong enough to handle that.

Still, she couldn't deny she missed the intimacy of a relationship. Having someone to talk to, someone to hold. Someone to share her joys and sorrows with. She didn't want to rule those things out either, or the possibility of having a family. She hoped the day would come when she could imagine being with someone else, someone that wasn't Damien. But not now. Not yet.

Her long silence must have worried Piper, because she spoke again, her voice sad. "I love you, Lexie, and I want you to be happy. Please just tell me you'll keep your mind and heart open to different possibilities, that's all I'm asking."

"I will, Piper, I promise." She hoped her friend couldn't hear the ambivalence in her voice.

Lexie breathed a sigh of relief when the conversation moved on to general chat about the upcoming tour, and then to what else was happening in their lives. Before they hung up, she promised Piper she'd come and visit as soon as her work allowed.

***

The next morning, Lexie went through her camera kit to take inventory of what she needed before she left in a couple of weeks. She was running low on some essentials, so she headed out to her favorite camera store.

When she got there, she made her way to the back of the store, smiling when she saw the store owner, Eric, serving a customer. She waited until he was done before wandering over to say hello.

She and Eric had become friends when she'd started coming here regularly after her business began taking off. Although the friendship hadn't come until after he'd asked her out, and she'd had to rebuff him gently. Luckily, the rejection hadn't fazed him. Instead, they'd fallen into an easy friendship centered around their ability to talk all things cameras and photography.

Stepping up to the counter, she gave him a warm smile which widened at the sight of the Fractured tour t-shirt he was wearing. His eyes lit up, and he returned her smile with a broad one of his own. "Hey, Lexie, long time no see. What've you been up to?"

"Oh, you know, this and that. I got back on Monday from photographing the Badlands National Park in South Dakota for a travel magazine. That was awesome."

"Sounds like fun. Do I get to see any of the photos?"

"Oh sorry, I didn't think to bring any of them with me. Next time?"

"Well, I suppose that's a good excuse for you to come back in and see me soon." He grinned at her, then raised a questioning brow. "So, what brings you here today, then?"

"Well, I've got a new job coming up, and I need to grab more memory cards and batteries. Plus, I wanted to pick your brain a bit."

"Oh really? What's the job, then?"

"You'll never believe it, but I'm going to be a tour photographer."

He gaped at her. "Really? That is so not your thing!"

She laughed at his response. "I know! I was shocked too, but they liked my work, I guess. It'll be an interesting experience, that's for sure."

He raised his eyebrows. "What band is it? Anyone I would know?"

Lexie debated how much to tell him. Connor hadn't asked her to sign a nondisclosure agreement, and she could use Eric's advice since he had more experience in this area than she did. Plus, she'd already told Piper, so there wasn't any reason not to tell him.

Leaning forward, she pointed at his shirt. He followed the direction of her finger, glancing down and then back up at her with round eyes, before mouthing, "Fractured?"

She nodded, smiling widely at his stunned expression.

"Oh my God, that is incredible! They're my favorite band, I've been to five of their concerts! Have you ever been to one? Do you know what you're getting yourself into?"

She shook her head and grimaced. "That's one reason why I'm here. I have a fairly good idea of what I need to do, but I want to check I'm not missing anything. I know you did some concert photography back when you were freelancing."

Eric motioned one of his sales assistants over, before turning to her and saying, "Let's go grab a coffee, and we can talk about it."

A few minutes later they were sitting down at a nearby

café. After their coffees were served, Eric started talking.

"So first of all, from what I've seen, Fractured has lots of lights and lasers during their shows, but not a lot of crazy pyrotechnics. Their sets are usually simple because they like to keep the focus on the music. They have those massive video screens around the stage, but not much over-the-top theatrics."

"Right, thanks." She nodded. "I was planning to use my fastest lens and bump up the ISO. The images will probably end up grainy, but hopefully there won't be any blur. And I can always edit out any grain and noise during post-processing."

Eric nodded. "Make sure you're always there for the sound and lighting checks so you can get a reading on the spotlights. Particularly for Connor since he'll be the main person being lit up. That way you'll save time in adjusting your camera during the concert. It will be easy to adjust your shutter speed to compensate for darker areas, like when you're shooting the drummer—that's Noah—since drummers aren't in the spotlight as often. Once you have a thorough understanding of the stage and lighting setup for the concerts, you'll need to do fewer adjustments on the fly."

Lexie had started making notes on her phone. She knew most of this stuff, but it was always good to get a sanity check and make sure she wasn't overlooking something obvious. "I figured I'd take two cameras with me to each concert. That way I'll have a wide-angle lens ready to go if I need it, just to get shots of the entire band together, as well as the crowd."

"Yep, that's always a good idea."

Lexie bit her lip. "God, I hope I don't screw this up."

"You won't screw it up, Lexie. You're insanely talented,

which is why they want you. Trust your instincts. You know what you're doing, and you've got a fantastic eye."

She nodded, still uncertain.

"The best piece of advice I can give you is to watch a lot of videos of their previous concerts. That way you'll get an idea of what they tend to do, how they move around the stage, that kind of thing." Eric reached over the table and placed his hand over hers. "And finally, Lexie, have fun, okay? You deserve it."

Tears pricked the back of her eyes. Eric knew about Damien. She'd told him everything over coffee one day, a few months after they'd started hanging out. He was right though. She needed to stop being nervous about this opportunity and see it for what it was—another chance to live life to the fullest for Damien's sake. Just as she'd vowed she would when she was working through her grief.

She turned her hand over to hold Eric's and gave it a squeeze. "Okay, I promise I'll have fun too."

He nodded, his expression serious. "Oh, and make sure those rock stars don't take any liberties with you. Otherwise, they'll have me to answer to."

That made her laugh. "I don't think that'll be an issue."

He raised a skeptical eyebrow. "For someone whose job involves seeing the beauty of the world through a lens, you can be surprisingly oblivious to what's in front of you."

She rolled her eyes. "Whatever."

Back at Eric's store, she stocked up on memory cards and batteries, something you could never have too many of on the road where stuff got left behind or lost all the time. After making her purchases, she kissed Eric on the cheek. "Thanks for the advice. I'll give you a full rundown when I get back."

"You'd better." He mock scowled at her. She laughed and turned to leave but stopped before opening the door when he called out to her. "Don't forget, have fun!"

She was smiling as she left, feeling far more confident than when she'd arrived.

Chapter 5

Three weeks later, Lexie joined the monster of a convoy in Las Vegas. They had sent a car to pick her up at the airport and Drew met her at the drop-off point before taking her suitcase and leading her through the parking area toward the band's tour bus. As they walked, he pointed out different people and pieces of equipment.

Lexie looked around, her heart starting to thump. Everything was chaotic. Members of the crew yelled to each other as they loaded pieces of kit onto trucks, and the engines of several buses rumbled as they idled, filling the scorching air with the pungent smell of diesel.

The shrill screams from the crowd of devoted, mostly female, fans that had gathered to get a glimpse of the band grated on her nerves. For about the thousandth time since she'd agreed to do the job, Lexie regretted her decision. This was not her usual scene and she felt completely out of her comfort zone.

She fished her camera out of its case, uncapped the lens, and started taking shots as they walked. The familiar weight of the camera in her hands calmed her and allowed her to focus. The order behind the chaos finally emerged, and she framed up and shot a few decent pictures as they walked.

Before she knew it, they'd reached the tour bus at the far end of the lot. It was massive, all black, and had the band's name written in large neon blue letters along the side.

"Subtle," Lexie muttered.

Drew laughed as he knocked on the door of the bus. "You'll soon learn that nothing these guys do is subtle."

A giant of a man, dressed all in black, swung the door open. Drew introduced him to her as Don, one of the band's security detail, before leading her up into the cool, air-conditioned interior. As far as vehicles went, this one was huge, but Lexie could imagine how the cramped quarters might become stressful after months on the road.

Drew led her straight into the open living area at the front of the bus. Wood paneling lined the walls between the big tinted windows, and plush black leather couches extended down both sides of the bus. At the far end of the long space was a kitchenette and a small built-in dining table with bench seats on either side.

Glancing around, Lexie took in the four large and very good-looking men lounging on various seats throughout the space. It was the first time Lexie had seen the whole band together, and it was kind of overwhelming.

Unbidden, her eyes jumped to the end of the room where Connor's long, lean form was sitting at the table. He'd been looking at his phone when she walked in but glanced up as her gaze landed on him. His piercing green eyes met hers, and for what felt like minutes but must have only been a second, she couldn't look away.

Finally forcing her gaze elsewhere, Lexie realized Drew was introducing her to the rest of the band. She gave herself a mental shake and concentrated on Drew's words.

She recognized the three of them from the research she'd done over the last few weeks. Tex was the band's lead guitarist, and resembled a huge Viking, with muscles for days, long sun-bleached brown hair and whiskey-colored eyes. Noah, the drummer, was the blond, blue-eyed one currently wearing a charming but devilish smile on his face. He looked more like a hot Californian surfer than a member of a rock band. Zac Donovan, the band's bassist, sometime keyboard player, and backup vocalist was as tall and muscular as the others. He had close-cropped brown hair and soulful-looking hazel eyes with long dark lashes that would be the envy of any woman.

"Lexie, you've already met Connor, but this is Tex, Zac, and Noah. Guys, this is Lexie, your photographer for the next few months." Drew put his hand on the small of her back and propelled her gently forward.

Lexie gave the three of them a shy smile and a half-wave. It was overpowering being in such a confined space with so much testosterone. All three of the guys grinned at her, frank male appreciation obvious in their gazes. A blush heated her cheeks. She was used to a certain amount of attention from men, but nothing that could have prepared her for this.

The sound of a throat clearing from behind her drew everyone's attention. She glanced over her shoulder to see Connor had come up alongside her and was glaring at the other three. After a long few seconds during which Lexie once again considered pulling out the contract, ripping it up, and bolting from the bus, Tex finally spoke up.

"Nice to meet you, Lexie," he drawled in a deep, gravelly Southern accent.

With the ice broken, Zac and Noah chimed in with their

own greetings, and Lexie felt some of the tension leave her.

"If you come this way, Lexie, I'll show you to your room. It's down the back here," Drew said.

Lexie's eyes widened. "I'm not going to be staying on this bus, am I? Isn't there a bus for employees?"

Before Drew could answer, Connor spoke up. "I decided you'd be better off here than on the crew bus, and you'll have better access to us for photos. You don't have to worry though, we're well behaved. Most of the time." The corners of his mouth curved up, but the expression wasn't exactly reassuring.

"Oh, right," she said, her voice weak. How had she got herself into this again?

"Drew, you'd better check on the crew and see if they've finished packing up," Connor suggested. "I'll show Lexie to her room."

Drew raised his brows at having been dismissed, but he didn't argue, giving Lexie a wave and smile as he left.

"Your bedroom is down here." Connor grabbed her suitcase from where Drew had left it and ushered her through the aisle leading from the living room toward the back of the bus. They passed several bunks stacked two high on both sides of the aisle. Was that where the guys slept? If so, where was he taking her?

As they reached the end of the aisle, Connor stopped and turned. Distracted by her thoughts, Lexie only stopped herself from crashing into him at the last minute by bracing her palms against his chest. For the few seconds she had her hands pressed against him, she lost herself in the feel of hard muscles, before coming to her senses and snatching her hands away in embarrassment.

"Sorry!" she gasped, mortified to have almost mowed him down. She stared up at him where he towered above her, surprised when something like heat flashed in his eyes before his expression cooled, and he stepped back from her. She must have imagined it. A rock star like Connor, who had the world's most beautiful women throwing themselves at him, wasn't likely to be excited by a lowly photographer almost knocking him over.

Connor reached past her and opened the door, letting it swing inward. Peering past him she saw a compact room with a comfortable-looking double bed in the middle, a big tinted window with black curtains drawn to the side to let the sun in, and cupboards lining one of the wood-paneled walls.

She frowned. "This is mine?" she asked in confusion, looking up at him.

The corners of Connor's mouth quirked upward. "It is."

He stepped slightly backward so she had space to move past him and into the room, but it was still a tight squeeze. As she brushed past him, she caught the scent of something crisp and fresh, like just-washed linen, his aftershave perhaps. A wave of awareness shivered down her spine. It was the same unsettling feeling she'd got when she first met him.

Shaking it off, she stepped into the room and looked around. The late-afternoon light streamed in the window, and it seemed about as comfortable as a bedroom on a bus could be. Turning back to him she asked, "This looks a lot nicer than those bunks. Who normally sleeps here? I don't want to kick someone out of their bedroom."

"It's a second living area which converts into a bedroom.

Sometimes when we can be bothered, we'll take turns sleeping in here when we're sick of the bunks. Or if one of us… needs it for a night." His slight pause and emphasis on the word gave her a good idea what needs he was talking about.

She took another look around. Great, she'd be sleeping in the band's sex den.

Turning back to argue about appropriating the only proper bed, she found him standing disconcertingly close. Since the bed was directly behind her, she couldn't step back. He didn't seem inclined to give her more space either, so she had to tip her head back to meet his eyes. Standing this close to him — close enough to feel the heat rolling off his body — scattered her thoughts. She blinked up at him for a second before remembering what she was going to say.

"I don't feel right taking this room just for me. Surely you should all have access to a comfortable bed when you… need it." She inadvertently put the same emphasis on the word as he had, and her cheeks heated.

His mouth curved upward. "Are you offering to share?"

Lexie's breath caught. As much as she didn't want it to, her body reacted to the suggestion in his tone.

Trying to shove her libido back down where it had been hiding out for the last few years, she licked suddenly dry lips. Connor's gaze dipped down for a second, then rose back up to meet hers again. The atmosphere in the small room felt charged. He ran his hand through his hair before stepping back out of her personal space.

"Don't worry about us, Lexie. We'll manage fine in the bunks. There'll be a few hotel stops along the way as well for when we need a break. Settle in and when you're ready, come on back up the front, and we can go through your plan for the book."

He held her gaze until she nodded, and then turned and left, closing the door gently behind him. Lexie's breath left her body in a rush. She felt completely out of her depth.

Chapter 6

Connor stopped outside the bedroom door and took a deep breath, trying to dispel the not unpleasant tension coursing through his body. The breath wasn't as helpful as it should have been since he could still smell the lingering light floral scent of Lexie's perfume.

It surprised him how strongly he'd reacted to being close to her. He was normally able to remain aloof from the women he associated with, taking only what he needed from them and giving them exactly what they wanted in return. But when Lexie had bumped into him, put her hands on his chest, and gazed up at him with wide, guileless eyes, he'd felt a surge of lust and something more, something he couldn't quite put his finger on.

Trying to shake off his reaction, Connor headed back up the aisle to the front living area. He paused when he heard hushed voices and laughter, certain he knew what was being discussed. He tensed when he heard Lexie's name mentioned, then strode back into the room, catching the smirks on the guys' faces.

"Nobody touches her," he growled.

His friends gaped at him in surprise. Noah spoke up first. "What the fuck, man. We were just talking. She's hot."

"I don't want her to feel uncomfortable. She's a professional, and she's here to do a job."

"Maybe you should have mentioned she was gorgeous before springing her on us, then." Tex narrowed his eyes at Connor. "You kept that close to your chest. Were you hoping we wouldn't notice?"

"It wouldn't be an issue if you weren't all a bunch of man-whores," he grated out.

Tex stared at him and then burst out laughing.

"What's so funny?"

Tex pointed at him. "You're as big a man-whore as any of us! And I'm sure I remember you screwing one of the wardrobe girls, then breaking her heart a few years back."

Connor gritted his teeth but had no defense against that accusation. He had slept with one of the wardrobe girls, and she hadn't taken it well when he didn't want to keep it going. That debacle had ended up with her leaving the tour, and Drew hadn't been happy.

"And I learned my lesson. I just want to make sure Lexie is happy and comfortable so she can do her job. So, I need you all to agree not to try anything with her."

Tex raised his eyebrows and crossed his arms over his broad chest. "And let's be clear—that includes you, right?"

Connor's eyes narrowed. Was Tex deliberately goading him? Perhaps he was as surprised by Connor's response to Lexie's presence as he was himself. The whole band was constantly surrounded by beautiful women, so what made Lexie any different? He nodded in response to Tex's question but didn't say the words out loud.

"All right, man, we can agree to that. We'll be nothing but gentlemen." Noah grinned, putting his hand on his heart.

"Though you could have made it easier on us and hired a man. Now I'll have to stop walking around naked."

Zac laughed. "Looks like Lexie's done us all a favor, then. No one wants to see that every morning."

"I beg to differ. There are many ladies that would be more than happy to see me naked in the morning." Noah smirked, leaning back in his chair and stretching out his long legs.

As the banter continued, Connor relaxed. He wasn't sure why he'd reacted so strongly to the guys talking about Lexie. She was a beautiful woman, so it would be more surprising if they hadn't said anything. And it wasn't like him to overreact like that. He was usually the one everyone relied on to maintain control and not let emotions get in the way.

He settled back in his seat at the table and went back to thinking about the more pressing problem. It was getting harder and harder to maintain the pretense that everything was okay with him. After years of touring, he no longer got the same sense of fulfillment he used to. The thrill of performing to a packed stadium, which had been all he'd dreamed of as a teenager, was getting old.

He hadn't mentioned it to anyone yet. None of the others seemed to have the same issue, and he had no idea what to do about it, anyway. Most of the money was in touring these days. Album sales alone weren't enough to keep the record label happy anymore.

Sometimes he even fantasized about giving it all up and doing something else with his life. He loved writing music, so maybe he could get into songwriting for other bands. But every time he caught himself thinking too much about it, he reminded himself that he had a responsibility to his best friends, and to Drew, who'd also become a good friend over the last few years. Connor was the frontman for the band for fuck's sake. It wasn't like he could up and leave and they would continue without him. Plus, he'd miss being with everyone. Since he didn't have a relationship with his father, and rarely had time to visit his aunt Maureen, the band, Drew, and hell, even the crew regulars had become his family.

He exhaled. Hopefully, this was just a phase he was going through. He just needed something to reinvigorate him, and then things would go back to the way they used to be. The way they should be.

His eyes were drawn to the aisle leading to the back of the bus. What was taking Lexie so long?

Chapter 7

Lexie had unpacked all her clothes and hung them up in the cupboards lining the wall. A tiny bathroom with a shower led off the bedroom, and she'd put her toiletries away in there. She wondered if the bus had another shower, or if she would end up having to share this one with the band. Her mind conjured up a picture of Connor standing under the shower spray, water sluicing down his lean muscles…

She stopped the thought in its tracks, but guilt surged through her, anyway. What was wrong with her? She hadn't had a lustful thought about any man since Damien, and now, of all people, she was imagining a rock star naked. How clichéd could you get? All the lovely men that had hit on her over the last few years hadn't been able to entice the slightest interest from her. And now her mind seemed to have picked the most inappropriate man on the planet to fantasize about.

She wandered over to the bathroom mirror and stared at her reflection, trying to see what had changed, but saw only the same long wavy brown hair and too-big gray eyes that she always did.

Why was she having these feelings now? Did it mean she'd started to forget Damien? A sharp pain sliced through her at the thought, and her reflection blurred as tears welled up in her eyes. While she didn't want to forget Damien and everything they'd had together, she couldn't bear the thought of harboring this pain for the rest of her life. Was she really betraying him by thinking about another man, or was Piper right, and she should be forcing herself to move on?

The frisson of desire she'd felt at the thought of Connor withered and died, leaving only a familiar emptiness in its place. This was a job, nothing more. A once-in-a-lifetime experience, and another way to keep herself busy and help fill the hole Damien's death had left in her life. One day, when she was ready, she could consider acting on that sort of attraction. But not now and not with someone like Connor. She needed someone as sweet and kind as Damien had been...

She gave her head a slight shake at the thought, then brushed the tears from her cheeks and laughed quietly to herself. It wasn't as if Connor would be interested in her, anyway. Dismissing the entire thing, she left the bathroom, bracing herself to head back out into the lion's den.

Returning to the living area at the front of the bus, Lexie held her laptop to her chest and glanced around, not quite sure what to do. All four of the band members were still there, chatting idly to each other or playing on their phones. When Connor noticed her, he gestured her over to the table where he was sitting. She slid onto the bench seat opposite him, placing her laptop on the table between them and giving him a tentative smile.

He smiled back and Lexie blinked at the sight before realizing he was asking her a question.

"Everything okay with the room?"

"Oh, yes, thanks. It's very, um, cozy." As she said it, she remembered what the guys used the room for, and her face flushed. Cozy probably wasn't exactly what they were going for.

The dimples in his cheeks appeared as his smile deepened, almost like he'd read her thoughts.

She shook off her embarrassment and got down to business. "So, I've got a general idea of how I think you want the photos to turn out. Would you like me to go through it with you now?"

He nodded. "It'll be another thirty minutes or so until we're ready to get on the road, so we might as well do it now. Hey, guys!" he called out to the others. "Lexie's going to go through her plans for the photos, so get over here and listen in."

With minimal grumbling, the guys stopped what they were doing and converged on the table. Tex slid in next to Lexie, his large muscular frame dwarfing her. Well, that wasn't intimidating at all. Noah slid in next to Connor, and then Zac pushed in next to Tex, forcing him to press so closely against her she almost ended up in his lap. She glanced up, noticing Connor glaring at the two men.

"Zac, why don't you pull up a chair. I don't want to have to find another photographer because Tex's inflated muscles smothered this one."

Lexie laughed. "Don't worry about it. I'm tougher than I look."

Zac got up from the table anyway and dragged a chair over, positioning it backward at the end of the table before straddling it and resting his arms on the back.

Now that everyone was settled, Lexie opened the laptop

and turned it on. "So based on what Connor and I discussed, I'm aiming for a mix of candid behind-the-scenes shots of all of you, and the obvious things like action shots during your concerts and photos of you interacting with your crew and fans. I also want to make sure I catch what you like to get up to after your shows and in your downtime."

Lexie paused for a second, waiting to see if one of them would make an inappropriate joke about what they liked to "get up to" in their downtime, but they all just nodded seriously. Okay, maybe her idea of the stereotypical rock star had been wrong all this time.

"I also want candids of the crew setting up. What's happening backstage while you guys are preparing to go onstage, or once you're actually up there? What's Drew doing while you're performing? What about the sound and lighting technicians; what are your concerts like from their perspective?

"I also plan to get out among the crowd to capture the energy and those intense emotions from the audience's point of view. So, I'll need to use your first show to check out how your stage is configured and what lighting you have going on, that way I can figure out how to get the best shots, and where I need to set myself up to shoot without getting in the way or blocking the crowd's view."

She paused again to check if anyone had any questions, but they seemed fine with what she'd told them, so she kept going. "I'd also like to use some of your extended stops during the tour to get some conceptual portraits of all of you, either together or individually."

Tex's deep voice broke in. "What are conceptual portraits?"

"Well, conceptual photography tells a story. It's all about conveying an emotion, idea, or message, as opposed to candid photography where you shoot what's happening organically around you. So, when I talk about conceptual portraits, I'm talking about trying to convey something about the person, not a straight snapshot of them like a normal portrait. For example, I could take you all out to some location, somewhere out of the way in one of the cities we stop at, or even out to the beach, somewhere like that. Then we could experiment with different setups. I'd like to take photos that show your unique personalities in an environment that people wouldn't necessarily expect to see you in."

"So, you want us to go down to the beach, strip off, and splash around in the water?" Noah asked with a grin. Lexie laughed, while the others rolled their eyes.

"What is it with you and stripping off?" Zac asked.

"Hey, I don't get to prance around at the front of the stage during our gigs like you do, so I've got to show off all this awesomeness somehow." He gestured down at his admittedly fantastic physique.

Lexie laughed again. "While I'm sure that would make many women very happy, having you all frolicking naked in the water wasn't quite what I had in mind. Here, I've got some examples of what I'm talking about."

She clicked an icon on the laptop and then spun it around on the table so they could all see the photos on the screen. She'd chosen several portraits of musicians to help them envision what she was thinking, and as she clicked through them, she noted which ones they each liked.

One seemed to catch Connor's attention. It was black and

white and showed a man in profile, sitting at a piano with his fingers hovering over the keys. The light was behind him, casting his face in shadow so you could see the outline of his features but not make out his expression. Motes of dust hovered in the air around him, caught by the light streaming in the window.

It was one of Lexie's favorites. The composition was so simple, you couldn't even see the man's expression. Yet his posture and the way he held his hands—poised just over the keys—conveyed a strong sense of melancholy.

Connor stared at the photo, his eyebrows drawn together above his black-lashed green eyes and a small furrow between his brows. Lexie watched him, wondering what he saw in the photo that made him react that way. When he glanced up and caught her eyes on him, his expression shuttered, and he looked away out of the bus window.

Lexie pushed aside her curiosity about his reaction and continued. "Anyway, those are just to give you an idea what I'm talking about. We can do anything you want, but I thought it might be nice to try to express something about you all, either individually or as a group, that says something about who you really are. As long as everyone's happy with that idea."

Murmurs of agreement came from around the table. Noah and Zac immediately began throwing around ideas which became increasingly inappropriate as they tried to outdo each other. Tex reached for her laptop, surprising her by politely asking, "May I?" and at her nod, flicking through the rest of the photos she'd saved. Connor had said nothing and was still staring out the window, rubbing the back of his neck with one hand as if deep in thought.

"Connor?" she asked quietly.

He turned to look at her, his eyes shadowed, and she had a strange urge to reach over the table and cover his hand with hers. Instead, she asked, "Are you okay with all of that?"

Connor looked around the table at Noah and Zac in fits of laughter as their ideas got even more outrageous, and Tex, who was still clicking through photos, and his expression cleared.

He turned back to her, his mouth tipping upward at the corners, and nodded. "I think that'll be just fine."

His deep, smooth voice with its Irish lilt washed over her, and as their eyes caught, tension filled the air between them again.

The sound of the bus door opening and someone climbing aboard broke the spell. Lexie blinked and turned away, flushing. Great. By staring at him for what must have been an inappropriately long time, she'd probably given him the impression she was mooning over him like every other woman out there.

Luckily, she was distracted from that embarrassing thought by a tall, muscular woman strolling into the living area with a broad smile on her face. "Good to see you boys again!" she called out. All four men stood and strode over to her, taking turns hugging her.

Curious who she was, Lexie slid out from the table and stood up. The woman's eyes widened when she noticed Lexie, and a grin spread across her face. "So, which of you four has finally wised up and found himself a pretty lady to call his own, then?"

Lexie had to giggle at the terrified looks on the guys'

faces. Since they all seemed too stunned at the idea of her being a girlfriend to introduce her, she did it herself, smiling up at the woman as she stepped forward and held out her hand.

"Hi, I'm Lexie. I'm the tour photographer."

She shook Lexie's hand, giving it a squeeze before letting go. "Hi, Lexie. I'm Maggie and I'm the boys' driver. It's my job to get them all safely from here to there. They'll try to convince you it's also my job to wait on them hand and foot, but I can guarantee you that's not the case." She threw a mock dirty look at the guys, who had recovered enough to put on expressions of wide-eyed innocence.

She turned back to Lexie. "So, are you going to be traveling with us too, then?"

Lexie nodded. "Looks like it."

"Well, that'll be nice. The boys are big enough and ugly enough to look after themselves. But if you need anything, sweetheart, give me a shout and I'll see what I can do. And don't let these four fool you. They may try to act like badass rock 'n' roll stars, but they're all teddy bears at heart."

"That's enough, Maggie." Tex fake growled at her. "You can't give away all our secrets, or we won't have any credibility."

Lexie laughed. "Too late, your secret's out. There's no going back now."

Maggie smiled cheerfully at her, and then being completely unsubtle, turned and gave the guys a wink and a thumbs-up before letting them know they'd be setting off in about five minutes. Then she headed to the front of the bus to get herself sorted.

Feeling much more relaxed about being on the bus now,

Lexie smiled to herself. Glancing up, she caught Connor's eyes on her, a pensive expression on his face. He turned away, joining in with the conversation the others were having about what they would have for dinner.

Lexie frowned at his serious expression, wondering if she'd done something to annoy him. She shrugged. He'd seemed happy enough with her concept for the photo book, so he was probably just practicing his brooding rock star look.

The bus rumbled to life as Maggie started the engine and Lexie sat back down at the table. Time to get to work.

Chapter 8

Lexie's first night on the tour bus was a bit of a revelation. She'd been nervous about spending time with a bunch of egotistical rock stars, but they were all surprisingly down-to-earth. She'd spent an inordinate amount of time laughing at their antics and taking photos. It was unlikely she would use any of the shots in the photo book. It was more to get the guys comfortable with her being around them, and to give her an idea of how they all acted in front of the camera. The thing that struck her the most was their complete lack of self-consciousness. There was something undeniably appealing about men that were so comfortable in their own skin—with who they were.

Noah was the clown, always hamming it up. He was quick to smile and laugh, and a terrible flirt, but had her in stitches half the time. Zac was more reserved but had a wicked sense of humor. His dark, soulful eyes were watchful, and it took him longer to warm up to her, but when he did, he was a lot of fun to be around. Tex was the epitome of a rock god, with his shoulder-length, sun-streaked brown hair and tattoos covering his muscular arms and chest. She found him intimidating at first, since he towered over her, but when he pulled out a paperback novel, they had a great conversation over a shared love of books.

Connor was the most difficult to get a read on. There was a sense of restraint about him, as if he was always holding part of himself back. After dinner, which Maggie picked up from a roadside diner, Tex, Noah, and Zac settled down to watch a movie on the large flat-screen TV. Instead of joining them, Connor went to the back of the room and pulled out an acoustic guitar and notepad. He bent his head over the instrument and quietly strummed it. She could see his lips moving though she couldn't hear what he was saying. Now and then he'd stop and make notes in the pad.

Lexie couldn't help herself from centering him in the viewfinder of her camera. She focused on the graceful line of his spine curving over the guitar, his dark hair falling over his forehead, and the long lashes that brushed his cheeks when he closed his eyes to concentrate.

Through the camera, she watched the muscles in his arms flex under his tanned skin as he played the instrument. She glimpsed a tattoo on his left arm, the edge of it partly visible below his t-shirt sleeve, and wondered what it looked like without his shirt covering it. What *he* looked like without his shirt. That sense of attraction whispered through her again, and she frowned, lowering her camera without taking the shot.

As she started to turn away, he tilted his head to the side, his gaze colliding with hers. Caught staring. Again. For a few breathless seconds, she held his gaze, the attraction ratcheting up a few notches as she lost herself in his green eyes. Then she came to her senses. This was not happening, she told herself.

Forcing a stiff smile, she broke his gaze and turned back to the others, raising her camera for a few last shots. It had been a long and overwhelming day, and she was tired. Time to go to bed.

She packed up her camera, wandered up to the front of the bus to say good night to Maggie, then back through the living area to say good night to the guys. Tex, Zac, and Noah smiled and chorused out their good-nights as she waved to them where they were sprawled out watching the movie.

Connor didn't appear to have moved since he'd caught her watching him. Feeling self-conscious as his eyes tracked her progress toward him, she gave him a small smile and a wave good night. He didn't return the gesture, but as she was almost past him, he reached out and grasped her wrist. Startled, she stopped and turned, meeting his eyes.

"Sleep well, Lexie" he murmured, and she felt his thumb skim the back of her wrist before he let her go and turned back to his guitar.

Lexie stood frozen for a second before pivoting and heading down the aisle to her room at the back of the bus, the faint sound of his guitar following her. Although she was exhausted, it took her a long time to fall asleep.

***

By the time she woke the next morning, they'd arrived in Seattle for the first stop of the tour. The bus had pulled up outside the stadium, and chaos seemed to reign again as everything was unloaded. Lexie could already hear the squeals of overexcited women, and she gritted her teeth, imagining the shrill sound would get very old, very quickly.

She got up, had a quick shower, and dressed in a pair of denim cutoffs and a fitted green V-neck t-shirt, then slipped on a pair of Converse sneakers and pulled her hair into a ponytail, ready for a busy day ahead. Yesterday had been her day to get used to everything, but today her job really started. She'd carry her camera with her everywhere to make sure she got as many shots as possible.

Lexie left the bedroom and wandered into the living area, only to be stopped in her tracks by the sight of four hot, shirtless rock stars lounging around eating breakfast. *Oh my God*. She blinked a couple of times, but they didn't disappear, so she took a deep breath and got her feet moving.

Tex noticed her first. "Mornin', darlin'. Did you sleep okay?" The rest of them turned around to smile at her and say good morning too.

"Yes, thanks. Surprisingly well considering I've never slept on a bus before. How were the bunks?"

Tex shrugged. "Not too bad. Ask me again in a week though; I'll probably give you a different answer."

Feeling bad again about stealing the only proper bed, she opened her mouth, about to offer it up, when Connor locked eyes with her. As if he knew what she was going to say, he gave her a frown and a tiny shake of his head.

She closed her mouth, then turned to busy herself with making a coffee at the kitchenette counter, because seeing Connor shirtless first thing in the morning was far too disconcerting. It had given her a chance to check out his tattoo though, which turned out to be a striking black Celtic-style tribal pattern extending from his bicep, over his shoulder and collarbone, and finishing over his heart.

As she absentmindedly stirred creamer into her coffee—

trying very hard not to picture smooth, tanned skin inked with stark black lines—she felt someone come up behind her. Before she had a chance to turn around, she heard Connor's low, husky voice over her shoulder.

"Excuse me," he said and then stretched his arm up over her head to reach the cupboard above her and retrieve a coffee mug. As he did, his bare chest brushed against her back, and the scent of warm-bodied man enfolded her, causing her senses to go on full alert. Her breathing quickened, and a hot flush swept over her body.

She angled her head back to look at him. He was looking down at her with a lazy smile on his face, his green eyes glinting with something that seemed an awful lot like amusement. *Damn him*. He was doing this on purpose to get a reaction from her, so sure of his effect on women.

Annoyed that he thought he could play with her, she reacted without thinking. Smiling sweetly, she turned so that her breasts brushed against his chest, trying hard to ignore how her nipples hardened at the contact. She put a hand on the smooth, bare skin of his ribs as she eased out from between him and the counter. That was a mistake because his warm skin felt a little too good against her palm. Her movement had the intended effect though. Connor's eyes darkened, and he looked a lot less amused than before.

"Let me just get out of your way." She kept the fake sweet smile plastered on her face as she moved away from him, unable to help trailing her fingers against his skin slightly longer than she needed to. But it had been such a long time since she'd touched a man's bare chest, and she'd forgotten how good it felt.

The thought brought her back to her senses. She wasn't

here to remember how good it felt to have her hands on an attractive man. She was here to do a job and do it well. That couldn't happen if she was being distracted by one of her employers.

Clutching her coffee mug, she wandered over to the dining table where the other three were finishing up breakfast. She lifted an eyebrow in amusement. Toast and cereal appeared to be on the menu. Not quite what she'd expected rock stars to eat for breakfast.

"So, what's the schedule for today?" she asked.

Zac answered. "After breakfast, we'll head into the venue to make sure the setup is going smoothly and there aren't any surprises. Then we'll head to the hotel for a few hours to relax, have lunch, and be back here this afternoon in time for soundcheck."

She nodded, trying to plan her photos. "Okay, well, I'll head out when you do and get some photos of everyone setting up. I'll just go and get my camera ready."

As she turned to leave, she couldn't help glancing over at Connor. He remained where she'd left him, leaning back against the counter with his muscular arms crossed over his chest, green eyes watching her. The sight of him like that did nothing to diminish the attraction thrumming through her veins.

"Get a grip, Lexie," she muttered to herself.

She didn't know if she'd spoken louder than she'd intended to, or if he could read her mind, but the corners of his mouth curled up in amusement.

Shaking her head, she turned and headed back to her room.

Chapter 9

A little later, Lexie followed the now fully dressed band members out of the bus. Two of the band's security detail stood guard outside. As they exited, one of the big guys peeled off to escort them into the stadium, while the other stayed behind to keep an eye on the bus.

Lexie took a few steps and then stopped to look around. There was so much activity. Equipment was being unloaded from trucks and taken into the venue, people were rushing around frantically, and a crowd of screaming fans was being held back by a fence and several security guards.

Lexie wanted to capture the beehive of energy, so while the band kept walking toward the venue, she stopped to snap some photos, spinning in place to make sure she got the full picture.

"Lexie, you coming?" Noah had turned and was now walking backward as he spoke to her.

"I might stay out here for a bit," she called back.

Noah nodded, then turned back to follow the others. Connor stopped and spoke to the security guy that was escorting them, who then headed back toward her, while Connor turned and continued into the venue.

She lowered her camera as the big burly guy approached her, looking up at him questioningly.

"Mr. Byrne wants me to stay with you until you're ready to go inside."

Lexie raised her eyebrows. "Oh, that's not necessary. I'm sure they need you more than I do. I'm not the one with hordes of screaming fans trying to get to me." She smiled up at him, but he looked back at her expressionlessly.

"Mr. Byrne told me to stay with you, so that's what I'm going to do."

Lexie blew out a breath. Not quite what she was used to, but it was what it was. Now she needed to get to work.

When she eventually made her way inside, she saw the band sitting in a row on the edge of the stage. She waved goodbye to Will, the security guard who had been escorting her outside, and he headed off to take up his assigned position.

Lexie spun in a circle again, taking in the sheer size of the stadium and the amount of activity underway. She'd never realized how much was involved in the setup of a major concert. The stage itself was very simple—all black with risers for Noah's drums and a piano. On stage, equipment and speakers were being set up, while the lighting crew hoisted trusses that would hold all the lights. Huge video screens were being lifted behind and around the sides of the stage, and a catwalk was being assembled at the front. In the secure area underneath the stage, the sound mixing and support techs were setting up. Dozens of men and women pushed pieces of equipment and cases on wheels around the floor of the stadium.

Lexie wandered around for over an hour, absorbed in her

work, and trying not to get in anyone's way while she took photo after photo of the organized chaos. She was taking a close-up of Noah's drum set—which had at least twelve microphones arrayed around it—when she felt a presence behind her. Without even having to hear his voice, she knew it was Connor.

She kept taking shots for a few more seconds, not wanting him to know how much his presence unnerved her. Then, taking a deep breath, she let her camera drop on its strap and turned to face him with a smile pasted on her face. "Hi, Connor."

The fact that at the first glimpse of his face her heart rate sped up meant she had to stop denying how attractive she found him. While she felt the sharp stab of guilt, she braced herself against it. She was a widow, she wasn't dead. This was what she wanted, wasn't it? To start moving on.

It wasn't as if her attraction to him was unusual; most women in the world would find him as sexy as hell. But just because she was attracted to him didn't mean she had to act on it. She was a grown woman, a professional, and more than able to control herself around a man. Even if he was an incredibly sexy rock star. She just needed to admit it and allow herself to admire him from afar.

"I wanted to see how it was going. Are you getting what you need? Is there anything you'd like to know about or want to get a photo of in particular?" His eyes were intent on hers.

"There's so much to capture. A lot of these initial shots won't end up getting used unless I get a lucky candid. At the moment I'm getting a feel for everything that's going on, so I know how best to prepare for the next time. Same goes for the concert tonight. Tomorrow is when I'll hit my stride."

"Have you been to one of our concerts before?" he asked.

Lexie shook her head. "I saw some videos on the internet; they looked amazing. I'm excited to see it tonight."

"So, you're telling me you're not a fan?" He frowned and appeared so serious, she tripped over her words as she tried to reply. "Oh, uh, no I…"

A smile slowly spread over his face, his gorgeous lips tilting up at the corners. "I'm teasing you, Lexie. I like that you're not a fan. This way everything is new to you and you can see us as we really are, not just what you expect to see."

Lexie's heart skipped a beat at his smile. He stood close to her in the dark corner, and she could smell the faint crisp, citrus scent of whatever he was wearing. It made her recall how he'd smelled this morning when he'd pressed up behind her, the fresh, clean scent of him when he'd just rolled out of bed. Those were not good thoughts to be having now. Or ever. Playful Connor was just as sexy as brooding Connor.

To break that train of thought, Lexie pulled herself up to her full five-foot-four height, stared him straight in the eye, and said with feigned indignation, "So you're saying you don't think I could be professionally objective?" She tried very hard to suppress her smile.

Connor's eyes flicked backward and forward between hers, checking to see if she was serious or not. His smile didn't budge an inch, letting her know she hadn't fooled him for a second. He leaned down, put his lips close to her ear, and said, "Maybe I'm hoping you won't be quite as professional as you should be."

Heat flashed through Lexie's entire body, her recently

resurrected libido rising up and hammering at her. This was not good. Of all the men in the world, why did it have to be him that finally got a reaction from her? A man that no doubt lived by the motto "bang a groupie a day to keep the doctor away." She didn't want him to be the one that pushed Damien out of her thoughts, but the heat still ricocheting through her told her that her body had other plans.

She took a deep breath and slowly stepped back from him. "Um, well, you're the boss!" It was an inane comment, but she needed the reminder that he was her employer.

"Actually," he said, his Irish lilt strengthening, "the record label is your employer. I just have creative control." He paused. "Which means you're not my employee, but you do have to do *anything* I want." His deepening smile, and the flash of his dimples, made his innuendo clear.

Oh no, this was not happening again. He thought he could get his flirt on with her because he wasn't her actual employer. She guessed he was bored and had decided to have some fun at her expense. He obviously knew the effect he had on women and probably flirted out of habit. She was sure he was enjoying watching her squirm.

She had two choices. She could go full-on ice queen and put him in his place or show him he wouldn't get the reaction he expected out of her. The first choice was the right way to go. Which was why she surprised herself by stepping forward, rising up on her tiptoes, and bracing herself with one hand against his firm chest so she could whisper sultrily in his ear.

"You may have creative control, Connor, but that doesn't mean you can control *me*. You can ask me to do anything you want…" She tilted her head back to look him right in the eye.

"And maybe I'll do it for you." She dropped back down on her heels and stepped back from him, then turned to leave, throwing over her shoulder as she walked away, "Probably not though. If you have a problem with that, I guess you can take it up with my employer."

He stood there watching her walk away, his eyes dark and a faint smile on his lips. Now he knew she was onto his little game, he'd turn his attention elsewhere, and she could go back to trying very, very hard not to think about him naked.

She was strolling toward the steps leading down from the stage feeling pleased with herself when he strode up beside her. In a casual tone of voice, as if nothing had happened, he asked, "Are you hungry? We're going to head out soon and grab some lunch. We've got a hotel suite we can all hang in for a few hours and get some room service before we have to come back for soundcheck. Want to come along?"

Lexie considered. While she would have liked to have walked off and enjoyed her win, she was actually starving since she'd jumped right into her work without having any breakfast. She had plenty of shots already, and she was happy she knew the basic photos she'd aim to get over the next few weeks. And it was her job to spend her time with them and get photos of everything, so it wasn't like she could avoid it.

Okay, well, she could be as casual as he was. She smiled up at him. "Thanks, that'd be great."

He nodded to where the three others stood waiting for them. "Let's go."

Chapter 10

Several hours later, Lexie was in the green room with the band as they prepared for the show. She could hear the screams of the crowd and feel the vibration from the opening act's bass notes, even from here. The muffled roar had her adrenaline spiking, but none of the guys were nervous at all. They were sitting around playing cards, drinking beer, and generally goofing around. Contrary to her expectations, there hadn't been any crazy preshow rituals either.

They did look exactly how she expected a rock band to look though—tight black jeans, tight t-shirts, leather cuffs, and chunky silver rings. Not to mention all the sculpted muscles and various tattoos on display. Very sexy. In fact, she could kind of get used to this, she thought as she snapped another photo of the four of them, mid-laugh at an off-color joke from Noah.

A knock sounded, and Drew poked his head around the door. "Connor, your guests are here."

Connor looked up from his cards. "Thanks, Drew, we'll be there in a minute."

Drew nodded and disappeared, closing the door behind him. Lexie wondered what was going on, as Connor stood, grabbed his guitar, and wandered over in her direction.

"Hey, Lexie, we've got some preshow visitors we're going to hang out with for half an hour or so. While you're welcome to join us, I'd prefer you don't take any photos."

Lexie's eyebrows rose in surprise, but she nodded, and without thinking said, "Of course, you're the boss."

He gave her a pointed look. "I thought we'd already had that conversation."

A blush heated her cheeks, but before she could reply she noticed the others had already left the room. She jumped up from the stool she was sitting on, not wanting Connor to be late for his visitors.

He led the way out of the green room and down a small side hallway. Lexie was curious about who the band was meeting with. Since Connor had asked her not to take photos, she couldn't help but be suspicious about what was going on. Maybe this was where she'd be confronted with the crazy rock 'n' roll lifestyle she'd heard so much about.

Lexie saw the others waiting with Drew outside a door at the end of the hallway. As soon as Connor and Lexie joined them, Drew opened the door and went in. The band followed and Lexie slipped in behind them, nervous about what she was going to see.

Looking around the room, there was a group of around a dozen kids, ranging in age from about ten to sixteen years old. There were a few adults as well, but they were sitting in chairs set up along the back of the room. All the kids, and most of the adults, had huge grins on their faces, and their eyes were bright with excitement.

Drew appeared at her side. "Hey, Lexie, come and sit next to me." He led her off to the side of the room where more chairs were set up.

After sitting down, Lexie turned to Drew and asked quietly, "What's going on?"

"You might not be aware, but the band supports several charities that focus on providing music therapy for disadvantaged youths and kids that have suffered emotional, physical, or mental trauma."

Lexie blinked in surprise. "I didn't know. But that's really great."

Drew nodded. "Connor tells me that music has significant benefits for promoting mental health and helping kids to release repressed emotion. It's a cause that's always been close to Connor's heart, and the other guys have gotten involved too. So now whenever they go on tour, Connor lets the local children's charity groups know when they're going to be in town and offers up free tickets to the show and the chance to meet the band beforehand for a chat and a small private concert. Most of the kids are massive fans, so getting to meet their idols is kind of a payoff for the work they put into trying to overcome their difficulties."

Lexie had never even considered the guys would take time out of their preshow schedule to do something so... sweet. She watched them with a new appreciation as they talked to the kids, shaking hands or giving hugs. The kids couldn't hide their excitement, and hero worship radiated from their faces.

After spending about five minutes chatting, the guys pulled up some chairs and asked the audience to call out some of their favorite songs. A few different titles were thrown out before the guys nodded, murmured to each other, and then began to play an acoustic version of one of their slower songs.

It was beautiful. Just the harmony of their voices, the guitars, and the small hand drum that Noah had brought with him. Emotion unexpectedly flooded through Lexie, especially when she saw the joy radiating from the faces of the kids watching. Several of them were crying as they watched their idols singing and playing for them.

Several times Lexie caught herself raising her camera to take a photo, before remembering she wasn't supposed to. The photographer in her desperately wanted to capture this moment, but she understood why Connor didn't want her to. This wasn't for publicity. It was about giving these kids an experience that would shine a light during what was a dark and difficult time in their lives. A memory that would hopefully provide inspiration and hope for a happier future.

After several more songs, the guys had to wrap it up because they needed to get ready to take the stage. Lexie brushed away a few tears of her own that leaked out when some of the younger kids cried as they got to give their idols a final hug.

"Come on, almost time for the show," Drew said.

Lexie got up and followed him out. As he led her back down the hallway, she glanced over her shoulder to see the band filing out of the room, broad smiles on their faces. These guys just kept on surprising her.

Fifteen minutes later, Lexie stood at the side of the stage. The opening act had exited a few minutes ago, and the crowd was going wild in anticipation of Fractured's appearance. The same anticipation coursed through her as the thump of the intro music and the flashing lights hyped everyone up even further. Soon the crowd was chanting the band's name, before erupting into an ear-splitting roar as the whole arena went dark.

The video screens at the back of the stage lit up with red and orange ribbons of light, silhouetting the band who'd come up on stage while the lights were off. The screams reached a crescendo as a figure detached itself from the shadows and stalked forward. Connor reached the edge of the stage and raised one arm high in the air.

Lights flashed on as the deep driving beat started. Connor lowered his arm, wrapped his fingers around the microphone on the stand in front of him, and began to sing.

His voice washed over her, low and sensuous, with just enough grit to send goosebumps rippling over her skin. It was a completely different experience from the soundcheck that afternoon or even the acoustic set they'd just done. Nothing could compare to the full impact of the lights, the music, the screams of the amped-up crowd, and the sheer sex appeal of the man on stage.

She was supposed to be analyzing the concert and figuring out how best to photograph the band and the crowd, but she was finding it hard to pull her gaze away from the mesmerizing sight of Connor on stage. He reminded her of some large, dangerous jungle cat—all lean muscles and fluid grace.

The other band members were killing it too. Tex's fingers moved smoothly over the fretboard of his guitar, weaving the melody through Connor's singing, Noah had a huge smile on his face while he beat out the rhythm on his drums, and Zac played the bass with his eyes closed, the deep resonant notes somehow linking the rhythm and the melody together. The sound was incredible, the bass notes reverberating through Lexie and filling her with a tension and energy that seemed to demand some kind of outlet.

Forcing herself away from the stage she moved around the stadium, through the mass of singing, screaming fans, taking establishing shots and making notes on her tablet. All the while, Connor's voice wove its way through her senses. When she'd done what she needed to do, she gave in to temptation again and made her way back to the side of the stage to watch the performance.

The music was fantastic, and the energy of all four of them playing together was explosive. But she couldn't take her eyes off Connor. At one point he made his way to the side of the stage close to where she was watching, and one of the crew tossed him a water bottle. He took a few gulps, then upended the rest over his head. Lexie could understand why the crowd went wild; with his slicked-back hair and white t-shirt now molded to his abs, he looked practically sinful.

Almost as if he sensed her gaze on him, he glanced her way and Lexie felt an almost physical shock as their eyes met. Time seemed to slow to a crawl, and she was so close she could see the lights reflecting off the water beads clinging to his dark lashes. He threw her a quick smile, and when he turned away to finish the song, she let out a long, shuddering breath.

As she attempted to pull herself together, Drew stepped up to stand alongside her. "Impressive, aren't they?" he said, loud enough she could hear him over the pounding beat of the music. Embarrassed that he might have caught her ogling the talent while she should've been working, she made a small sound of agreement and started to edge away.

Before she could, Drew turned to her. "Lexie, just a word

of warning. You're going to be in close quarters with these guys for several months. They're good men—the best—but when it comes down to it, they're rock stars, and they're used to getting what they want. You're a very attractive woman, and I wouldn't put it past any of them to make a move on you. While they don't mean any harm, well, hearts have been known to get broken. I want to make sure you're conscious of that."

Lexie stared at him aghast, then drew herself up, feeling defensive. "I appreciate the warning, Drew, but I'm not fifteen, so I think I'm more than capable of not fangirling all over them."

Drew sighed. "Look, I didn't mean to offend you. But charisma like these guys have is a potent force, especially if one of them sets his sights on you. I'm sure *you* will keep it professional; the problem is I can't guarantee the guys will. They know how to use their looks and charm to get what they want. I don't want you brokenhearted, and since I can't rely on the guys to show restraint, then I'm relying on you. I'm sorry again if I've offended you." He gave her a tight smile and walked off.

A wave of exhaustion flooded over Lexie. All the noise, the chaos, the unfamiliarity of the situation was too much. She wanted to go home and curl up in her bed. But as Drew had reminded her, she was a professional. She was here to do a job, and she was going to get it done.

Throwing one last look over her shoulder as she turned to leave, her gaze once again met Connor's. His eyes were narrowed, brows drawn together. Mortified that he might have seen her being told to keep her hands to herself, she turned away and headed backstage.

Chapter 11

Connor tracked Drew down at the end of the show and grabbed his arm. "I saw you talking to Lexie. She seemed upset—what did you say to her?" he asked, with more anger than intended.

Drew glanced down at where Connor's hand gripped his arm and then back up at his face, his eyes round. Connor knew it was because he was usually the cool, calm, and collected one of the group. Drew wasn't used to having Connor's anger directed at him.

"Calm down. I just wanted to reinforce the fact that since you're all traveling together, things needed to stay professional. It's hard to say something like that without it sounding offensive, but honestly, it needed to be said. To her and to you guys. Don't think I don't know why the band asks for the 'no fraternization' clause to be left out of your contracts."

He tried to shake off Connor's tight grip, and Connor let him go, raking his fingers through his hair. Drew's brows pinched together. "Are you okay, mate? It's not like you to get worked up like this. Tex mentioned you had a go at them yesterday over this girl. Tell me she's not going to be a problem."

Connor couldn't blame him for being concerned. It was Drew's job to keep the band operating smoothly. Anything that might cause tension between the band members was his priority. Connor knew he'd been acting erratically, even before Lexie's arrival. It was obvious that Drew and his friends sensed something was bothering him, because everyone in their own way had tried to get him to talk about what the problem was. But Connor didn't want to talk about it. Not until he could figure out what, if anything, he wanted to change. So, it was no wonder Drew was trying to do something about an issue he could actually address.

"Well, you don't have to worry, I think everyone's got the message now. No funny business with the photographer. I just hope she isn't too pissed off. I'd hate to see the compromising photos she could take if she is." He tried to laugh off his unusual behavior and hoped Drew would buy it.

Drew chuckled, looking relieved. "Yeah, good luck with that," he threw over his shoulder as he strolled away.

Connor smiled back but didn't feel any happier. His reaction to Lexie was disconcerting, and he hoped hiring her wouldn't end up being a big mistake.

Heading to the green room, Connor found Lexie already taking shots of the band members as they wound down from the show. He was late, so everyone else had already had showers and were hungrily devouring the catered food that had been brought in for them. Although he was starving after performing his ass off for the last two hours, he desperately wanted a shower to wash off the sweat, and to bring his heart rate down.

Lexie noticed his arrival as he made his way through to

the dressing room. She lowered her camera and smiled at him, and damn, once again he was struck by how gorgeous she was. Unable to fight the urge to talk to her, he detoured in her direction. As he approached, he saw her gaze almost involuntarily sweep down his body. The way her eyes widened slightly and a flush warmed her cheeks made a smile tug at his mouth.

"So, what did you think of the show?" he asked as he stopped in front of her, realizing that he honestly cared about her opinion. He'd performed in front of millions of fans throughout the band's career, but for some reason, he wanted to know that *she* had enjoyed it.

Her face broke into another gorgeous smile, and his stomach did a slow cartwheel in response.

"I loved it; you guys were phenomenal! I don't know if I've ever felt so much energy contained in one place before."

He smiled down at her. Millions of albums sold, sellout world tours, and one woman telling him she'd loved the show had made him happier than he'd felt in a long time. Or maybe it was the way the sparkle in her gray eyes made them appear almost silver. Or the way her lips looked so soft and inviting. Or the way her tight t-shirt and cutoffs clung to her curves... Okay, now he needed a shower for a completely different reason. A cold shower.

"Well, I'm glad you enjoyed it. I'm going to hit the shower, so I'll see you back out here when I'm done. Drew will be bringing back some VIP guests soon for a meet and greet, then the after-party. Be warned though, sometimes it can get a bit crazy, especially when they break out the alcohol."

She nodded, looking mildly apprehensive. "I can

imagine. If things get too debauched, then I'll head back to the bus. I assume there are some things you don't want memorialized on film."

Connor had a good idea what she thought was going to happen. Like most people, she probably bought into the whole sex, drugs, and rock 'n' roll thing. And there was no doubt in the early years when they were just taking off, partying hard and picking up groupies after every show was standard.

But eventually, the novelty had worn off and now most of the craziness that happened at the parties was on the part of the fans. Women asking for various body parts to be signed, taking their tops off, propositioning band members or the crew, even the security guys—yeah, that happened. He and the others weren't saints—sometimes they took what was being offered, though they usually waited for a night when they were staying in a hotel. While they had been known to use the bedroom on the bus if needed, in those cramped quarters it was hard to let loose and really enjoy yourself.

Now with Lexie staying with them, he doubted there'd be any action going on outside of a hotel room. Having to listen to your friend have crazy-loud sex in the bunk next to you wasn't high on any of their to-do lists.

"I'm more worried about you getting trampled in the stampede." He smirked at her.

"Well, I was caught in the middle of a stampede of wildebeest when I was on a job in Africa, but I imagine hordes of screaming, half-naked female fans might be more dangerous." She smiled back up at him, eyes sparkling.

Shit, he was enjoying being on the receiving end of her

smiles a little too much. "Well, how did you escape the stampeding wildebeest?"

"Climbed a tree." She made a show of looking around the room before turning back to him. "No trees here though. I might be in trouble."

"I guess you'll just have to climb the tallest thing in the room, then." He copied her, making a show of scanning the room, before looking back into her eyes. "Looks like that would be me."

Fuck, was he flirting with her again? From the way she parted her lips and blinked at him, it was obvious he was. He wondered if she was going to shut him down this time, or flirt back like she had before. Either way, he knew he was pushing his luck with her. Knew it, but couldn't seem to stop.

She bit her bottom lip, drawing his attention to her pretty mouth. When he dragged his gaze back up, her silver-gray eyes had darkened, and she paused before saying, "I think that would be the most dangerous thing I could do, don't you? I'm pretty sure getting too close to you will guarantee I'll get hurt."

Connor froze. He wasn't sure if she meant the fans would hurt her trying to get to him, or if he would end up hurting her if the two of them got too close. Either way, it was true. He needed to keep himself in check when it came to Lexie. She wasn't the right person to play with, and she definitely did not give off the vibe she'd be up for a one-night stand. There were plenty of women out there that would be more than happy to take only what he was willing to give them. No need to mess with a woman who was going to be living with him for the next three months.

"You're right. Bad idea. You could try climbing Noah; you'd be in no danger there," he said as Noah came up alongside her.

He sounded more flippant than he felt, and had to grit his teeth as Noah put his arm around Lexie's shoulders and asked, "Why are you going to climb me? Not that I have an issue with that, just curious."

As Lexie turned and smiled up at the drummer, one of those cute blushes spreading across her cheeks, Connor backed away and headed for the bathroom. One cold shower coming up. Maybe that would knock some sense into him. What had he told the guys the day before? No one touches the photographer. Especially not him.

Chapter 12

Four days later, Lexie was sitting in the front of the bus keeping Maggie company as they drove toward Colorado. They had driven overnight, and the sun was starting to rise. Shafts of light were beginning to break through the heavy clouds, casting long shadows across the road in front of the bus.

Since Lexie was used to rising early for her job, she was often the first one up. She'd started making her way to the front of the bus to sit in the comfortable passenger seat across the aisle from Maggie, keeping her company as she drove. Maggie seemed to enjoy having someone to chat with. She'd already regaled Lexie with several stories of her time in the Navy, where she'd been responsible for training and maintenance on the navigation equipment.

"What was it like living on a ship for months at a time?" Lexie asked.

Maggie grinned. "It was great to experience the comradery, and getting to visit so many other countries was amazing. Every day was a challenge, both in a good and bad way, but overall, I enjoyed it. Watching the sun rise from the deck of a ship in the middle of the ocean was one of the most beautiful and peaceful things I've ever experienced."

Lexie smiled, her photographer's mind immediately visualizing the scene and working out how she'd capture it on camera. Giving her head a slight shake, she brought herself back to the conversation. "So how did you end up with this job?"

"I got my bus license after I got out of the Navy. Used to drive Greyhound buses but got a bit bored going backward and forward on the same route. I saw an ad in the paper to be a tour bus driver one day, applied, and here I am!"

"How long have you been driving these guys around for now?"

"This is the third tour I've done with them, so almost four years." Maggie couldn't hide the affection in her voice.

"Do you enjoy it?"

"I do. This job can be a bit hit or miss depending on which artists you're driving for. Some are nicer than others. But I love these guys—they're fun without being so crazy they make my life miserable. And they're respectful, which makes the job much more pleasant."

Lexie smiled to herself. She'd only been with the band for just under a week, but she already knew she liked them all a lot.

Maggie glanced over at her, a broad smile on her face. "They're good men, all four of them." A pause. "Single too."

Lexie turned surprised eyes toward Maggie, then squirmed uncomfortably at the knowing look on her face. "Oh, um, well I'm sure that's the way they like it."

"Maybe. Could be they just think they like it that way."

Lexie fidgeted in her seat. She might like all the guys, but there was one that filled her thoughts more than the others. She hoped it wasn't too obvious, though the way Maggie was looking at her made her think she wasn't as good at hiding her feelings as she might hope. She schooled her features into an expression of pleasant inquiry, hoping her blush wasn't too visible.

Maggie chuckled and turned back to the road. "Now, if I were a few years younger, and as pretty as you, I'd be picking one of those boys to have some fun with."

Lexie's mouth fell open, and she checked over her shoulder to make sure none of the guys had come out and overhead Maggie. "I'm not here to have fun. I'm here to do a job." Even to Lexie's ears, her protest came across less emphatic than it should have.

Maggie nodded. "Yes, you are. But I'm not convinced the two are mutually exclusive."

Lexie shook her head in denial, and Maggie chuckled again. "Now, I don't have any favorites—all of those boys are something special—but..." She looked over at Lexie speculatively. "I think you and Connor would be a good match."

This time Lexie knew her blush would be visible. Oh God, did everyone know about her inappropriate attraction?

Looking back at the road, Maggie nodded decisively. "Yeah, he's the one. I'm not quite sure what it is, but there's something about the two of you together that fits."

Lexie tried to laugh it off. "I don't think so, Maggie. Connor and I have nothing in common."

"Really? I think you're more alike than you realize. You're both artists, passionate about your art. You both have big hearts, although you wear yours on your sleeve and Connor hides his away. And I could be wrong, but I think you've both experienced a great deal of pain in your lives." She looked over at Lexie and gave her a sympathetic smile. "Maybe the two of you together could ease each other's pain." She gave Lexie a wink. "Or you could just get frisky."

Lexie cringed with embarrassment. As much as she found Connor attractive, she knew it was superficial. No matter what Maggie thought, the two of them didn't have anything in common. He was a world-famous playboy rock star, and she was just a photographer. She wasn't sure if he was in pain or not, but even if he was, she was in no position to help him. They'd been thrown together by circumstance, and in a few months, they'd go their separate ways and never see each other again.

All she wanted was to do justice to Connor's vision for the photo book and then get back to rebuilding her life. Maybe one day she'd be able to consider trying to find someone to share that life with, but regardless of whether she ever got to that point, having a fling with someone like Connor wouldn't be a good idea. Now or ever. Plus, she was fairly sure the idea of doing anything more than casually flirting with her hadn't even crossed his mind.

"The guys will be up soon. I'd better go and get the coffee going." She jumped up and made her escape.

***

Not long after the guys had woken and joined Lexie in the living area, Maggie stopped for gas. She pulled the glaringly obvious tour bus behind the gas station so they wouldn't be mobbed by fans. Lexie let Maggie know she was getting off to stretch her legs while they were pulled over. The last thing she wanted was to be accidentally left behind.

Grabbing her camera, she stepped down from the bus and walked a little way off. She turned as she heard the others getting off as well, all of them stretching after sitting on the bus for so long. She watched as Connor stretched his arms over his head, his shirt riding up and giving her a glimpse of hard, tanned abdominal muscles. Warmth suffused her and she dragged her eyes away.

Trying to distract herself, she turned and gazed off into the fields of corn that stretched out to the horizon on either side of the road. The day was overcast, but the rising sun turned the underside of the clouds almost violet, while the corn rippled like a green ocean in the light, fresh breeze. Inspired by the view, she raised her camera and took a couple of shots, then checked the results on the screen.

The sound of footsteps behind her caused her heart rate to spike, as if her body already knew how to tell Connor apart from everyone else.

"How does it look?"

His deep voice sent a shiver down her spine; she hoped it wasn't obvious. Turning and looking up into his vivid green eyes, she kept her camera held up between them as if it somehow offered protection from the effect he seemed to have on her. She smiled and looked back down at the screen. "Not bad. The nice thing about overcast days is there isn't much contrast, so the details are more visible. See?"

Before she could turn the camera around so he could see the screen, he moved next to her, his arm pressing against hers as he leaned down to look. Her traitorous heart skipped a beat, apparently not having received the memo that he wasn't the kind of man she should want.

"It's nice," Connor said. "A bit dark though." He raised

his brows at her, his eyes glinting with mischief.

"Well, I haven't done any post-processing yet."

"I don't know, Lexie; I think I could do better with my cell phone camera." His dimples appeared along with a teasing smile.

"Is that so?" she asked, pretending to be offended, but sure that the smile twitching at the corners of her mouth gave her away.

He nodded, his smile growing wider.

"Okay then," she said with mock seriousness, running her eyes up and down him as if assessing him. "Show me what you've got."

Deliberately misinterpreting her, he threw her a smoldering look. "Well, I'm not usually into exhibitionism, but I can make an exception if you really want to see—"

He laughed as she rolled her eyes and slapped his arm, which ended up backfiring as the feel of his rock-hard bicep made the skin of her palm tingle.

Still, two could play at the innuendo game.

She smirked at him. "Don't tell me you're all talk and no action. Whip it out and show me what you can do."

He raised one brow and eyed her up and down. "Well, if you insist gorgeous."

His hands went to the button of his jeans, and Lexie realized she wasn't going to win this one. From the grin on his face as he popped the button, he wasn't planning to be the first to back down. She stifled a slightly hysterical giggle as his fingers slowly started pulling the zip down, his eyes sparkling as he challenged her to react.

For a second, she couldn't stop her eyes tracking the movement of his hand, a breathless, curious part of her temporarily beating out her more sensible side. She wondered if he was wearing underwear or if he went commando. The overwhelming urge to let him keep going so she could find out, warred with the knowledge she should be stopping him before the joke went too far. The internal conflict made her bite her lip, eyes still locked on to where the zip was edging downward.

His hand stopped moving, and her eyes darted back up to his, which were now glittering with something other than humor. Tension flashed in the air between them as she realized she'd been staring at him like some sort of sex-starved groupie, which was embarrassing considering he'd just been messing around with her.

Coming to her senses, she shook her head and hoped she managed to come across as completely unaffected as she conceded defeat. "I meant your phone, Connor. There's no chance you'll take a better photo than me with what you're about to pull out."

The humor returned to his eyes, and he winked at her before pulling his zip back up and redoing the button. "Well, you should be more specific if you're going to say things like that. Right, let's see, then."

He pulled his phone out of his back pocket and tapped the screen to activate the camera, then squinted at it for a few seconds before taking the shot. He brought the phone back down so he could check the photo, and she saw him frown.

"How does it look?" she asked, as if she didn't know.

He glanced over at her, and she smiled innocently. He cleared his throat. "Just going to take another one. You know, to make sure I get the right atmosphere."

"Take as many as you want." She kept her expression

serene as he glanced at her out of the corner of his eye before snapping a couple more photos. When he checked those, he didn't appear any happier.

"Can I have a look?" she asked.

He mumbled something under his breath and then walked over to where she was standing watching him.

"Sorry, I didn't hear you. What did you say?" Lexie didn't try to hide her smile this time.

"I said it might be a bit harder than I thought."

She couldn't help but laugh when he thrust his phone under her nose. The photo was flat and dull, the colors muted. She looked up at him, ready to be a gracious winner, but her breath caught as they locked gazes. He was standing so close she could see tiny flecks of gold in the deep green of his eyes.

All it would take was for her to rise up on her tiptoes and for him to bend his head a little and she could press her lips to his. It was almost like he had the same thought because his eyes broke from hers and dropped to her mouth. The urge to do it was so strong she swayed toward him before she became aware of what she was doing. Flustered at her reaction, she took a small step backward.

His eyes met hers again, but his expression had shuttered, and she couldn't tell if he'd figured out what was running through her head. Regardless, she needed to pull herself together. She cleared her throat. "I can show you how to edit these if you want. Overcast lighting is really good, but it does need a bit more post-processing afterward to make it look great."

Something that looked strangely like uncertainty flashed across his face, but as she held his gaze and smiled in as friendly a manner as she could manage, he nodded. "It'll be a few more hours until we get to Denver, and I'd like to see you work your magic."

Maggie called out then, letting them know it was time to get on the road. Back at the bus, Lexie realized they were the last two to return. Everyone else was already ensconced in various areas of the living room.

"I'll get my laptop and I'll show you what we can do with those photos."

"Sounds good."

She returned a few minutes later and slid into the seat next to him at the table. "We'll do mine first, then yours. That way you can see what works best."

She transferred the photo from her camera to the laptop and opened it in Lightroom, the photo editing software she used. "So, the best thing about clouds is that they're basically a big sun diffuser. It makes the light soft and even, and there aren't any harsh shadows. But as you just found out, that also means photos tend to be duller, so you have to play with color and saturation in post-processing."

She played around with the sliders, explaining to Connor what she was doing and why. She always enjoyed teaching people about photography, especially when they seemed as interested as Connor did.

She worked on the photo for a couple of minutes, until she was happy with the deep green of the cornfields and the dramatic purple-gray of the clouds overhead. "What do you think now?" She turned to Connor and couldn't help the smile that bloomed across her face as he looked at the photo and then at her, admiration clear in his gaze.

"Stunning," was all he said, keeping his eyes locked on

hers.

She looked back down at the screen so he wouldn't see her blush. He was talking about the photo, not her, she reminded herself.

She could still feel his gaze on her as she went about saving her edited photo. His attention made her breathless, which was why it sounded even worse when she said without thinking, "Do you want me to do you now?" She closed her eyes when she realized how it sounded, particularly coming out all breathy the way it had. His low laugh ensured she knew he'd heard it too.

"I thought you'd never ask." His deep voice was full of deliberate innuendo, unlike hers which had been completely accidental.

Oh God, why did this keep happening to her? What was it about him that she couldn't seem to keep her physical reactions in check?

She shook her head at her own stupidity and then had to laugh. "Obviously, what I meant to say was how about I do your photos now?"

She peeked up at him and her heart rate accelerated at the smile that was curling his gorgeous lips. His eyes were warm as they did a slow perusal of her face, seeming to pay particular attention to her mouth, before landing back on her eyes.

"I think I liked it better the way it sounded the first time. But either way, I'd like to see how it turns out."

She rolled her eyes but smiled at him. He was way too sure about the effect he had on women, a total flirt, and far too sexy for her peace of mind. She was a grown woman though, and she could handle his teasing. Even enjoy it. It had been a long time since she'd felt the flush of attraction. Although she'd rather it hadn't been Connor that caused it, it was probably a good sign for her that she was able to feel it again.

She took his phone and loaded the photos onto her computer, then pushed the laptop toward him. "Actually, why don't you give it a go."

He didn't hesitate, and when he started playing with the different sliders, it was obvious he'd been paying attention to what she'd been showing him. While he was making adjustments, Noah strolled up and peered over his shoulder.

"Hey, that's pretty good. Don't tell me you're planning on a career change. There might be one or two fans who'd be a bit disappointed if you give it all up to run off and be a photographer."

Connor shot him a look Lexie couldn't interpret but then went straight back to editing the photo without replying. At Noah's words, Tex and Zac wandered over to watch as well. They all started commenting and making suggestions, but Connor seemed to tune them out, concentrating on the task at hand. She liked that about him. He knew his own mind; no bowing to peer pressure for him. Eventually the others wandered off again, leaving him to it.

He was doing a good job. It wasn't quite how she would have done it, but this wasn't about what she would do, it was about what he wanted. After all, that was the best thing about art—it was all about how it made *you* feel, not what other people thought of it.

When he was done, he sat back. "It's better than it was, but not as good as yours."

"Well, you did take it with a cell phone. As good as they

90

are these days, they're still not as good as a DSLR camera, particularly in low-light conditions like today. A DSLR has better resolution, better focusing, a bigger sensor, and a manual zoom instead of a digital zoom, among other things. All of which give better image quality."

"Yeah, yeah, I get it. I'll concede, you won." His mock grumbling tone shouldn't be sexy, but it was. Unfortunately, everything he did seemed to be sexy.

She was about to respond when his cell phone sitting on the table rang, and she saw Drew's name flash up. Drew was in one of the other buses traveling ahead of them. He didn't often call while they were in transit, preferring to talk to the guys in person once they got to the venue.

Connor leaned back against the bench seat as he answered. He stretched his arm out along the top of the seat, behind where she was sitting, his hand casually brushing the nape of her neck. She shivered. While the urge to stay still and enjoy his inadvertent touch was strong, she knew it wasn't a good idea. Instead, she leaned forward to save his photo and then close the editing program. She couldn't help but overhear Connor's side of the conversation as she did.

"Why can't he make it?"

"Shit, that fucking sucks."

"How far away is the hospital?"

"I don't want him to miss out—we'll make time before the show to go. We're almost there now, so bring the schedule forward, and we'll take a car. We'll make it back in time."

"Hang on a minute."

He covered the phone with his hand and called out to the others. "Hey, one of the kids can't make it to the show tonight; he's in hospital with a broken arm. Are you guys happy for us to head to the hospital before the show and see him? It'll be a little tight, but we should make it in time."

Tex, Noah, and Zac agreed, and Connor was straight back on the phone to Drew to let him know.

Lexie stared at him with wide eyes, a warmth in her chest which had nothing to do with how good-looking he was, and everything to do with the kind of man he was turning out to be. Physical attraction was one thing, but an emotional connection was something altogether different. She didn't want to start thinking of him as anything more than a rock star client who was easy on the eyes and fun to be around. She *definitely* did not want to start developing anything like feelings for him. She was still trying to get back on her feet when it came to men, and the last thing she needed was to develop an inappropriate crush. Her heart had been broken enough; she wasn't willing to have it happen again. And if there was one man in the world that was guaranteed to break a woman's heart, and had likely done so a thousand times before, it was Connor.

She closed her laptop with a snap while he was still talking to Drew. His eyes met hers, and he gave her a questioning look. Trying not to show how unsettled she felt, she flashed him a bright smile, then slid out of the booth and headed back to her room.

Chapter 13

Three weeks into the tour, and usually by this time Connor was starting to struggle with it all. Over the last few years, tours had started to become one big blur: concert after concert, city after city, interviews, and PR events. As much as he loved the music, he hadn't been able to shake his restlessness. The band had reached the peak of success, the kind of fame he'd always dreamed of, he just couldn't figure out why he felt so unsatisfied.

So far this tour, he hadn't felt anywhere near as frustrated as he had on previous tours. A soft laugh caught his attention, and he glanced across the bus to where Lexie was talking to Zac. And there was the reason. One very attractive, very off-limits photographer.

Her presence was effectively distracting him from his thoughts, and he was genuinely enjoying having her around. She was like a breath of fresh air and was amazingly tolerant of being stuck in a confined space with a bunch of arrogant and, he'd admit it, occasionally childish rock stars.

She could chat for hours with Tex about books, trade surprisingly inappropriate jokes with Noah, and sit in contented silence with Zac while he played his bass guitar and she edited photos on her laptop. Sometimes she'd go up to the front of the bus and curl up in the chair across from Maggie, keeping her company while miles of road passed under the wheels of the bus.

Unfortunately, he was finding himself more and more fascinated by her. He kept finding excuses to be near her, to talk to her, and increasingly he was finding excuses to touch her. Innocent touches, for the most part, an arm slung across the back of her chair, his fingers lingering on hers when she passed him something or sitting closer to her than strictly necessary.

He liked being around her. And it wasn't just how fucking sexy she was, or the way her smile lit up the room, it was also how smart and talented and compassionate she was. Lexie was one of those rare people that radiated warmth like sunshine wherever she went. But he was thinking about her way too much, spending far too much time imagining the things he'd like to do to her, how she'd feel naked underneath him, what would make her call out his name as she came.

Connor raked a hand through his hair and frowned as he watched Lexie standing next to Zac and talking to him as he tuned his bass. She was wearing a flirty green sundress that showed off her long, toned legs and dipped down across the top of her full breasts. She laughed at something Zac was telling her, before raising her camera and snapping a photo of him as he grinned lazily up at her. Unreasonably jealous, he gritted his teeth as Zac stood up and gave Lexie a one-armed hug.

Fuck.

This attraction was getting out of hand. He needed to get laid, and soon. Maybe then he'd stop thinking about her. It had been a while since he'd gone this long without sex, and it was doing his head in. While they'd stayed at hotels several times over the last few weeks, something had held him back from taking up the offers he'd received from fans and groupies. That something being this ridiculous infatuation with Lexie, which had so far been a huge mental cockblock.

He couldn't have her, but that didn't mean he had to be celibate for the rest of the tour. Maybe if he could release some sexual tension, it would reduce the lust he felt constantly when she was around. He forced his eyes away from Lexie and Zac. They were staying at a hotel the next night, and this time he was going to get laid.

***

Connor turned off the water, ending his post-concert shower. The buzz of conversation from the room next door told him it was already full of crew and fans. *And Lexie*, his mind whispered, knowing she'd be out there with her camera in hand, distracting him and making him want what he couldn't have.

He wrapped a towel around his waist, then wiped the condensation off the mirror over the sink and studied himself. He looked tired. He *felt* tired. And there were still two months of this to go. Well, time to get dressed and find someone to screw, he thought cynically.

Quickly dressing in dark jeans and a black fitted t-shirt, he left the dressing room and headed next door. It was packed as always, and he stopped to grab a beer before making his way over to where Tex was standing next to the food table, a half-naked red-haired woman hanging off him. A ripple of excitement washed through the room as he passed. Fans that had been waiting to see him jostled for position to approach or tried to maneuver into his line of sight.

"Hey, man." He stopped next to Tex and took a swig of his beer.

"Hey, dude. You're fashionably late. Did you just want to make a grand entrance?"

He shrugged. "Got to keep the fans waiting."

"Hi, I'm Amanda." The red-haired woman next to Tex held her hand out to him while she fluttered her fake lashes. He shook her hand but didn't introduce himself. She knew who he was; the way she held on to his hand a little too long proved that.

It was another thing he was starting to dislike about this life. Most of these women didn't care which band member they ended up with, as long as they got to tell their friends they'd fucked someone famous. If they couldn't get one of the band into bed, they'd go for the crew next. He knew he was a hypocrite because he took advantage of their willingness to be used, but there wasn't really much of an alternative, particularly when they were on the road.

As various fans sidled up to him to ask for his signature, his eyes scanned the room. He deliberately didn't look for Lexie, which had sadly become his normal modus operandi when he entered any room these days. Now he was just looking for someone hot enough to take his mind off her.

A dark-haired woman was standing off to the side and giving him serious eye. Hmm, maybe she'd do. Noticing his interest, she smiled seductively, but he averted his gaze when he realized she vaguely resembled Lexie. *Okay, looking for a blonde woman now.* Someone who looked nothing like Lexie.

His green eyes met a pair of sultry brown ones at the other end of the room. The woman was tall and stacked, with long blonde hair that tumbled over her shoulders and draped over her considerable cleavage. She stared him straight in the eye and skimmed her tongue across her lips in blatant invitation. Excusing himself from Tex and Amanda, who apparently saw his departure as the signal to start getting hot and heavy, Connor moved purposefully through the room toward the blonde.

By the time he arrived in front of her, she was almost hyperventilating in excitement, her breasts heaving with every breath. He kept his eyes firmly on her brown ones, trying not to stare at all the jiggling going on below her neck.

Up close, he could see she was quite pretty, if heavily made up. Her red dress was so tight it left absolutely nothing to the imagination. That wasn't something he'd ever thought he'd have a problem with, but images of flirty sundresses and slender, toned legs kept flitting through his mind.

"I'm Tiffany," she said breathily, holding out her hand.

He took it and squeezed. "Hi, Tiffany, how's it going?" Not the best pickup line he'd ever come out with, but she didn't seem to care. Her lashes fluttered, and she wet her lips with her tongue again before answering.

"It's going great now." She smiled flirtatiously.

"Did you like the show?"

"It was great. You were so fucking hot, if I'd been closer to the stage, I would have thrown my panties at you."

Connor gritted his teeth. This wasn't going quite as he'd hoped. He wouldn't normally have a problem with this kind of inane conversation, knowing they both knew where it was heading. But tonight, it wasn't quite doing the trick of getting his mind off a certain photographer. Who he still hadn't spotted in the crowd, though that was probably because he was forcing himself not to look for her.

He'd need to figure out the logistics of getting Tiffany back to the hotel with him too. Usually, the guys all got a limo back to the hotel together, along with any women they were bringing with them. They'd all been fairly restrained so far on this tour, with only Noah and Zac bringing women back the first time they'd stayed in one place overnight.

Having Lexie in the limo with them hadn't been great. In fact, it'd been embarrassing for everyone, except the two girls apparently, who'd been practically climbing all over Noah and Zac. Lexie had put the lens cap on her camera and stared resolutely out the window for the whole ride back. Which had been great for Connor, because he'd been able to stare at her pretty profile until he noticed Tex looking at him with raised eyebrows, so he'd quickly turned his attention elsewhere.

The next hotel stay, Lexie had suggested she could get a lift with Drew, but since none of them had ended up taking anyone back, they'd insisted she ride in the limo with them. No one had hooked up since, which must be some kind of record for all of them.

Well, the way Tex and Amanda were going at it in the corner, he might not be the only one breaking that dry spell tonight. Connor would have to have a word with Drew before they left to make sure he could give Lexie a ride back because he didn't want to have Tiffany climbing all over him while Lexie was sitting opposite.

Part of him didn't want Tiffany climbing all over him at all. But that part needed to shut the fuck up.

Okay, so he needed to get things moving here. He grabbed a chair that had become vacant next to him and pulled Tiffany down to sit on his lap. She giggled and nuzzled up against his throat. He ran his hand up her leg, skimming it under the hem of her skirt. She inhaled sharply and then reached down and grabbed his cock, rubbing and kneading enthusiastically.

Christ. He gritted his teeth. The manual stimulation was doing the job, but it was hardly the most erotic experience he'd ever had.

Suddenly, the crowd in front of him parted, and he saw Lexie for the first time that night. She was standing next to Noah, who had his arm draped over her shoulders. She was mid-laugh at something he'd said to her, her eyes shining, and her camera held halfway up to her face as if she'd been about to take a photo when he'd made her laugh.

He should have looked away, but he didn't, and as she turned her head slightly, their eyes met. Her laugh started to morph into one of her heart-stopping smiles when she suddenly noticed what was happening on his lap.

Her smile faltered as her eyes dropped down to where his hand was currently located under Tiffany's skirt, and then to where Tiffany's hand was. Lexie's eyes widened and shot back up to his, a flash of what looked suspiciously like hurt crossing her delicate features. She quickly plastered a smile back on her face, then turned away, raising her camera and taking a photo of what appeared from his angle to be some random person's back.

Connor froze after seeing the expression on Lexie's face. She *had* looked hurt; he wasn't imagining it. There was only one reason for her to be hurt by what he was doing—she wanted him too. His mind started to race.

Fuck it. He didn't want to go through with this plan anymore; didn't want to try to distract himself from Lexie. Screw doing the right thing. Screw his agreement with the other guys. That'd been before he'd started wanting her so much. If he explained the situation to her—if she knew they could only have one night—then maybe he could actually have *her*.

His cock, which had reluctantly risen to half-mast under Tiffany's ministrations, surged to rock hard in an instant at the thought.

He'd have to do some damage control after what she'd seen, but he figured Lexie wouldn't be too upset as long as he didn't take Tiffany back to the hotel. After all, having fans and groupies all over you was one of those things you couldn't avoid, right?

He yanked his hand out from underneath Tiffany's skirt, then grabbed her hand where it was wedged between them and pulled it away. "I'm so sorry, gorgeous, I've just seen my manager waving me over. He probably needs to talk business, so I've got to go. You understand, don't you?" It was times like this he purposefully made his Irish accent stronger. Women seemed to find it irresistible, and as much as he'd lost any interest he'd had in Tiffany, he also didn't want to hurt or embarrass her.

She nodded up at him, her big brown eyes looking disappointed, so he pressed a quick kiss to her lips to make up for it. Some women would have made a huge scene if he tried to leave them, so he'd got lucky. He lifted her off him, gave her hand a final squeeze, and began moving through the crowd to try to find Lexie. He searched for a few minutes, but when he couldn't find her, he grabbed Noah instead.

"Hey, where did Lexie go?"

"Drew asked her if she wanted a lift back to the hotel. I saw them head out a few minutes ago," he said, not noticing the frustration on Connor's face.

The adrenaline of the last few minutes seeped out of Connor's body, and he started coming back to his senses. What was he thinking? The reasons he hadn't wanted to mess with Lexie in the first place were still valid. What were the chances she'd want to hook up for just one night? Slim to none; she wasn't the type. He was fairly sure he could talk her into his bed if he tried, but he didn't want to fuck around with her and then potentially have it ruin the rest of the tour. It was too late to get another photographer, and he loved what Lexie had done with her photos so far. She was easy to be around and had developed a great rapport with everyone. She was one in a million, and he'd be stupid to throw that all away just to have her for one night.

He scrubbed his hands over his face and groaned. He couldn't even be bothered trying to track Tiffany down again. His plan to distract himself from Lexie by screwing another woman had just crashed and burned. At least for tonight, anyway.

"Do you want to get out of here?" he asked Noah, who nodded and finished off his beer.

"Let's go."

Chapter 14

Drew walked Lexie back to her hotel room. "Is everything okay? You were pretty quiet on the way back." Concern pinched his brows together.

"Just a long day." She rubbed her temples where they'd started throbbing.

"Do you need any painkillers? We carry a whole stash with us."

She shook her head. "No, thanks, I've got some in my room. I'll take a couple and go to bed. It should be gone in the morning."

Drew studied her face as she rummaged for her room key. He cleared his throat. "Lexie, do you remember what I told you during the first concert?"

Finding the key, she pulled it from her purse before turning to him. "Yes," she said warily.

"Look, I know you were upset about what I said then, which I'm sorry about. But I hope you know that I was looking out for you, as well as the band." Lexie nodded slowly, wondering where he was going with this. "These guys are my friends. I've got to know them well over the last few years, and they're good guys. But when it comes down to it, they're still rock stars. They're not used to being told they can't have something. Which sometimes means their inner toddler comes out. If you tell them they can't have something, it just makes them want it more."

"I understand," she said, just wanting him to stop talking so she could retreat to her room.

He sighed. "What I'm saying is, just look after yourself, okay. Don't let the guys get to you, or at least don't let them know they're getting to you. They'll just want to do it more."

Finally, he finished, gave her a swift kiss on the cheek, and wandered back down the hallway to his room closest to the elevator.

Gratefully, Lexie opened her door, switched on the light, and then closed and locked it behind her. She walked over to her bed and slumped down on it, toeing off her shoes.

She didn't want to think about why she'd reacted so badly to seeing Connor with that woman. Yes, she found him very attractive, and yes, she enjoyed being around him. But she enjoyed being around all the guys; they were a lot of fun.

Maybe it was because she hadn't seen him do anything like that since she'd been on tour with them, and she'd become complacent. Spending so much time around him, she'd almost started seeing him as just a man—an incredibly hot man admittedly—but that wasn't who he really was, was it?

Too tired to shower, she changed into her pajamas and then wandered over to the bar to pour herself some water to take her painkillers. When she heard voices in the hallway, she paused, straining to identify who it was. It sounded like Connor and Noah.

She listened hard to see if she could hear any female voices, but there was nothing. Did that mean he hadn't brought that woman home with him? Or had she just been rendered mute by the anticipation of sleeping with Connor?

She held her breath as she heard Noah's door open and close and then what sounded like a single pair of footsteps getting closer. So, Connor hadn't brought the woman back with him.

His footsteps slowed as he approached her door, and Lexie's heart rate sped up. Was there a chance he was going to stop and knock? She wasn't sure if it was a good idea to have him in her bedroom right now. Her pajamas didn't leave much to the imagination, and she was still figuring out how she felt about what she'd seen tonight.

She didn't end up having to make the decision though, because he kept on walking, and then she heard his door open and close. Letting out a deep breath, she switched off the lights and climbed under the bedcovers.

The fact that she felt happy about Connor coming home alone—and let's be honest, slightly disappointed that he hadn't knocked on her door—did not bode well for her sanity. She still had two more months of this tour to get through.

Closing her eyes, she willed herself to go to sleep, but her brain kept insisting on replaying the image of Connor with that woman sitting on his lap. She knew it was wrong to feel jealous. There was nothing between them except a working relationship, and maybe the start of a friendship.

She shouldn't be feeling this attracted to him, but it was hard not to. If he was just a gorgeous face and a hot body, then she could have dealt with it. But he was more than that. He was talented and funny and generous, which ridiculously unfair. And the way she felt when she was around him? Like everything inside her lit up. When he pinned her with his green eyes, that intense look on his face as if he could see all her innermost thoughts and feelings, it made her breathless.

She needed to get rid of those feelings and get her jealousy under control. There was nothing between them, and she didn't want to spend the rest of the tour getting upset whenever he touched another woman. Confused and frustrated, it was a long time before she managed to get to sleep.

***

The next morning, after having tossed and turned all night as a result of vaguely remembered dreams, Lexie told herself that she needed to get a grip and stop putting Connor on some kind of pedestal. He was a man, like any other. Well, that wasn't exactly true considering how he'd been genetically blessed in both the looks and talent department. But he had the same wants and needs as any other man, and imagining that he would somehow be above messing around with the willing women that threw themselves at him was extreme naivety on her part.

What he did, with whomever he wanted to do it with, had nothing to do with her. She needed to keep that fixed in her mind and not let her feelings about it change the relationship between them.

So, when she saw him down at breakfast, she made sure her smile and greeting were as warm as normal. After grabbing some fruit from the buffet, she wandered over to the table the guys were sitting at. Since there was only one empty seat, she didn't have much choice but to slide in next to Noah, and opposite Connor. Tex and Zac were sitting on the same side as Connor, while Drew sat on the other side of Noah.

The ever-affectionate drummer immediately draped his arm around her shoulders and kissed her on the cheek. "Good morning, beautiful!"

"Morning, Noah." She couldn't help but smile back at him. He was such an outgoing guy, as excitable and enthusiastic about everything as a golden retriever puppy.

Sliding her eyes back in Connor's direction, she found him staring resolutely out the window at the end of the table with a stormy expression on his face, his jaw noticeably tense. She craned her neck to see out the window, curious as to what had upset him, but couldn't see anything obvious.

Without thinking, she reached across the table and lightly placed her hand over his, which he'd clenched in reaction to whatever had pissed him off.

"Connor, is everything okay?" She said it quietly, not wanting to draw the attention of everyone at the table, who'd all gone back to talking animatedly about something or other.

Connor's gaze went to where her hand rested on top of his. For a second, he didn't say or do anything, and she couldn't get a good look at his expression because his eyes were hidden by his dark lashes.

Worried that he was annoyed at her touching him, she was about to pull back when he suddenly turned his hand over and clasped hers. At last, he raised his gaze so that his now clear green eyes met hers and held, as his thumb began stroking the soft skin on the back of her hand. The slight roughness caused by the guitar string callouses on his fingers enhanced the sensation.

She couldn't help the shiver that ran through her. He stilled briefly before resuming the movement and she knew he'd noticed her reaction.

Oh God. She really needed to pull her hand away from his. Especially after last night and her resolution from this morning, but she couldn't quite bring herself to do it. Connor's eyes began making a lazy perusal of her face, as if cataloging every inch of skin, every freckle on her nose, before dropping to her mouth. His intense scrutiny was nerve-wracking, and without thinking about how it might look, she licked her lips to moisten them. His eyes flashed back up, burning into hers.

Not sure what to do, Lexie froze, her heart hammering inside her chest. Part of her wanted to run and hide from the intensity in his eyes, and part of her wanted to climb over the table and crawl into his lap.

The visual of that scenario shocked her back to reality, especially with the vivid memory of another woman sitting in his lap just last night. A woman almost the complete opposite of Lexie. Had that woman felt the same as she did right now? Had he made her feel like she was the only person in the room, just like he was doing to her?

Feeling exposed, sure that her wide eyes must be broadcasting her every thought and feeling, she broke his gaze and looked down at the table. She tugged her hand out of his and placed both of her hands in her lap, so he wouldn't notice them tremble.

After taking a deep breath, embarrassment swept through her. She was acting like a naïve virgin having her hand held by a boy for the first time. She was a strong, smart woman. She'd been married for God's sake! She remembered what Drew had said the night before, about the guys wanting something more if they thought they couldn't have it. Was that what was happening here?

Frustrated at her overthinking of the whole situation, she jerked her eyes back up to face him, only to see him looking out the window again, this time with a small smile on his infuriatingly gorgeous face.

Lexie blew out a breath, gave herself a mental shake and a stern talking-to about keeping her hands to herself from now on, then tuned back into the conversation underway at the table. The guys were trying to decide what to do for the rest of the day. Since everything had been set up at the venue the day before, they only needed to be back in time for the final soundcheck later that afternoon, so they had several free hours. Noah, Zac, and Drew were tossing around ideas, but both Tex and Connor were silent. Connor, because he was still staring out the window with a smug expression on his face, and Tex because he had pulled out one of his books and started reading.

An idea popped into Lexie's head, and she smiled to herself. "Hey, Tex?"

Everyone stopped what they were doing and turned to her. She made sure not to let her eyes stray to Connor's. "Can I steal you for a few hours this morning?"

Tex's eyebrows rose, and he blinked at her lazily. "You can do anything you want with me, honey."

She could see the humor in his whiskey-colored eyes, so she knew not to take him seriously. Sensing the sudden stillness emanating from Connor's direction, her devilish side made her smile seductively at Tex and purr in her huskiest voice, "Then I need you to take me somewhere we can be all alone."

She couldn't stop the giggle that escaped her at the five shocked faces staring back at her. Then a big grin spread over Tex's sinfully handsome features as he stood, pushed his chair back, and walked around the table to hold out his hand to her.

"What are we waiting for then darlin'? I'm all yours."

Lexie gave everyone still sitting at the table a big smile as she stood up, then looked directly at Connor as she reached for Tex's hand. If she'd been a better person, the confusion in his eyes wouldn't have been quite so satisfying, but no one's perfect, right?

Chapter 15

Tex had scrounged up a car from somewhere, and he and Lexie were driving around the seedier downtown area looking for something that Lexie had told him she'd know when she saw.

Drew had tried to insist they take security with them, but Tex had firmly declined. She'd noticed a distinct glint in his eye as she gave him a list of things she needed him to do before they left. The list included getting changed into leather pants and a white shirt, finding a spare guitar to take with them, and bringing one of his books. He seemed to be enjoying himself, even though she wouldn't tell him what she was planning.

Now, as they cruised the back streets, Tex regaled her with crazy stories of the things the band had got up to when they were younger. Lexie loved hearing all about their meteoric rise to fame, and the escapades they'd all got up to. They also talked about favorite movies and books. And when Tex confessed his guilty secret to her, she made an immediate emergency stop at the first bookshop she found.

Eventually she spotted what she was looking for: a grungy bar that appeared to have just opened for the day. Parking out the front, Lexie told Tex to stay in the car while she scoped the place out, but he ignored her, saying he didn't want her wandering around in that kind of dive on her own. Shrugging, she figured it wasn't the most likely place for him to get inundated by fans wanting him to sign autographs. They both got out of the car, made their way to the bar, and pushed through the swinging door into the dingy interior.

"It's perfect!" Lexie grinned, looking around at the dirty walls and carpet, stained wooden tables and chairs, and the light practically having to force its way through the dirt-encrusted windows. A rough-looking older man was behind the bar eyeing them curiously. Lexie went over to talk to him.

"Hi, I was wondering if you could do me a huge favor?" He just raised his eyebrows at her and kept on chewing a toothpick sticking out of the corner of his mouth. Lexie pulled some cash out of her purse. "Since there's no one else here yet, how would you like to earn $50 for letting me take a few photos of my friend?"

The man glanced over at Tex in his leather pants and white shirt, buttons open almost to the navel. "This porn?" he grunted. Lexie's shocked laugh caught Tex's attention, and he wandered over.

Still laughing, Lexie replied, "No, just an impromptu photo shoot for my friend." She lowered her voice conspiratorially. "He's a musician."

The man gave Tex a once-over. "Would I know any of your music?"

"Probably not." Tex smiled smoothly back at him.

The man stopped caring at that point and plucked the money from Lexie's hand. She then set about moving tables and chairs around, trying to get things set up just right. She asked Tex to go out to the car and bring in his guitar and her tripod that she'd put in the back seat, as well as the book she'd purchased on the way there. By the time he'd come back, she'd bought a cheap bottle of whiskey and put it on the table next to a glass.

After he gave her the tripod, she set it up facing the table and chair which she'd moved to sit in the single shaft of light coming in the dirty window, so that they almost seemed lit by a spotlight.

Finished fiddling with her camera, she turned with a big smile on her face to get Tex and ran smack into a wall of muscle. Shocked, she stared up into Tex's tawny eyes. His serious expression made her smile fade, and before she knew what was happening, he'd put his hands on her upper arms and tugged her closer so that her body was flush against his. Surprised and confused, Lexie didn't resist, but when his eyes dropped to her mouth and he moved one hand up to cradle the back of her head, she realized what he was intending.

Frozen and unsure how to respond, unable to deny she was curious as to how it would feel, she didn't resist as he tipped her head back. He paused, giving her time to protest, and when she didn't, he leaned down and pressed his mouth to hers.

Lexie didn't move except to bring her hands up to his chest, though whether to push him away or pull him closer she wasn't sure. He'd taken her completely by surprise. She thought he'd been joking every time he made a comment about getting her alone. The devilish glint that always seemed to reside in his eyes probably hadn't helped.

It was her first kiss in three years, and she braced herself against the familiar pang of guilt, but when it came, it wasn't as strong as she expected. Instead, she focused on how nice the intimacy felt. This was one of the things that she'd missed since Damien's death. The touch of a man, the feeling of being desired, things she'd experienced every day since she and Damien had started dating.

And she wasn't going to lie, the man could kiss.

A slow warmth spread from where Tex's lips were pressed against hers, radiating right through her body. But that's all it was—the warmth of being touched and held close by an attractive man. There was no fire in it, no static on her skin, nothing sparking deep inside her.

Tex was a very sexy man, and an incredible musician, but he wasn't the man that made her breathless with one look, whose touch caused goosebumps to break out on her skin. Tex must have realized it too, because he broke the kiss quickly, looking down at her face with his gorgeous eyes sparkling.

"Sorry, darlin', I didn't mean to take you by surprise, but I had to know."

She shook her head in confusion. "Had to know what?"

"You're a beautiful woman, Lexie, inside and out. I like being around you. One day I'm planning to meet the love of my life, get married, and have a family. I just needed to find out if you might be the one." He shrugged, his deep voice a little wistful. "But you're not mine, are you?"

She put her hand on his arm and squeezed. "You really are a romantic, aren't you? I'd love to meet her when you find her, Tex. She's going to be quite a woman. I think she'll be someone I'd like to know." Then she felt stupid for saying that, since she'd be ancient history by the time he met her.

Saddened by the thought, she wrapped her arms around

his broad chest and hugged him. "I'm flattered you considered me though."

He nodded. "At least it was worth the black eye I'll probably get for kissing you."

"What do you mean?"

"Connor will probably punch me for kissing you."

Lexie's heart sped up. Did he mean that Connor would be jealous? But Tex's next words disabused her of that notion.

"Yeah, I shouldn't really mention it, but Connor made us all agree that none of us would make a move on you since you're kind of important for the photo book. He doesn't want any of us messing with you."

Feeling stupidly deflated that Connor would only care because they'd made some kind of boys' club promise not to bang the photographer, she started to turn away from him to recheck her camera.

Tex was obviously more attuned to her emotions than she thought because he caught her arm and turned her back toward him. He looked into her eyes and must have seen something because he nodded to himself. "Connor's had a rough life. It means he keeps people at a distance. Something's had him down for a while, and he won't tell me what it is. I've seen a change in him recently though, there's more of the old Connor there. Not the one from a couple of years back, but the one I remember as a kid. He's all fired up about something. The photo book's important to him for some reason, which makes you important to him too." He paused, still studying her eyes. "Your photos might not end up being the most important thing about you though."

"What do you mean?" she asked, a frown creasing her brow.

But he'd apparently said all he was going to say, because he just shrugged, grinned, and strolled over to the table and chair. "Let's get this done before the regulars show up."

Feeling frustrated, but realizing he was right, she got him posed.

He was sitting in the chair, which was tilted back, with his long legs propped up on the table. His guitar, the bottle of whiskey, and a half-full glass were on the table next to him. With his long golden-brown hair, two-day growth, and thickly lashed bedroom eyes, he looked like a sexy pirate king, lit by the shaft of light coming in the window.

The best part was the book he was reading as he reclined lazily in the chair. It wasn't the one he'd brought with him from the hotel because the guilty secret he'd revealed to her on their drive was that he enjoyed reading good old bodice rippers. The cover of the book that he held in his large hand showed, fittingly, a swarthy dark-haired pirate holding a petite black-haired, blue-eyed maiden hard against his chest as they stared lustily into each other's eyes.

The setup was perfect—his fans were going to die when they saw this photo. Lexie couldn't stop smiling. She was happy, doing what she loved doing, and she was finally able to push thoughts of Connor out of her mind. Well, mostly.

Chapter 16

Connor was trying to write a song in his hotel room but couldn't concentrate. Every time he heard voices, or the elevator door open, he would pause head up, ears straining to hear if it was Tex and Lexie coming back from wherever they'd gone that morning.

When he heard Tex's deep drawl and Lexie's soft laugh, he shot to his feet and strode to the door. He was about to throw it open and demand to know where they'd been but realized just before he did exactly how irrational he was being. He had no claim on Lexie. No right to tell her she couldn't spend time with Tex. So instead of barging out into the hallway demanding answers, he stood as close as he could to the door without actually pressing his ear against it. Because it wasn't eavesdropping if you just happened to be standing in earshot, right?

He heard the deep rumble of Tex's voice. "Thanks, Lexie. I had a real good time with you. Though I still think it would have been better with less clothes on."

He tensed at Tex's words and edged closer to hear Lexie's soft reply.

"Well, sometimes the more clothes you keep on the sexier it is. Don't worry, you gave me exactly what I needed."

Connor's eyes widened. Son of a bitch! Irrational or not, he was about to break Tex's fucking nose.

He was just about to throw open the door and take a swing when his brain processed the rest of what Lexie was saying. "I can't wait to see how the photos turn out."

Connor sagged against the wall. He was a fucking idiot. Of course they had just been taking photos. He scrubbed his hands over his face. What the hell was wrong with him? He could hear Tex and Lexie's low voices still talking, and while he wanted to hear what they were saying to each other, he forced himself to walk away and go back to his futile attempt at songwriting.

A few minutes later, there was a banging on the door. He knew from the heavy thumps that it was Tex, so he took his time going over to answer it. Opening the door, he kept a neutral expression on his face and tried to keep it cool, while surreptitiously checking the hallway for Lexie, who wasn't visible. "Hey, man, what's up?"

A big grin spread over Tex's face. Apparently, he hadn't been successful at appearing uninterested.

"So, are you going to invite me in, or do you want to do this in the hallway?"

Connor frowned. "Do what?"

Tex just waited in silence, still with that shit-eating grin on his face. Sighing, Connor stepped back from the doorway, letting Tex walk past him into the room. After closing the door, Connor turned and followed him into the living area, then stood with his arms crossed, waiting for Tex to say whatever it was he wanted to say.

Instead of spilling, Tex reached down to the coffee table where Connor had left his guitar, picked it up, and started casually strumming it with his head lowered.

Connor's jaw clenched. What the hell was Tex's deal? Just as he was about to demand to know what was going on, Tex raised his head, and with a small smile on his face said in his deep Southern drawl, "I kissed Lexie this morning. Just wanted to let you know since we had that agreement and all."

There was a roaring in Connor's ears, and the slightly murderous feeling he'd had when he was listening at the door came back full force. His eyes narrowed, and his fists clenched.

Tex held up Connor's guitar and continued. "Thought this might be insurance against you punching me."

A dull pain cut through Connor's fury. If he didn't know better, he might have thought it was hurt. He clenched his hands harder to stop himself giving in to the anger and landing a fist right in the middle of Tex's face. "What the fuck, Tex?" he gritted out from between clenched teeth.

Tex searched his face as if he could read on it exactly what Connor was feeling. Then he said, "She didn't kiss me back. I'm not her type, I guess. She was cool about it though. I'm not going to lie, I was hoping something might come of it, but I guess she's not meant for me."

Connor's tense muscles unclenched as relief washed through him. She hadn't kissed Tex back? Did that mean she didn't want him, or just that she was more professional than Tex was? He tried to tell himself that his anger was just over concern that Lexie would get hurt and break her contract by leaving, but that was a lie. He wanted her for himself. Knowing Tex had already made a move and been knocked back didn't help the situation.

There was no way he could have her. He already knew he couldn't offer her the things a woman like her needed. A night in his bed might be enough for most of the women he associated with, but someone like Lexie would want more, and he wasn't willing or able to give it. He just needed to screw his head back on, suck it up, and get through the rest of the tour keeping his hands to himself. Then when she was gone, he'd finally be able to put her out of his mind, and things would go back to normal.

"So, are we cool, man?" Tex asked.

Connor rolled his eyes, the tension leaving his body. It was hard to stay mad at his best friend. Especially now that he knew Lexie hadn't been interested.

He smirked. "Hopefully the sting of rejection will teach you a lesson. But from now on, keep your fucking hands to yourself!"

Tex nodded and raised both hands in the air. "Hands off, I promise."

Shaking his head, Connor wandered over to the bar and poured them both a drink. Newly found resolve or not, there wasn't enough alcohol in the world that was going to make it easier to get through the rest of the tour.

***

A week later, they were in Indianapolis. Connor was watching Lexie take photos of the catwalk being set up from where he sat on the drums' riser. She was dressed in a pair of frayed cutoffs that cupped her ass, and a silky white tank top that clung to her full breasts. Just watching her moving gracefully around as she worked had him half hard.

Things hadn't improved over the last week. All he could think about was walking over there, pinning her up against the nearest vertical surface, and kissing the living hell out of her. He could almost imagine the noises she'd make when he finally got a taste. Groaning, he scrubbed his face with his hands. Being around her—wanting what he couldn't have— was becoming torture.

He wasn't used to feeling this way, like a schoolboy lusting after his high school crush. Normally, he just took his pick of the women throwing themselves at him. Just a way to scratch an itch. With Lexie, he could look but not touch, and it was driving him mad. He couldn't remember the last time he'd spent a long period with a woman he liked, as well as wanted to sleep with.

Whenever they were in the same room, his eyes were drawn to her. When she wasn't in sight, he wondered where she was and what she was doing. During their concerts, he looked for her in the crowd.

Since she'd joined them on tour, he hadn't had a single hookup, and things were starting to get dire. His attempt to sleep with a random woman to get rid of some of that pent-up lust had failed and trying again now just seemed wrong, since he knew he'd be thinking of Lexie the whole time. The shower was getting a good workout that was for sure, either for taking care of his needs or just hosing himself down with cold water.

Now he was watching her when he should have been using his downtime to work on the new album. So, he noticed when Joe, one of the lighting techs, wandered over to talk to her. Lexie turned as he approached her and gave him one of her trademark gorgeous smiles. Connor clenched his jaw; unreasonably jealous it wasn't him she was smiling at.

From this angle, he couldn't see Joe's face, so he wasn't able to take a guess as to what the man was saying, but the expression on Lexie's face caused him to sit up straight. Her smile dropped, and she gave a tiny shake of her head. He couldn't hear what they were saying, but he saw Joe reach for her hand. She let him take it, but her body stiffened. She shook her head again and then gently tugged her hand away.

Connor stood.

He didn't know what the conversation was about, but Lexie looked upset, so he was going to find out and put a stop to it if he needed to.

As he started toward them, Joe gave a slight shrug, then turned and walked off, looking disappointed. Lexie put her fingers up to her mouth, her eyes wide and hurt. Before he could get to her, she spun on her heel and walked quickly to a side door, pulling it open and slipping through.

Connor broke into a jog, grabbed the door just before it swung shut, and followed her through. They were in one of the large rooms used to store various pieces of sports equipment. There were no windows, the only light coming in through the cracks around several doors.

"Lexie!" he called out to her. "Lexie! Where are you, baby?" The endearment came out without any thought on his part, but he didn't care. He just wanted to find her and try to fix whatever was wrong.

He heard a muffled sob from the back of the room and made his way through the equipment until he found her sitting against the wall, head hanging, her dark hair hiding her face from him. Crouching down in front of her, he reached for her chin, lifting it gently so he could see her face. Her eyes were closed, but her eyelashes were spiked with tears and her cheeks were wet.

"Lexie," he murmured, "what's wrong, sweetheart?" At last, her eyes opened, and she gazed up at him. His heart stuttered. She looked like she'd been wounded, her eyes large silver pools of misery. Even as he watched, fresh tears welled up and overflowed, dripping down her cheeks. In a low voice, he gritted out, "What did he say to you, Lexie. If he said something to hurt you, I swear I'll walk out there and kick his ass right this minute."

Looking aghast, she shook her head quickly. "Connor, no, please it wasn't anything he said."

"Then what is it? I want to help, baby, but I need you to tell me what's wrong."

She shook her head again and tried to look down, but he wouldn't let her. "It's my husband," she whispered.

His heart stopped and then began pounding in his chest. Her husband? *What. The. Fuck*? "You're married?" Connor's voice rasped as he asked.

She nodded, then immediately shook her head. "No, not anymore."

His heart finally started working properly again. He kept silent and let her keep talking.

"I don't usually like to tell people—it's difficult for me to talk about. But sometimes it just hits me hard. He died. Damien, my husband." She brushed a tear away from her cheek. "Three years ago. It was a car accident."

Jesus Christ, she was a widow. Connor felt like he'd been sucker-punched. Letting go of her chin, he moved to sit on the floor next to her, putting his arm around her shoulders and gathering her against him. The irony of the fact that he was finally getting to hold her, and it was only to comfort her over the death of her husband, wasn't lost on him.

From the protection of his arms, Lexie kept talking.

"I loved him more than anything in the world. We'd only been married two years when it happened, but we'd been together since high school. After he died, I felt like the world would never be the same again, that *I* would never be the same again. I was so grief-stricken I could barely function, and it felt like there was nothing good left for me in this life." She sighed and wiped at her cheeks. "But then I started to realize that I owed it to him to live my life to the fullest. To have all the experiences he wouldn't be able to. I pulled myself out of it and started trying to fully experience every moment.

"That's why my photography is so important to me. It lets me travel to places I never would have thought to go, meet people I'd never have a chance to meet, and try to capture it on film for everyone else who doesn't have the same opportunity. It helps me cope." She paused, then took a deep breath. "But I haven't been able to…" Another pause. "To be with anyone since he died." She sniffed and wiped her cheeks again.

"I keep telling myself that I'll be able to move on soon. That I just need a bit more time, that I'll say yes, the next time a man asks me out. But every time someone does, all the pain and heartbreak come rushing back and I panic."

She tilted her head to look up at him and smiled sadly, the sheen of tears enhancing the soft gray of her eyes, and his heart thumped hard in his chest. Shit, this woman was dangerous. He didn't want to start developing feelings for her. And he absolutely did not want to complicate his life with something that would inevitably end up messy. Particularly since she was obviously still in love with her husband.

"So, is that what happened with Joe? He asked you out?"

She nodded. "He was very sweet, the kind of guy I should go out with, but I just can't bring myself to say yes. And I worry that maybe I'm broken, that I'll never be able to be with anyone ever again, and it terrifies me. I don't want to be alone for the rest of my life."

Connor sat quietly for a few minutes, just holding her and gently stroking his hand up and down the soft skin of her arm. When he'd gathered his thoughts, he started to talk.

"You're not broken, Lexie, not by a long shot. I've got to know you fairly well over the last few weeks, and I can honestly say I've never met a person with more love to share with the world than you. But grief, it's not something that you can control or put a time limit on. People talk about the stages of grief as if you can just step through them one by one, and then when you reach the end, you'll feel better. That's not how it works. It's different for everyone, and sometimes it can last months and sometimes it can last years. And sometimes it does leave scars that will never fully heal."

He paused, and her stillness told him she was listening closely to his words. "I don't know if you know this, but my mom died when I was eleven."

She flinched slightly, and then she was babbling. "I'm so sorry, Connor. I did know that, and I can't believe I was crying all over you when you went through—"

She tried to move away from him, but he didn't let her go. He pulled her back against his chest and stroked his hand down her silky hair. "Shh, baby, that's not what I was getting at." He waited until she relaxed back against his chest.

Connor didn't know why, but being in the dark with Lexie nestled against him felt almost like being in a confessional. Like he could finally share something that had weighed him down for the last seventeen years. "I've never told anyone this before, but when my mom died, I wanted to die too. It was cancer that killed her. Seeing her struggle to stay strong for me and dad while she faded away, broke my heart. When she died, my grief was so bad, I prayed to God to take me too." Lexie made a small noise of sympathy but didn't interrupt him. "And what made it worse was that when I needed my dad the most, he turned away from me; too caught up in his own grief to want to deal with mine."

Connor felt rather than heard Lexie suck in a sharp breath, but he kept going, needing to get it out. "His love for her was so consuming, he didn't have room in his heart for anyone else, not even me. He completely shut me out."

He could hear the pain and bitterness in his voice and clamped down hard on the emotions, annoyed that his father's rejection still had the power to hurt him after all these years. "I think I reminded him too much of my mom, especially when I started playing music. She was a music teacher, and I played to feel closer to her, but I had to practice outside the house so he couldn't hear me. He hated it."

As he spoke, Lexie's fingers had begun gently stroking over the skin of his bicep, just under the edge of his t-shirt sleeve. He didn't think she even knew she was doing it; it was just a subconscious soothing gesture. The feel of her fingertips smoothing over his skin was doing crazy things to his body, but he tried to concentrate on what he was saying.

"When I was about thirteen, I fell in with the wrong crowd. It could have gone pretty badly for me then, I won't lie, but my dad shook off his self-absorption enough to do what was, in hindsight, the very best thing he could've done, which was pack me up and send me to the US to live with my aunt. Luckily, she's amazing. She helped me pull myself out of the pain I was in at what was basically the loss of both of my parents."

Suddenly he realized that the tremors he could feel coming from Lexie's slender frame in his arms were caused by fresh tears.

"I'm not telling you this to make you cry, baby. I'm trying to show you that you're not broken, not at all. Unlike my dad, you've picked yourself up and made sure that you're living your best life. You're paying tribute to your husband's life, not letting his death destroy yours. Your heart is so full of love to give that it spills over into everything you do—that's why everyone loves being around you. And when the time is right, when your heart is healed enough, when the perfect man comes along, you'll give all that love to him. And I'm sure he'll spend the rest of his life counting his lucky stars."

When he finished, Lexie raised her head and looked into his eyes, her own beautiful gray ones looking almost luminescent in the faint light. He would have given almost anything at that moment to bend his head and press his lips against hers, but he couldn't. As much as he might desire her, he wasn't the right man to help her get over her broken heart. He had nothing to offer her other than a night in his bed, and that would probably only end up hurting her more, which was the last thing he wanted.

Even as he tried talking sense into himself, he was fast losing his resolve not to kiss her. Just when he was about to throw caution to the wind, she raised her hand and rested her cool fingers on the side of his face. Her eyes searched his, a small furrow between her brows. "Connor, have you been in love before?"

He flinched in shock. Had he somehow given her the wrong idea? Did she think he was falling in love with her? His heart rate accelerated. That was a complication he didn't need. His tone was sharp when he answered. "No, I've never been in love. What's the point when I can have a different woman every night?"

His arms, which had been wrapped around her, loosened in preparation of her pushing away from him. But she didn't. Instead, she cocked her head to the side, her eyes still searching his, then she nodded to herself.

"I'm so sorry for what you went through, Connor. I'm sorry you lost your mom. And I'm so sorry that your dad hurt you. Love should never be selfish like that. Thank you for being so kind to me tonight. It means a lot."

Reaching up, she gave him a soft kiss on the cheek and then used his shoulders to push herself up to stand. She held out her hand to him, and without thinking, he stood and took it. They walked back to the door with her still holding his hand, but when they got there, she just gave it a quick squeeze before dropping it, opening the door, and slipping out.

He stood there in the dark for a second, wondering why he suddenly felt so hollow. He didn't know if it was reliving the pain of his childhood, or because he missed the feeling of Lexie's hand in his. *Fuck*, he did not need this. Whatever it was between them had to stop. Right now.

Chapter 17

Lexie didn't know if her conversation with Connor changed things for better or worse. He'd started acting differently around her since they'd shared the details of their painful pasts. Now he seemed intent on keeping his distance from her. There was no more casual brushing of his hands along her skin. No draping of his arm along the back of her chair if they sat next to each other. In fact, he didn't even sit near her much anymore. It wasn't until he stopped doing those things that she realized how his constant presence, those oh so casual touches, had started to mean something to her.

She wasn't sure what had caused the change in him. Maybe he regretted telling her about his parents. Or maybe knowing she was a widow was making him keep his distance. Whatever had caused it, the feeling of loss hurt. And that frightened her.

Something had begun to change inside her. Her heart still ached when she thought of Damien, but now there was a glimmer of hope. Because maybe Connor was right, and she wasn't broken; she just needed time, and to meet the right man. That man wouldn't be tall and dark with piercing green eyes, but it was Connor who had given her the first taste of desire in years. He'd made her yearn for his touch, even though she knew she shouldn't. All he would ever want from her was one night. As much as she might have started fantasizing about how a night like that would feel, she knew she'd end up risking her still-scarred and fragile heart.

So, Lexie let him keep away from her; she didn't push the issue or try to recapture what might have been between them. If they both needed to keep their distance from each other for their own reasons, it probably meant it was the right thing to do.

Lexie sighed and stared out of the bus window. It was morning, and the convoy was rolling into Pittsburgh for their next stop. Unsettled and jittery, Lexie decided she needed to get out in the fresh air. So far, she'd only done Tex's portrait, so this would be as good a time as any to knock another one over. Scanning the bus, she noticed Noah playing around on his phone. Lexie smiled to herself. Spending a few hours with the easygoing drummer sounded like just what she needed.

***

Later that morning, Lexie was sitting in the passenger seat of a car that Noah was driving. Her decision had been a bit premature since she didn't really have a good idea what she wanted to do for Noah's portrait yet, but she was hoping inspiration would hit. Plus, it gave her a chance to chat with him, which often helped spark ideas. The only thing she'd asked him to bring was his drumsticks since she wanted to incorporate those into the photo somehow.

Noah had specifically asked to drive since he enjoyed it

and didn't get much chance while they were on tour, and she'd been happy to oblige because it gave her a chance to study him and try to decide what she wanted to do. There was no doubt that like all the other band members, he was very attractive. With his long, surfer-blond hair and sparkling blue eyes, she could easily imagine him on a Californian beach, but his high cheekbones and strong jaw gave him an edgier look.

Looking over at him, she noticed him tapping his fingers on the steering wheel, even though there was no music playing in the car. It must be a drummer thing, since he was constantly tapping on objects with his drumsticks, hands, or anything else that was lying around. She smiled, wondering what it was like to constantly have a beat running through you that you had to express in one way or another.

"So, tell me what it's like to be the drummer for the world's hottest rock band?" She wanted to get him talking to see if anything he said would trigger an idea.

He glanced at her out of the corner of his eye, and his lips quirked up. "Well, as the drummer, I'm obviously the most important person in the band."

"Of course." She smiled at him.

He laughed. "You think I'm joking? Well, maybe I am a bit, but it's partly true."

"Okay, I'll bite. Tell me why you're the most important person in the band."

He grinned at her. "A lot of people don't realize that the role of the drummer isn't just to look cool while playing sick beats." He arched an eyebrow and smiled when she giggled. "It's to keep the rest of the band in time. I need to keep the rhythm so that the others can stay on beat. If my timing is off, everyone's is off. Plus, I control the intensity and speed of the music. The others have to follow my lead, or the song will fall apart."

He glanced at her intrigued expression. "Didn't know that, did you?" he laughed.

She shook her head. "I didn't. But now you've explained it, it makes perfect sense. So, you're kind of like the heart of the band?"

"Hmm, I like that analogy." He grinned, taking one hand off the wheel to rub his chin. "I'll make sure to tell the others that's what you called me."

Lexie laughed and shook her head. Looking over at him, an idea started to emerge. The heart, hmm. A heart. Something to do with a heart…

Just then a light rain started to fall, raindrops spattering on the windscreen. Hearts, rain, drumsticks. She ran her eyes up and down him, her mind working, and then a picture popped into her head.

"Noah, I need you to pull over at the next lot of stores we get to." He raised his eyebrows but nodded without asking why.

At the next mall, he pulled into a parking lot. He stayed in the car with a cap pulled down over his face so he didn't get recognized, while she jumped out and raced into the building before she got too wet in the rain. She was smiling to herself when she came out a few minutes later, her purchase tucked into her purse.

"Got what you needed?" Noah asked when she got back into the passenger side of the car.

"I did. Now I need you to drive until we find a park or open space where there aren't too many people around."

"Your wish is my command." Noah started the car and pulled out, driving for a few blocks until they found a small park with a stream running through it. It was deserted due to the weather, so was perfect for what Lexie was planning. Noah pulled the car into a nearby parking spot.

"I just need the weather to hold," Lexie muttered to herself, looking up at the cloudy sky.

Noah turned to her. "Okay, what do you need from me?"

"Take your top off."

He raised a brow and smirked at her before pulling his shirt off over his head. "I thought you'd never ask, babe."

She rolled her eyes at him, before pulling out the item she'd just purchased from her purse and waving it at him. It was a temporary tattoo of a red heart, about two inches across.

"Okay, I kind of see where you're going with this. Where are you planning to put it?"

"On your back." She smiled, twirling her finger in the air. "Turn around please."

He twisted around in the driver's seat so that she had access to his back. Wow. He had a very nice back to go along with the rest of him—smooth, golden skin stretched over hard muscles. She shook her head. It was ridiculous that all the guys were so attractive. Nice too, which made it even worse. She was going to get spoiled spending so much time with them all. For the first time, she considered how much she was going to miss hanging out with them after this was all over. She pushed the thought away. There was still plenty of time to enjoy their company before they all went their separate ways.

She smoothed her fingers on the left side of Noah's lower

back, just above the waistband of his jeans. He shivered slightly, then glanced over his shoulder at her, brilliant blue eyes sparkling. "That's nice. Feel free to keep going."

Shaking her head at him, but unable to stop her smile, she peeled the backing off the temporary tattoo, then paused. She'd forgotten she needed to apply moisture to get it to transfer to his skin. "Do we have any water in the car?" she asked.

Noah shook his head. Realizing what the problem was, he looked over his shoulder at her again. "You can always use your tongue. I won't complain."

She laughed. He was such a flirt. "I bet you wouldn't."

Looking around the car for something to use to wet the tattoo, she suddenly realized what was staring her right in the face. Twisting in her seat so that she could keep holding the tattoo in place, she pressed the button to wind down the window and stuck her other hand out into the rain. When it was wet enough, she turned back and ran her wet fingers all over the tattoo. She had to do it a couple of times before she judged it was wet enough and then slid the paper away from his skin.

"Did it work?" he asked, unsuccessfully craning his neck to see if he could see it.

"Yep. Now put your shirt back on."

He turned to look at her, confused. "But then you won't see the tattoo."

She raised her eyebrows at him. "Don't tell me you've never seen a wet t-shirt competition, Noah, because I won't believe you."

Realizing what she meant and glancing out of the window at the rain still coming down, he laughed. "Right.

Lucky I wore a white shirt, then."

"Yep, it was meant to be. Now let's go get wet!" She jumped out of the car and stood for a second, looking up at the clouds. The light rain was warm, and she closed her eyes, taking a deep breath as the drops fell steadily but softly on her face.

"Earth to Lexie!" Noah called. She turned to look at him and let out a small sigh of appreciation on behalf of every woman in the world, admiring the way the rain had already started to mold the t-shirt to his body.

She realized he was staring at her too, a slightly dazed expression on his face. Noticing where his gaze was directed, she glanced down and realized her own outfit wasn't immune to the rain. While she wasn't wearing white, the pale pink shirt with a sheer lacy bra underneath wasn't much better and didn't leave much to the imagination. She used the excuse of needing to get out her camera bag to sidestep behind the car and break Noah's admiring gaze.

Not embarrassed at all to have been caught staring, he grinned at her shamelessly and shrugged. Lexie rolled her eyes. He was incorrigible. Although, she couldn't really get upset considering she was about to take photos of his very hot body for the gratification of women everywhere.

Once she was set up, she got Noah to get his drumsticks out of the car. She arranged them in the back-left pocket of his jeans so that they crossed over each other just below where she'd applied the red heart, framing it.

When she moved back from him and checked the composition, she smiled happily to herself. His blond hair was slicked back, and he was leaning forward with his hands braced on top of a small stone wall overlooking the stream.

His head was turned to the right, so you could see his profile, and his wet shirt was plastered to his body, perfectly outlining the defined muscles of his back. The red heart, framed by his drumsticks, showed perfectly through the now translucent material. Perfect.

It didn't take long for Lexie to get the shots she needed, and shortly after they were back in the car and heading to the hotel. They sat in companionable silence for a bit, but when thoughts of Connor began to intrude, Lexie looked for a topic of conversation to distract her.

"So why don't any of you have girlfriends?" she blurted out. Not the best question to ask, but it was too late to take it back now. Noah didn't answer straight away, and Lexie started to fidget. "Sorry, I didn't mean to pry."

He flashed her a quick smile. "No, that's okay. I suppose it's not an easy question to answer because there's a variety of reasons. In the beginning, it was because we were young and there was just too much… attention, I guess you could say, to want to maintain a girlfriend. I actually had a girlfriend when we first started getting well-known. It didn't end well." His hands clenched slightly on the steering wheel, and he paused for a second, a rarely seen frown on his face. Then he seemed to shake it off and kept going.

"Going from being a nobody to a superstar in such a short period, well, it's hard to explain what it does to you. Everything you ever thought you wanted is thrown at you, and you can't believe your luck, so you take it all, without even thinking about it. Then, when the novelty eventually wears off, you find yourself stuck with a certain persona, which ends up being fairly hard to shake."

He glanced at her, and she nodded to show she

understood what he was saying. Looking back at the road, he continued. "A couple of times I tried having a girlfriend. But either there were trust issues when we were out on tour that got too difficult to work through, or because she expected me to play around on her, she thought that meant I wouldn't care if she did too." He grimaced. "Just to be clear, I'm not a cheater, and I don't appreciate anyone cheating on me."

Lexie wasn't used to Noah being so serious, and she felt bad about bringing up the subject. But he seemed happy to keep talking, so she let him, figuring that perhaps he didn't have much of a chance to talk about things like this with other people.

But when he continued, it wasn't about him. "The others have their reasons too. Tex is a not-so-closet romantic, happy to play around until he meets the love of his life." Lexie blushed, not mentioning that Tex had tried her on for size in that role.

"Zac dates, but only for a month or two at a time, and never while we're on tour. He doesn't really talk about why he does that. And Connor..." Noah paused, and Lexie suddenly felt sick. She didn't want to know why Connor didn't have relationships. She wished she'd never asked the question in the first place.

"Well, Connor is just Connor; he's got no interest in falling for anyone. I guess he's happy enough just being loved by all our fans and, well, there's no shortage of women to fulfill the physical aspect."

Lexie's stomach twisted. Of course there wasn't. He could have any woman in the world. His flirting was just second nature to him, part of who he was, and she'd reacted to it the same way every other woman in the world would. But she couldn't afford to let it affect her. She was already too mixed up and confused about her feelings when it came to him. She couldn't let him screw with her head and heart just when she might be getting back on track.

Realizing Noah was still talking, she turned her attention back to him. "I know you won't tell anyone else what I just told you, Lexie; you're not that kind of person. Just make sure you don't mention anything to the guys. They'd kill me." He grinned at her; all seriousness gone. "And I kind of like my life."

She pulled herself together and returned his smile. "Cross my heart."

"Speaking of hearts. It's going to be hard for me to reach my sexy tattoo in the shower. Want to help me wash it off?"

Lexie laughed. Yep, completely incorrigible.

A few minutes later, they were back at the hotel. They dropped the car off in the basement to avoid a group of fans waiting out the front of the hotel and rode the elevator up to their floor to change out of their still-wet clothes.

As Noah was saying goodbye to Lexie outside her room, Connor's door opened, and he walked out. Lexie's heart skipped a beat. He was as sexy as ever in faded jeans and a soft, gray t-shirt that stretched across his broad shoulders and firm chest.

Glancing over at them, his eyes narrowed as he took in their disheveled appearance, both with hair still dripping, wet clothes only just starting to dry. His eyes swept down Lexie's body, gaze catching where her shirt was still clinging to her breasts. Lexie's nipples hardened in response to the heat that flared in his eyes, and she flushed in embarrassment when he looked back up at her face. He glanced at Noah, standing next to her, and his expression cooled, turning impassive.

"Hey, Connor. Lexie and I spent all morning getting wet together. Now I'm trying to convince her to give me a sponge bath," Noah joked as Connor walked toward them.

Lexie cringed at the cold look in Connor's eyes as he approached. She held up her camera case and waved it in his direction to give context to Noah's comment. Connor nodded at them as he passed. "Good luck with that." His smile was sardonic as he headed past them to the elevator.

Lexie glanced up at Noah, who had a frown on his face at Connor's uncharacteristic terseness. He looked back at her and shrugged in confusion.

Not wanting to keep staring after Connor, Lexie quickly said goodbye to Noah and opened her door. She heard the elevator open and couldn't help turning her head to look at Connor before she went into her room. He was leaning against the back of the elevator staring at her, arms crossed and jaw tense as the doors began to shut.

Turning away from him, she slipped into her room. Shutting the door behind her, she leaned against it, face burning and heart racing from the fierce look he'd given her. She'd been denying it to herself, but who the hell was she kidding? She wanted him so badly it was like an ache inside her. He wasn't the man who would eventually fill the hole that Damien had left in her heart, but he might be the only man that could give her what her body needed.

Chapter 18

As the elevator descended, Connor couldn't stop the whirl of thoughts running through his head. What the hell was going on with Lexie and the other guys? Did they all have a thing for her? First Tex and then Noah—they were all like moths fluttering around her flame. Now all he needed was for Zac to start mooning over her, and she'd have the complete collection.

A horrible thought occurred to him. Was there a chance that she'd slept with any of the others? Anger raced through him at the thought. Tex had already admitted to kissing her—would he admit it if they'd slept together? And what about Noah? That guy was the biggest flirt he knew, and they'd been standing pretty close together when he'd come out of his room.

Connor ran both hands through his hair, breathing deeply as he tried to control his anger at the thought of the others touching Lexie.

The elevator door opened when he got to the parking garage, and he strode out, jumping in the back of the car that was waiting to take him to the venue. He was heading there early so he could fine-tune some of the songs he'd been writing using his electric guitar rather than the acoustic he kept in his room.

He'd also been hoping to take his mind off Lexie—a plan which had been pretty much shot to pieces now. The whole thing was getting intolerable. Something was going to have to give, and he didn't know when or what it would be.

***

Connor extricated himself from the clutches of another scantily dressed woman, this one seeming to assume that because he'd signed her ass cheek as requested, it meant he was going to take her back to his hotel room. She was hot enough that not too long ago he might have considered it, but tonight he had no interest in her or any of the other women that kept pressing themselves up against him. He would have been quite happy not to be at the after-party at all, except he needed to make an appearance for the benefit of all those VIPs that had paid for his presence.

As he wound his way through the room, he noticed Lexie sitting on a couch in the corner, looking at the LCD screen on her camera. Fuck this. He didn't want to talk to any of these strangers, he wanted to talk to her. He was sick of holding himself back from doing what he wanted when it came to her.

Making his way over there, he glared at the douchebag sitting next to her who was checking her out while she was working. She was wearing one of her sexy little sundresses, and while part of him wished she'd stop wearing them because they were so distracting, another bigger part of him loved seeing all her smooth golden skin on display.

So did everyone else apparently. When the douchebag

dragged his eyes away long enough to notice Connor's hard stare as he approached, he quickly got the message and stood, pretending he desperately needed to grab himself a beer.

Connor sat down next to Lexie, and she glanced up with a distracted smile on her pretty mouth. When she realized it was him, her pupils dilated, and she bit her full bottom lip. Hoping she didn't glance down at his suddenly too-tight jeans, he casually stretched his arm out along the back of the couch behind her shoulders.

"I feel like I haven't spoken to you for ages. How are those photos going?" Smooth, he thought to himself in disgust.

She glanced down at the photo currently on her camera screen, then back up at him. "It's going really well. I've got lots of great shots already, so the problem is going to be culling them all down to get the best ones for the book."

"Can I have a look?"

She passed the camera over to him and showed him the button to push to scroll through. Man, she had a good eye. There were some photos of that night's performance that looked fantastic, though it was hard to see much detail on the small screen. He said as much, and she paused for a beat before replying.

"I can show you on the laptop when we get back to the hotel. If you're not too tired, that is." Her voice was quiet, and she stared down at her camera as she spoke, but he saw pink stain the side of her cheek as she said it.

Holy shit. Was she suggesting what it sounded like she was suggesting? So many thoughts flashed through his mind, but the one that stuck was that he had no idea what was going on in her head and couldn't afford to make any assumptions. What might happen if she came to his room would have to be up to her.

As much as he wanted her—and his dick was currently letting the world know just how much he did—he wasn't going to take advantage of her. But he was sick of fighting this attraction, so he leaned toward her, watching in fascination as her breathing became erratic.

"Let's go. Now," he said.

Standing up, he reached for her hand, pulled her up, and then tugged her toward the door, only stopping to tell Zac they were taking the car and he'd send it back for the rest of them. Zac nodded. He eyed Connor's hand where it was wrapped around Lexie's but didn't say anything.

Once they were out of the room, he regretfully dropped her hand, because he didn't want all the crew seeing him dragging her along behind him, knowing exactly what they'd think. Feeling the urgency beating through his veins, he led her quickly toward the car, trying very hard to make small talk.

They were almost there when Drew came out of fucking nowhere, wanting a ride back to the hotel. Knowing he couldn't say no, Connor smiled stiffly and agreed, hoping that Lexie wouldn't reconsider on the way back. Luckily, Drew engaged her in conversation during the drive because Connor was in no state to say anything of value.

When they got to the hotel, Lexie excused herself to go back to her room and grab her laptop and memory card. Connor was in the middle of changing into something more relaxed when the knock came at his door. Anticipation hummed through his veins as he finished zipping up his jeans before opening the door for her.

Lexie's eyes widened, and he had to suppress a groan as she ran her eyes down his bare chest before dragging her gaze back up to meet his, cheeks flushed.

God, she was sexy. Her dark hair hung in loose waves around her slender shoulders, which were mostly bare except for the thin straps of her dress. He stepped back from the doorway so she could come in, the sweetness of her perfume wrapping around him as she moved past and into the room.

"I'll just finish getting changed," he threw over his shoulder as he went back into the bedroom. Quickly he threw on a plain white t-shirt, before heading back out to the living room. She was sitting down on the couch and had already set up her laptop on the coffee table. He sat down next to her, moving close enough that he could feel the heat emanating from her skin.

"I've got some great shots so far," she was saying, and he tried to focus his attention on something other than on how much he wanted to touch her. He still didn't know if she had a reason to be here other than to show him photos. He needed a sign from her to tell him what she wanted to happen tonight. Until that moment came, he needed to concentrate on her work.

"I like these ones," he said as she clicked through a series of crowd close-ups. The photos showed a mass of faces, mouths open, eyes glittering, lit up by the reflection of the stage lights. A forest of hands reached toward the stage as if desperate for just one touch.

"You can really see the emotions on your fans' faces." She smiled up at him. "That's a lot of love for you right there."

"Not love. Lust," he corrected her. He should know—it

was exactly how he was feeling right now. The irony wasn't lost on him.

She glanced up into his eyes, some emotion he couldn't identify flitting across her face before she averted her gaze. "I suppose so," she said slowly. "Either way, it must be pretty gratifying."

He shrugged. "It doesn't hurt."

She shifted on the couch, twisting around to look him in the eye again. "What's it like?" She seemed genuinely curious.

"What? Being lusted after by hundreds of thousands of women?"

"Millions I imagine," she said. Then added, "And plenty of men too."

He laughed. "Well, you're not wrong."

She cocked an eyebrow at him, and he realized she was still waiting for him to answer her question.

He wanted to be honest with her. "Well, I'm not going to lie, it's a rush at first. Women throwing themselves at you, offering you everything you could ever want, no strings attached. It's hard to say no to."

She nodded as if in understanding but then ducked her head down and started closing the photos she had open on the screen. "Well, it's getting late and you're probably tired—" she started to say but stopped when he leaned toward her.

He lowered his voice. "You didn't let me finish."

She stared up at him, her big gray eyes round as he intruded on her personal space.

"Sex with groupies and fans, it gets old after a while. There's no getting around it Lexie, I've been with a lot of women since we got famous. But I don't know how long it's been since I've wanted one woman in particular. Since I've gotten turned on just from sitting next to her."

He kept his eyes locked on hers, searching for something, anything to tell him she wanted him the way he wanted her.

Her pupils dilated, and he leaned in closer, pushing for a definitive response. He knew he had it when instead of moving back, she swayed toward him.

Fuck it, decision made. Reaching out his hand, he softly trailed the tips of his fingers down the side of her face. Her eyes widened and her lips parted slightly, but she didn't make a sound, so he kept going. He ran his fingertips slowly down the smooth skin of her neck until they rested over the pulse fluttering wildly at the base of her throat. He looked back up at her eyes, only to see they had drifted shut.

"Lexie," he murmured. Her eyelids fluttered open, and the dreamy expression in her eyes had all his blood rushing south. "Lexie, baby, I need to know what you're thinking. Is this something you want?"

She kept her eyes trained on his, and the pause before she responded seemed to stretch out forever, and then she nodded. Her pulse accelerated, beating like butterfly wings under his fingertips.

He needed more, to make sure she completely understood the situation. Particularly since he knew this was the first time she'd have been with a man since her husband's death. He wanted her—almost painfully—but he didn't want to hurt her.

"I can't give you anything more than tonight, you know that, right? I promise I'll make it good for you though, and I don't think either of us will regret it." It almost killed him to say it, knowing it could be a deal-breaker for her. He wanted her too much to do the right thing and leave her alone, but he needed her to know the reality of what it meant if they kept going.

She closed her eyes briefly and took a deep breath, before looking back at him and whispering, "I want this."

That was all he needed to hear, and before she had time to react, he reached out and buried his hands in the soft dark silk of her hair, bringing his mouth down on hers. Knowing she hadn't been with anyone for so long, he wanted it to be soft and restrained, but weeks of desire had weakened his will power.

She surprised him by only hesitating for a second before parting her lips under his. He took possession, thrusting his tongue into her mouth, loving the way she moaned and leaned into his kiss. God, she tasted just as sweet as he'd imagined.

He moved one of the hands that had been buried in her hair down her neck and to the small of her back, using it to draw her body tighter against his. She raised her hands and fisted them in the material of his shirt, and the feel of her pressed against him drove him crazy. Breaking the kiss, he stared down into her flushed face; her lips pink and swollen, her eyes heavy-lidded with desire.

"Bedroom," he managed to get out.

Standing up, he reached for her hand and drew her up with him and toward his room, stopping every few steps to kiss her, because he missed the taste of her when he wasn't. The little moans she made every time he stroked her tongue with his had him harder than he'd been in as long as he could remember.

By the time they finally made it to his king-size bed, he felt like he was going to die if he couldn't touch her skin to skin in the next moment.

Chapter 19

Lexie's heart was hammering so hard in her chest, she could feel it throughout her whole body. She stood next to his bed and looked up at him where he loomed over her, his green eyes glittering and muscles tense. He appeared to be a second away from picking her up and throwing her on the bed.

A part of her knew this was a bad idea, that it would change everything between them, but that part was drowned out by the part that wanted him. That wanted this. It was so strong that her body vibrated with it—the need to touch and be touched, to feel smooth skin and hard muscles moving over her. Every part of her that had felt so empty for so long wanted to be filled by him. She pushed everything else out of her head.

Unable to wait any longer, she reached for him, sliding a hand under his shirt and running her fingers over the hard, corrugated muscles of his six-pack. He jerked at her touch and she looked up.

His jaw was tense, his eyes narrowed, watching her intently. Then, as if a dam had broken, he moved, grasping the hem of his shirt and pulling it off in one smooth motion. The sight of his naked torso sent heat flashing through her.

Her fingers tingled with the urge to touch his smooth, tanned skin.

Reaching for him, she traced her fingers over the solid black lines of his tattoo, before drifting them down his chest, and over the ridges of his abdominal muscles, stopping only when she hit the waistband of his jeans. Connor was standing as still as a statue while she touched him, but when she raised her eyes back up to his face, she saw the strain of not moving, not touching, written on his face.

She reached around to her back and began unzipping her dress. Connor finally moved again, putting his arm around her and brushing her hand out of the way so he could take over. He dragged the zip slowly down until it reached the small of her back, then took his time trailing his fingers back up to her shoulder, hooking them under the thin strap of the dress, and sliding it off. He did the same on the other side so the dress slipped down and pooled at her feet, exposing her overheated skin to the cool air and his hungry gaze.

Because the straps of the dress had been so thin and the bodice fitted, she wasn't wearing a bra underneath. Her nipples, already peaked from the desire that raced through her veins, tightened even more under his scrutiny.

"So beautiful," he murmured. Reaching out, he cupped her breast, his thumb brushing her tight nipple, eliciting a soft moan from her. Wanting to feel the hard planes of his chest pressed against her, she stepped forward, raised up on her tiptoes, and wound her arms around his neck, almost whimpering at the feel of his rock-hard muscles against her sensitive breasts.

Groaning, Connor crashed his mouth down on hers, all restraint gone. He ran his hands down her back and cupped her ass, pulling her hips tight against his. She shuddered in anticipation as she felt the long, hard length of him through the denim of his jeans. Dropping her hands to his waistband, she fumbled with the button, desperate to touch every last inch of him.

Finally managing to get it undone, she drew his fly down and dragged his jeans and briefs down over his hips. As he stepped out of them, she took the opportunity to take all of him in. Her eyes swept up and down his incredible body, all hard planes, cut muscle, and a very, very large… Her eyes widened. Oh! The shudder of desire that went through her at the knowledge of what was about to happen weakened her knees.

He didn't give her long to admire him, pulling her close again for another deep kiss, his tongue sliding against hers, making her whimper. There was nothing between them now but her panties, and she could feel the entire hot length of him branded against her stomach.

He stepped back from her. "Lie down, Lexie." His voice was a low, dark rumble that almost seemed to vibrate through her body.

She sat down on the bed and then scooted up so her head was at the top. He climbed on next to her, bending over and grazing her nipple with his lips, before enveloping her in the wet heat of his mouth, swirling his tongue and sucking until Lexie couldn't help her body arching upward at the exquisite feeling. She reached up, clenching her hands in his thick, dark hair, not wanting him to stop. After a few seconds, he turned his attention to her other nipple, sucking it deep and making her cry out with pleasure.

Lexie's hands left his hair and trailed over his shoulders

to his biceps. She pulled at him until he moved over her. With his hips between her thighs, she was able to drift her hands down his back, unable to get enough of the feel of his smooth skin and the hard muscles that flexed under her touch. Connor alternated between her breasts, licking and sucking her nipples until she was writhing beneath him.

She ground herself up against him, feeling like she'd burst into flames if she didn't get relief from the pressure building inside her. Connor jerked against her and he groaned, reaching down with one hand to hold her hips still. With one last suck of her nipple, he dropped his head and began pressing soft, slow kisses between her breasts and down her stomach, her skin quivering beneath his lips. When he reached her panties, he sat back, tracing the line of them from one of her hip bones to the other. She squirmed, so aroused she thought she might burst into flames.

"Connor, please, I need you to touch me."

He glanced up at her and must have seen the desperation on her face because his lips curled up, and he hooked his fingers under the sides of her panties, dragging them down and off. Then he sat back again and just looked, his eyes roaming over her hungrily.

Lexie thought she should feel self-conscious, since he'd probably seen hundreds of gorgeous women naked. But she was so caught up in her body's reaction to him, so desperate to satisfy the long-dormant desire pulsing through her, that instead of trying to hide herself, she parted her legs in invitation.

"Christ, Lexie. You are so fucking gorgeous," he gritted out between clenched teeth as he stroked a finger lightly up and down where she'd parted for him, dragging it over her clit. The sensation on her sensitized skin caused her hips to jerk, and the slickness she could feel proved just how ready she was for him. He eased a finger into her, sliding it deep before withdrawing and adding another, stretching her, readying her to take him. When he withdrew them, she whimpered and shuddered in protest at the feeling of emptiness.

He made a noise deep in his throat. "Later I'm going to taste you here. But I need to be in you right now. I can't wait any longer." His voice was dark and low with lust.

"Yes," she panted. "Please, Connor."

He stretched to open the bedside drawer. Pulling out a condom, he ripped it open and rolled it down himself, before looking down at her with glittering, hungry eyes.

"Tell me you want this."

She nodded jerkily, her entire body vibrating.

"Say it for me, Lexie. Say you want me."

"I want you, Connor. I need you."

Satisfaction flared in his eyes, and he braced himself above her, pressing against her entrance before sliding partway in. She gasped at the sensation of being filled.

"Fuck, you're so tight," he murmured, jaw tense as he pushed slowly into her.

"Sorry, it's been a while," she replied breathlessly.

He huffed a small laugh. "Don't be sorry, baby, you feel amazing. I'm just afraid I'll hurt you. Or that this will be over before it's begun."

"You won't hurt me." She smoothed her hands down the hard muscles of his back, before gripping his hips and tugging. "And I want to feel all of you."

He searched her eyes, and seeing what he needed to see,

pressed his lips to hers, his tongue invading her mouth at the same time he gave one last hard thrust, filling her completely.

Lexie's body clenched tight, before relaxing as her muscles eased and stretched around him.

"Are you okay?" he asked, holding himself rigid above her.

She exhaled and nodded, adjusting to the feel of him inside her. "You feel incredible." She shifted her hips, moving against him tentatively.

He groaned. "Just hold still for a second, baby. You've got me about ready to blow. Then I'd have to wait at least one minute before I'd be hard enough again to do everything I want to do to you."

Unbelievably, considering how on fire she felt, he'd made her laugh. "One minute, huh? I definitely don't want to have to wait that long."

Her laugh caused her body to tighten, and Connor made an inarticulate noise, dropping his forehead against her chest. "This is ridiculous. You've got me feeling like a teenager." He tensed as she laughed again.

Finally, his muscles started to relax, and he began to move, sliding in and out of her in the most exquisite way, sending pleasure shuddering through her sensitive nerve endings. There was no more laughter after that.

"Oh my God, Connor!" Lexie gasped, bowing up against him as he grazed her nipple with his teeth. Her hips flexed against his as her pleasure built quickly. It'd been such a long time since she'd felt anything as good as this, she knew it wouldn't take long for him to send her over the edge. As he moved against her, the pressure inside her grew.

"Are you going to come for me, beautiful?" he said, before pressing a slow, hot kiss to her mouth. Then he turned his attention back to her breasts, sucking on one nipple while pinching and tugging the other. Lexie threw her head back as her pleasure peaked suddenly, bucking her hips up and feeling herself clench around him. She gasped his name, shaking at the sensations flooding through her body.

"That was a beautiful sight to see, Lexie." The Irish lilt in his voice had deepened, and he was holding himself rigid above her again. His eyes were almost black, his pupils blown wide with desire. "I want to see it again before I come."

She shivered. The aftershocks of her incredible orgasm were still rippling through her body, but his words, and the feel of him still so hot and hard inside her, started the pleasure building again.

Connor's thrusts began picking up speed, his hips flexing hard against hers. Lexie dragged her fingers down his back, feeling the tension in his muscles and reveling in all that strength above her, surrounding her, in her. She could feel her body tightening in a precursor to an orgasm that might be even more intense than the first if that were even possible. Connor pushed himself up above her and braced himself on one hand, reaching between them to stroke her clit.

"I'm so close," she panted.

"That's it baby. I need to feel you come again." His pace increased—hard, driving strokes—while his fingers worked their magic, until the orgasm exploded through her, so powerful her back arched up off the bed as she cried out his name.

"Fuck, Lexie," he groaned out through gritted teeth as he

made one last almost violent thrust, then held himself hard against her as he came.

Lexie's climax was still cascading through her, waves of pleasure flooding her, inundating her, reaching every part of her body, filling her so completely it was almost unbearable. Long moments passed as the sensation gradually ebbed. As she came down from that incredible high, her muscles quivering, reality began to intrude into her pleasure-saturated thoughts.

Connor relaxed against her, feathering slow, soft kisses along the side of her neck. It felt good. It felt... intimate. But she couldn't stop herself wondering how long it would be before he asked her to leave. Part of her wished the sex hadn't been as incredible as it had been. How much easier would it be to leave his bed and go back to normal tomorrow if it had just been good sex. But how did you go back to normal after sex like that? How did you not crave another taste? How did you watch him possibly take other women back to his room and not have it hurt?

Connor pulled out of her, dropped a soft kiss on her lips, then stood up to dispose of the condom in a nearby wastebasket She watched him, entranced by his graceful movements and the flexing of his muscles, but wondered if this was when he'd ask her to leave.

Instead, he returned to the bed and lay down next to her, pulling her lax body against his so that she was partially draped over him. He stroked his fingers lightly up and down her back and didn't seem inclined to rush her out. Lexie laid her head on his chest and drew soft circles over his smooth skin with her fingers. She could hear his heart, still beating fast, an echo to hers.

"That was fucking incredible," he said languidly.

"Mmmm," she agreed, before propping herself up slightly so she could see his face. His eyes were hooded, but the corners of his mouth tipped up when she looked at him. He was so incredibly gorgeous, with his tousled hair and those vivid green eyes sweeping over her face as if trying to memorize it. But even though she was lying naked in his arms, he still felt out of reach.

She knew this was when she should get up and leave, start distancing herself, so she could walk away with her head held high. But if this one night was all they got, then she didn't want to waste it. Tomorrow was going to hurt, there was no getting around it, so she might as well make the most of tonight. She wanted him filling the empty spaces inside her again and again because she didn't know when she would feel this way next. And maybe when she left him in the morning, she wouldn't go back to feeling so hollow all the time.

Returning his smile with a small one of her own, she raised herself above him and pressed her mouth to his. His arms came up immediately, drawing her down to him then rolling them over so she was on her back. He was already getting hard, and she rocked her hips against him in a silent plea.

"Is there something you want, baby?" he asked, his voice deepened with desire. He hovered his lips just above hers, waiting for her to answer him.

"I want you," she breathed against his mouth, causing him to growl low in his throat before he slanted his mouth over hers and proceeded to give her exactly what she'd asked for.

Chapter 20

L exie was having the nightmare again. The one she'd had almost every night for a year after Damien's death. Although she recognized the familiar dream, as always, she couldn't shake herself out of it.

In the dream, everything was black, and icy rain fell on her face. Two brilliant beams of light flared, burning into her eyes, blinding her. She flinched away from the light, raising her hands to protect her eyes. The next thing she heard was a terrible screeching sound, the noise like nails down a chalkboard. The sound of shattering glass, then nothing, silence, blackness. And always, just before she jolted awake, Damien's voice, whispering, "Lexie..."

Chapter 21

Connor was jolted awake by Lexie's anguished moans. A different sound from the moans of ecstasy she'd just been making in his dream. He propped himself up on one elbow and leaned over her, concerned to see her brow furrowed and her eyelids flickering. As he watched, debating whether to wake her, a tear leaked out from the corner of her eye and ran down the side of her face. That decided him.

"Lexie, baby, wake up. You're having a bad dream." He stroked the side of her face, wiping the tear away with his thumb. "Lexie, wake up."

Her eyes flashed open; the brilliant silver gray made brighter by the wash of tears that spilled over. She looked up at him, some unknown emotion flickering briefly in her eyes, then her mouth trembled, and more tears fell. The expression of loss etched on her face struck him like a blow.

He brushed away more tears. "It was just a dream, baby."

She shuddered and raised her hands to her face, wiping away the wetness on her cheeks. "A nightmare, always the same. Damien, dying, alone in the rain. I haven't had it for a couple of years. I thought it had gone for good."

Fresh tears spilled down her cheeks, and he tried to

gather her up and pull her toward him, but she resisted, bracing her hand against his chest. Hurt stabbed through him at the evidence that she didn't want his comfort. Instead, she sat up and looked away from him, seemingly unaware of her nudity. The moonlight illuminated the creamy skin of her full breasts, and his body stirred in response. *Now is not the time*, he told himself. He pulled his attention back where it should be and heard her mumble, "This was a mistake."

He tensed, disappointment hitting him hard. He was the one that had insisted this was just a one-off. But if he was completely honest, after last night he knew one night wouldn't be enough. He wanted more of her in his bed.

He took a guess at what she was feeling. "Lexie, God knows this must be hard for you, but I'm sure Damien wouldn't want you to feel bad about moving on with your life." He realized he'd said the wrong thing when he saw her stiffen.

"How would you know what Damien would or wouldn't want?" She jumped up and frantically started gathering and pulling on her clothes.

He got up and quickly donned a pair of briefs. "Because if I died, I wouldn't want someone I loved to spend the rest of her life alone. You must know he wouldn't want that, and I'm sure if it was the other way around, you wouldn't want him to be alone forever." His logic seemed to wash straight over her. She was dressed now and heading for the door of the suite, detouring to pick up her laptop. She still hadn't looked at him.

"Since you've never been in love, I don't put too much stock in your opinion. And I'm sure if Damien did want me to move on, it wouldn't be with some playboy rock star who decided to take a break from his groupies for one night."

Her words hit him like a slap in the face, and he stopped in his tracks just before he reached her. Maybe she was right. This entire thing seemed like one big mistake right now. He'd screwed up big time by sleeping with her, and now he might just be losing everything he'd gained over the last few weeks. If she walked from the tour, he'd be right back to square one. He felt like he'd been making progress. Apart from the distraction of lusting after her, he'd been feeling happier, but if she left, that could all come crashing back down.

Sudden iciness swamped him, and just as she opened the door, he called out to her. She looked over her shoulder at him, eyes swimming with tears. Even as the words came out of his mouth, he regretted them, but he couldn't seem to stop himself.

"Don't forget you signed a contract."

He knew the words sounded callous, but he'd frozen up inside at the thought of her leaving. Her spine stiffened as she realized what he was saying. He waited for her to yell at him or something—at least that would keep her from walking away. But instead, her eyes iced over, and she gave him a tight little nod, before turning and walking out the door. The click of the latch seemed to echo through the room.

"Fuck!"

He sank down on the couch, his heart beating hollowly in his chest. How did something go from so right, to so wrong, in the space of a few minutes? He slumped forward, elbows on his knees, and pressed the heels of his hands against his eyes.

His thoughts flashed back to the night before, and he

couldn't stop his body reacting to the vivid memories. He'd had his night with her, but one night wasn't anywhere near enough. He wanted more of her. Part of him had known that this was what would happen, which was why he'd tried so hard to resist the temptation.

His heart thudded dully in his chest at the thought she might leave, that she might walk away, and he wouldn't see her face or hear her voice, her laugh, again.

This was why he didn't do relationships. Who the hell needed this kind of turmoil in their life? That's why it was safer just to fuck random women and then walk away. No emotion, no confusion, and everyone ended up happy. Now he'd screwed himself by sleeping with someone he actually liked. And he hadn't just screwed himself. Lexie had looked devastated, and he hated the thought that what they'd done together had made her feel so guilty.

Thinking again about the night before, Connor groaned. He had never been so painfully aroused by a woman, never wanted to push himself into someone so hard, as if he could imprint himself on her skin. Her scent, the noises she'd made, the memory of her with head thrown back as she came, was branded into his mind.

How the hell was he supposed to go back to simply screwing whichever groupie was the closest now? How the hell was he supposed to see her in the morning and not reach for her, pull her toward him and crush his mouth to hers? Or pull her to the nearest vacant room, pin her against a wall, and thrust into her wet heat.

He looked at the clock. It was only 4:00 a.m., but there was no way he was getting any more sleep tonight. Picking up his guitar from where it was propped against the wall, he tried to ease the pain in his chest with notes and chords, just like he always had.

Chapter 22

Lexie stood in the shower, the tears dripping down her face washing away with the water. She didn't even know what was making her cry harder—the feeling that she'd betrayed Damien, or how unfair she'd been to Connor.

Now that the immediacy of the nightmare had passed, she knew she'd said things to Connor she didn't mean. She'd lashed out at him in guilt, and if she was honest, out of fear. Because being with Connor had stirred up far more emotions than she'd expected.

Waking up from that familiar nightmare and seeing him leaning over her, brows furrowed and concern filling his gorgeous eyes, her first instinct had been to reach for him. She'd wanted to twine herself around him, to lose herself in him.

Connor, not Damien.

The realization had hit like a sledgehammer, and a split second later, the guilt broke over her like a wave and took her under.

It hurt to admit, even to herself, that last night had been the most passionate night of her life. She'd had an amazing marriage with Damien, a wonderful and fulfilling sex life. If he hadn't died, she would have never looked at another man, never wanted anyone but him. But fate was cruel, and that life had been ripped away from her. Nothing she did would change that; no amount of guilt and pain would bring Damien back.

So why did it still feel like she'd betrayed him by being with another man? It was just one night. Just one night to feel that intense physical connection with someone again. To not feel so alone. It wasn't something she should feel guilty about.

She needed to move forward, and Connor had helped her take the first step. She just hadn't expected it to feel like more than that. But it had, and that was the problem.

She'd used her anger like a shield against the guilt and the hurt. Not that it had worked, because now the anger had faded, pain beat hard against her chest.

She owed Connor an apology for what she'd said to him. As hard as it would be to see him again after the incredible things he'd done to her body, the things he'd made her feel, she needed to see him and clear the air between them. He'd been completely up-front about the extent of what could be between them, and she'd freely taken what he'd offered.

She needed to keep smiling through the pain, just as she'd been doing for so long now, and finish the job she'd agreed to do. Then she could walk away, head held high, and eventually find a man she could have a relationship with.

The pain kicked her in the stomach again, causing her to curl her arms around her middle. Another chance at love, a family, being able to explore everything the world had to offer with those she loved, that's what she wanted. That wasn't something Connor could or would want to be a part of, so better to cut off any burgeoning feelings now and do damage control so she could finish the tour with her pride intact.

Lexie's tears finally stopped. She sighed and turned off the shower, stepping out and wrapping a towel around herself. She checked the clock. It was only early morning, but she knew she wouldn't be able to get any more sleep, so she got dressed in jeans and a tank top. She'd have to suck it up and see Connor later this morning to apologize, but until then she might as well get some work done. She set up her laptop and started editing.

***

Lexie knocked tentatively on Connor's door, half hoping he wouldn't be in. After a few seconds, during which her blood pressure skyrocketed, the door swung open. Connor stood before her, jeans on, bare-chested, his wet hair suggesting he'd recently got out of the shower. The sight of his smooth, tanned skin made Lexie's mouth go dry and images of the night before flash before her eyes.

She saw surprise register in his eyes when he saw her, but then his expression shuttered. He crossed his arms and leaned against the doorframe as he waited to hear what she had to say.

"Um, I just wanted to come and apologize for the way I reacted this morning." Connor's expression didn't change, and Lexie felt her face heat as she continued. "It's been a long time since I've had that dream, and I guess it shook me."

She saw his expression soften and rushed on, desperate to get it over with. "But that's no excuse for what I said to you. I want to make sure I haven't ruined things between us. Because this job means a lot to me, and I don't want what happened to affect our professional relationship. If you're happy to, I'd like to just go back to how things were before."

She was breathless by the time she finished, waiting with heart pounding to see how he would react.

Connor's eyebrows furled, and he lowered his eyes, hiding his expression from her. When he raised them back, his face was serious. "You haven't ruined anything, Lexie. It's hardly surprising you'd be upset after going through what you have. I'm sorry this is the way it ended up, but we already agreed it was only a one time thing, so no harm done, right?" He quirked an eyebrow at her.

Lexie nodded, trying to keep her face neutral. Connor had just told her exactly what she wanted to hear—that there were no hard feelings and things could go back to the way they were. So why did his words still hurt? She should be happy. He'd broken her sexual drought in the most spectacular fashion, and that was all she needed from him. They both knew there was no future here. They were adults and could work through any awkwardness, do the job, and then go their separate ways.

She smiled tentatively. "Okay. That's good, then. Um, I guess I'll see you later." She gave him a self-conscious half-wave, turned on her heel, and headed back toward her room.

"Lexie." He stopped her after a few steps, and she turned back toward him, gray eyes meeting green. "I don't regret it." His low voice sent shivers down her spine.

She bit her lip, and his eyes dropped to her mouth for a second before meeting her gaze again. "Neither do I," she whispered and then turned and walked back to her room.

Chapter 23

Lexie realized she'd been naïve to think things would go back to the way they had been after her night with Connor. Now when she looked at him, it was with a vivid new awareness.

During concerts when she was supposed to be photographing the crowds or the stage crew, she found it hard to drag her eyes away from him. When he sang, his voice sent goosebumps coursing over her skin.

Sometimes she imagined that he searched her out in the crowd, locking eyes with her, as he crooned seductive words into the microphone. His taut muscles, outlined by his tight t-shirts, caused flashbacks to the night they'd spent together. Images of his naked body moving over her sent full-body shivers through her, leaving her skin overly sensitive.

Three days after their night together, she was sitting at the tour bus dining table with Tex and Zac. They were scheduled to arrive in Boston in an hour or so, but there wasn't a concert until the next night, so it was a rare night off for the band.

"So, do you guys have any grand plans for tonight?" Lexie smiled over the table at Tex and Zac.

Zac answered. "Yeah, Drew has a beach house not far from here. We're going to head out there for the night, have a BBQ, some beers. It'll be great!"

"That sounds good. You all deserve a night to relax. I never realized going on tour was so full-on. I don't know how you do it year after year."

"It does get a bit much after a while. Unfortunately, it's where the money is these days, so it's in our contract with the label. We need to tour after any album we release."

She shook her head. "I guess it's lucky I'm not a rock star, then. It's fun to do this as a one-off experience, but I couldn't do it all the time."

"Don't you travel for your work?" Tex asked.

"I do, but most of the time it's only short trips if I'm in the US. Maybe a month at a time if I'm going overseas. I love traveling and seeing new places and meeting people. But I love being at home too. I get to have the best of both worlds."

Zac nodded and said almost wistfully, "It sounds great."

"Being up there onstage in front of thousands of people must be an incredible adrenaline rush though. I'm guessing it would be hard to give that up."

Tex shrugged. "It will happen one day; we won't be doing this forever. At some stage, we'll all get sick of it. Or of each other." He elbowed Zac in the ribs. Zac didn't react, other than rubbing the spot where Tex had elbowed him.

"When we started out, this was the one thing we all wanted. It was all we talked about," Zac said. "But we've been doing it a while. When you achieve all your dreams, you have to start looking around for new ones. Otherwise, you just stagnate. I'm still enjoying this now, but I've got some ideas of things I'd like to do in the future."

Before Lexie could ask what ideas he had, the bus slowed and pulled up outside the hotel they were booked into for the next few nights. Noah came sauntering out from the bunk area, looking adorably sleepy. "Thank God we're here. I can't wait to head out to Drew's and hit the beach."

Connor followed Noah out, and Lexie's pulse skyrocketed at the sight of him. He'd obviously just rolled out of his bunk and pulled on some jeans because he was shirtless, and his hair was mussed as if he'd just run his hands through it.

Lexie couldn't have stopped her eyes tracing the smooth lines of his chest down to his six-pack, even if she'd wanted to. And for once, she didn't. After their night together, her dreams had been filled with visions of him, naked and pressed up against her. She tried hard to suppress those memories when she was awake, to do exactly what they both wanted, which was to go back to the way things were before. But it was becoming increasingly difficult. Just this once, Lexie wanted to give in and indulge in those memories. She could feel her skin heating as she remembered his mouth on hers, his hands running over her skin, the feel of him inside her.

Dragging her eyes back up his torso, she saw he was watching her. His gaze was sharp, his eyes almost predatory as they locked with hers, and she realized that it must have been obvious from her erratic breathing and flushed skin what she'd been thinking about.

Embarrassed now, not wanting him to think she was just another one of the many women that couldn't let go after a night with him, she turned away, a sudden ridiculous urge to cry rising in her.

She should never have given in to the temptation to sleep with him. It was too much. *He* was too much. She should have waited until her heart was fully healed and she met a sweet, gentle, reliable man to sleep with. Someone that she might have the possibility of a future with. She should have known that with her emotions all over the place, sleeping with someone like Connor and then having to see him every day afterward was the worst possible idea she could have had.

She took a deep breath, trying to ease the tightness in her chest. The guys heading out for a night was exactly what she needed right now. She could stay in her hotel room and give herself a bit of space to try to sort out her thoughts. Because being around him constantly was becoming harder and harder.

She heard her name and realized Noah was talking to her. She jerked her head up to try to catch what he was saying. "If you didn't bring a swimsuit, we can stop off at a shop on the way."

She shook her head frantically when it became clear he was suggesting she go with them to the beach. "Oh no, thank you, I thought I'd just stay here. You know, give you all a break from me and my camera always hanging around."

A chorus of denials came from Noah, Zac, and Tex. But it was Connor who said, "You should come."

Zac chimed in. "We enjoy having you around, Lexie. Besides, who's Tex going to flex his muscles for if you're not there."

Tex cuffed the back of Zac's head. "We all know it'll be Noah doing the flexing. And he'll definitely want you to take photos of him half-naked."

Lexie interrupted the banter. "I should really do some editing work tonight, so it's probably better if I stay—"

"I want you there." Connor's voice was firm. Not giving her a chance to respond, he finished. "I want there to be photos of us outside of all the tour craziness. Doing things normal people do."

She opened her mouth for one more protest, but the hard gaze he leveled at her reminded her that he was technically her employer even if it was the label that had signed the contract. She closed her mouth and gave him a small nod.

Just what she needed, she thought miserably. Forced to spend time with the sexiest man she'd ever met as he cavorted around at the beach half-naked and wet. She already had enough fuel for her fantasies to last for a lifetime, she didn't need any more.

For the first time, she wondered if what had meant to be one night of passion had ruined her for other men. She felt the prickle of tears again and blinked rapidly to keep them at bay. She tried to picture Damien's face, but the memory was hard to hold. It kept slipping away—warm chocolate eyes replaced by vivid green. Guilt surged up in her again. What had she done?

Chapter 24

Connor was driving one of the cars to Drew's house. He enjoyed driving, particularly when he was heading out of the city and toward the beach. Unbidden, his eyes glanced up at the rearview mirror to find Lexie in the back seat, her face turned to gaze out of the window.

He frowned at her pensive expression. She hadn't wanted to come with them, and the right thing to do would have been to let her have some space. But he'd been a bastard and basically commanded her to be there with them. He didn't really care if there were photos from this getaway in the book or not; that had just been the only excuse he could think of at the time. He just liked being around her, even if the enjoyment he'd found in her presence before they'd slept together had been replaced by the constant pull of desire.

Dragging his eyes away from her pretty profile, he looked back at the road. The last thing they needed was to get in an accident because he couldn't focus.

Tex was lounging in the passenger seat next to him, a cap pulled down low on his forehead. Tex had offered for Lexie to sit in the front, but she'd declined, saying he needed more legroom than she did since he was so much taller. Connor hadn't pushed the issue. He'd told her she had to come with them, he didn't want to be a complete asshole and tell her where to sit as well.

He took one hand off the wheel and scrubbed it over his face. He didn't know how he would get through the rest of the tour with this constant desire thrumming through him. She was always on his mind, when he was onstage, when he was supposed to be writing songs, when he was lying in bed at night unable to get to sleep. That would be all right if he were on his own and could relieve the tension, but when they were on the bus, packed in like sardines, it became a little awkward. Suffice to say, the shower was becoming his favorite place to be these days.

Even worse, he couldn't get enough of her as a person, the way she viewed the world, the way she used her camera to share that view, the way the sound of her laugh made him smile.

He tried to push thoughts of her out of his mind because he was looking forward to this afternoon, and tonight, he desperately needed a break from the tour.

His uncertainty about his future kept dragging him down. No matter how you looked at it, he had a responsibility to his friends to keep seeing this through. None of them had ever given any sign they were ready to try something different. And leaving when the band had reached this level of success seemed like a real dick move. And even if they were all ready to move on, he didn't have a clear idea about what he wanted to do.

Music was still the most important thing in the world to him. It had been the one thing that had always made him feel closer to the memory of his mother, and the one thing that had eased the hurt of his father pushing him away. Even now, whenever he was upset, picking up his guitar and playing could soothe him like nothing else.

The reasons he had wanted to be in a band since he was a teenager were still real to him. Being surrounded by music, his friends, the adoration of fans had been all he ever wanted. The idea had been like a balm for his soul. That it felt like it wasn't enough for him anymore was difficult to deal with.

Frustrated, he flicked his eyes back up to the rearview mirror, hoping a glimpse of Lexie's profile would jolt him out of his unproductive train of thought. Instead, his eyes met hers in the mirror and caught. He saw the silver of her eyes go dark and stormy with some unknown emotion before she quickly looked away. He gave a tiny shake of his head as he returned his attention to the road stretching out in front of him. *She's a widow*, he told himself, *and she has definitely not moved on from the memory of her husband yet*. Even if she had, he wasn't willing or able to take the man's place.

A few miles later, he turned left down the road leading to Drew's beach house. As they crested a rise, the ocean appeared, spread out before them like a blue blanket sparkling in the sun. Tex let out a whoop at the sight, and when Connor glanced in the rearview mirror, he saw Lexie's face break into a broad smile, gray eyes glowing, and something shifted almost painfully in his chest.

He pulled in to park next to the car Drew, Noah, and Zac had driven down in, opened the car door, and got out, Tex and Lexie following suit. One deep breath of the salty air and he felt lighter, like the sound of the surf and the fresh air had lifted a weight from him.

Stretching his arms over his head, he turned toward Lexie. Unsurprisingly, she had her camera out and was snapping photos of the beautiful view in front of them, which meant he got a few seconds to watch her without her knowing.

The sea breeze fluttered her dark hair out behind her and molded her short dress to her body, outlining her breasts and the slight curve of her stomach. It also caused the short skirt to kick up, revealing almost the full length of her slender, toned legs. He let out a quiet groan at the memory of those same legs wrapped around him, closing his eyes against the sight, hoping to calm his arousal before anyone noticed.

Tex appeared next to him, his own bag and Lexie's slung over his shoulder, and his guitar case held in his hand.

"Nice view?"

Connor glanced at him out of the corner of his eye. The smirk on Tex's face and the direction of his gaze was good enough evidence he knew Connor wasn't looking at the ocean.

Well, apparently he wasn't hiding shit from Tex.

"Beautiful," he muttered, before turning back to the car and grabbing his bag and guitar case out of the trunk.

"Lexie, we're heading up to the house!" Tex called out to her.

Lexie dropped the camera from her face, letting it hang from the strap around her neck, and turned back to them. Her cheeks were flushed, and her eyes sparkled in the bright sunshine.

"I'll be up in a minute; I just want to get a couple more shots!" she called back.

Connor turned and headed up the stairs, taking them two

at a time. He needed to get away from her, from the desire that kicked through him every time she looked at him or smiled or just fucking breathed. He reached the top of the stairs and shouldered his way into the house, letting the door slam behind him. He should have just let her stay back at the hotel.

Chapter 25

L exie turned around at the sound of the slamming door. She wasn't sure what had got into Connor. Since he'd practically forced her to join them, he'd barely said a word to her. She'd caught his eye a couple of times in the rearview mirror on the drive up, but he hadn't once smiled, and she got the feeling he was angry at her, though she didn't know why he would be.

Turning back to the spectacular vista spread out in front of her, she took a few steps out onto the dunes the house sat above, taking photos as she went. She breathed in the fresh, briny sea air; the smell always left her calm and invigorated. But even the beach couldn't completely soothe her rattled nerves. She was so torn by her attraction to Connor, someone so completely wrong for her. That, along with her guilt over Damien, had her mind and heart in complete turmoil.

Not wanting to go into the house and keep pretending she was fine, she sat down in the sand, pulling her knees up to her chest and resting her chin on them. Looking out at the endless sparkling blue, she let the sound of the waves wash over her.

Finally, the chaos in her mind ebbed, leaving her more at peace than she'd been in days. She stretched her legs out and lay back on the sand, spreading her arms out to either side of her, closing her eyes and basking in the warmth of the sun kissing her skin.

A shadow fell over her, and she blinked her eyes open, bringing up a hand to shade them so she could see who it was. Her heart jumped for a second, thinking it might be Connor, but the bulk of the silhouette indicated it was Tex.

"Hey there, darlin'. Everything okay?"

She smiled up at him but didn't move. "Just enjoying the sun and the peacefulness."

"I might join you, then."

Without a second's hesitation, he whipped his t-shirt off over his head, dropped it on the ground, and lay down next to her.

She angled her head so that she could see his face, which was turned up toward the sun, his eyes closed. She skimmed her gaze down the hard planes of his muscular, tattooed chest and sighed to herself. How much simpler it would be if she was attracted to Tex instead of Connor. Inside that sinfully gorgeous, rough exterior, Tex was a romantic through and through. Lexie could imagine that whatever lucky woman he eventually fell in love with would get treated like a princess. What woman in her right mind wouldn't want to be with a man like that?

She blew out a breath of air in frustration. Apparently, she was not in her right mind.

At the sound, Tex turned his head to face her. His eyes leisurely scanned her face.

"You are one beautiful woman, Lexie. You know that, right?"

Lexie's heart pounded. He wasn't going to kiss her again,

was he?

Probably seeing the confusion on her face, he smiled his sexy smile and turned his head back up to the sun, eyes closing. "It's all right, darlin', we both know I'm not the man who's got you all tied up in knots." He spoke to her with his eyes still closed.

Even though he wasn't looking at her, Lexie felt heat flood her face. Oh God, was it so obvious?

As if reading her mind, Tex added, "Don't worry, he doesn't know. I think you two could be really good for each other, but Connor has… issues he needs to work through." He turned his head to face her again. "I don't want to see you get hurt, Lexie, so be careful with your heart, okay?"

The sympathy and concern in his gaze made something tighten in her chest. She didn't want to tell him that his concern was misplaced. Connor had been clear about what he wanted from her, and she was the one who had ended up saying hurtful things to him. Now they just needed to get through the rest of the tour, and they'd go their separate ways with the memory of their one night together. And she was sure it wouldn't take long for even that to fade from Connor's mind. After all, he was only the second man she'd ever slept with, but she was just one of the many women he'd been with.

Not wanting to say any of that to Tex, she just nodded.

After that, they both lay in the warmth with their eyes closed for a little while longer, before the hot sun got too intense.

"Are you ready to go inside? I think Drew's going to start the grill soon, and the guys want to get in a quick swim before lunch."

Grateful for Tex's support, she smiled at him. "Okay, let's go."

He stood up, grabbed his shirt, and then held his hand out for hers, pulling her to her feet when she gave it to him. Keeping hold of her hand, they walked to the house in companionable silence, with Tex giving her hand a quick squeeze before letting it go as they got to the door.

It took Lexie's eyes a few seconds to adjust to being inside after the brightness of the sun, but when they did, she gasped at the beautiful interior of the house. Cool, neutral tones with splashes of ocean blues and greens made for a perfect beachy vibe. Floor-to-ceiling windows extended across the back wall, perfectly framing the stunning view out across the ocean. The day was sunny, but Lexie could imagine how amazing it would be to sit in one of the comfortable chairs in front of the windows and watch a storm roll in across the ocean.

The others were all outside on the back deck, and Lexie followed Tex out.

"What took you two so long?" Noah asked.

Tex put his arm around Lexie's shoulders and squeezed before answering, "Just enjoying some one-on-one time." He aimed a big shit-eating grin right at Connor.

Lexie raised her eyebrows at the icy glare that Connor directed back at Tex. Was he angry? Surely not. She hadn't meant anything more to Connor than a one-off good time. Still, she didn't want him to think she was the kind of woman to just jump from one band member to the other. Her night with Connor might not have meant much to him, but it had been a big deal for her. Even if he didn't care, she didn't want to cheapen it by pretending it had meant nothing.

She put her arm around Tex's waist and gave him a gentle squeeze in thanks for keeping her company, but then disengaged and moved away from him. She wandered over to Drew, who was firing up the grill. "Your house is beautiful. I think I could live out on this deck."

"Thanks, I love it here. Whenever it all gets too much, I like to fly out here and decompress for a few days."

Noah wandered over and offered her a bottle of beer. She accepted it, giving him a grateful smile before taking a sip of the icy-cold beverage. "Once we finish these drinks, we're going to have a quick swim while Drew makes us lunch." Noah grinned and raised his bottle at Drew, who rolled his eyes in return. "You'll join us, won't you, Lexie?"

Lexie had bought a bikini from the store in the hotel, but she felt bad about leaving Drew on his own to cook. Not to mention a little nervous about wandering around half-naked in front of a bunch of guys used to being around supermodels. "That's okay, I might just wait until later. That way I can help Drew set up."

"Don't worry about me, Lexie. I'm only going to grill the burgers up and put out some condiments. It won't take me long, and I'll probably make some calls while I'm cooking, so head down with the guys. I'll give you a yell when lunch is ready."

"Okay, if you're sure," she replied a little reluctantly.

"Definitely. Hey, Noah, can you show Lexie where her bedroom is?"

"Sure. Come on, Lexie. We'll all get changed and then head down."

Lexie put her beer down and followed Noah back into the house. She glanced back at Connor as she went, but he was looking down at his beer, the sweep of his dark lashes hiding his eyes from her.

Noah led her down a hallway running off the side of the large, open-plan main room. Several doors opened off the hallway, presumably all bedrooms, but Noah led her right to the end.

"This one's yours."

Lexie opened the door and smiled at the large sunlit bedroom, done up in creams and blues, continuing the beachy vibe.

"I'll leave you to get changed. Just come back through when you're done."

"Thanks, Noah." She closed the door behind him and gazed around the room. Her bag was sitting on the bed, so Tex must have dropped it off here before coming back down for her.

A door at the back of the room led to a small bathroom which she used before digging through her bag to find her new bikini. She pulled it out, frowning and pursing her lips. There hadn't been an enormous selection in the shop, and it was a little skimpier than she'd normally buy. But it was a pretty turquoise color, and she'd thought she looked okay when she'd tried it on.

Shrugging, she pulled it on. After all, Connor had already seen her naked, and the other guys probably wouldn't care what she looked like one way or the other.

She wandered over to the full-length mirror on the back of the door and checked to make sure she wasn't falling out anywhere. Turning around, she peered over her shoulder to see how her butt looked, then laughed at herself. What was she doing? She was young and healthy, and Damien had always told her he thought she was beautiful. What did it matter what she looked like in a bikini? She wasn't going to see any of these guys again after the tour was over, so who cared what they thought! She felt good in the bikini, so damn it, she would have fun and not care that she didn't look like a supermodel!

Deciding to forego the cover-up she'd also bought, she made her way back out to the deck. She could see through the glass that all the guys had already changed and were waiting out there for her.

Her steps slowed as she caught sight of Connor in his swimsuit. He was facing away from her and leaning against the railing, so she could admire the broad expanse of his shoulders and the hard muscles of his back leading down to a pair of black board shorts that hung low on his narrow hips. Lexie's heart tripped, and a ripple of heat passed through her. She paused and took a deep breath to steady herself, before pushing the door open and stepping out.

At the sound of the door opening everyone turned, and five pairs of male eyes perused her appreciatively, which was not at all embarrassing. She felt a deep blush suffuse her entire body.

Drew cleared his throat. "Well, you guys head down. Lunch will be about half an hour, but I'll call you when it's time to come back up."

A few steps out on to the soft sand and Lexie realized it had heated up enough to sting the soles of her feet. Noah, Zac, and Tex took off at a sprint toward the water. Connor turned back and held his hand out to her. "Come on, you don't want to burn your feet."

She must have hesitated for a second too long because he

took two steps toward her, swept her up in his arms, and jogged down to the water.

"Connor!" She shrieked in surprise and then squealed when he waded out into the chilly water with her still in his arms. The contrast between the scorching sand and the water made her instantly break out in goosebumps. Unfortunately, it also made her nipples harden visibly through her bikini top.

Hoping he hadn't noticed, she glanced up at him, just in time to see his eyes zero in on her breasts.

Embarrassed, she muttered, "You can put me down now."

He nodded but kept going for a few more steps before letting go of her legs. He held on with his arm around her back, so that her body slid down his as he lowered her until her feet touched the sandy bottom.

Lexie's breath hitched at the feel of her breasts pressed against the hard muscles of his chest, and she couldn't guarantee her nipples were only responding to the water temperature now. Not wanting to look up at him and let him see what must be showing on her face, she stared at the stark black lines of his tattoo.

"Um, thanks?" Not her most original response, but he'd shocked her considering he'd barely spoken or come near her since the night they'd spent together.

His face was inscrutable. "Anytime, Lexie."

Then he let her go and headed over to where the other guys were splashing and goofing around like teenagers.

Lexie took a couple of deep breaths to calm her racing heart, which had decided to try to beat its way through her rib cage while she was pressed up against him. Then she gave herself a tiny shake and followed him out to the deeper water.

Chapter 26

Once Connor got out to where the others were splashing around, he dunked his head under the water, trying to get himself under control after having Lexie pressed up against him in her tiny bikini.

He should have just let her go when they got to the cooler wet sand, but the feel of her in his arms had just been too good to resist. Now he was sporting the hard-on from hell, but luckily the water covered him up otherwise the guys would have been all over him about it.

Lexie had followed him out, and Noah, the giant flirt that he was, had immediately gone over to her and thrown his arm around her shoulders. He must have made a joke because Lexie burst out laughing and shoved at his chest, which did nothing of course because Noah was twice her size.

Connor turned away, raking his hand through his wet hair. Was she really not affected by him the way he was by her? Here he was, torn up with still wanting her, and she seemed completely unmoved.

Tex waded over to him and nodded over at where Lexie was now laughing with Zac and Noah. "You did good with that one." Connor looked at Tex sharply, wondering how much he'd guessed of what had happened between him and Lexie. But his fears were allayed when Tex continued. "She gets on with everyone—makes it easy to have her around while she's photographing us. Easy on the eyes too."

Connor mumbled something noncommittal, not wanting to speak in case he gave away too much.

Tex smirked and started wading toward the other three, throwing back over his shoulder, "Now you just need to get that hard-on under control."

Fuck. Tex could always see right through him.

Half an hour later, Drew called them up from the beach to have lunch. Connor trailed behind the others, admiring the sway of Lexie's hips as she walked in front of him. It had gotten so hot that his skin had mostly dried by the time they got back up to the house.

Drew had set out some plates, condiments, and salad, and everyone tucked in ravenously. When they finished, they all pitched in to clean up while Drew sat down with a beer and put his feet up. There was a lot of good-natured joking around, and having Lexie there, rather than it just being the five of them as it usually was, gave it an added dimension that had him relaxing fully for the first time in what felt like years.

The afternoon passed in a haze of sun, sand, and swimming, with Drew joining them the second time they went down to the water. Once the sun started to set, they all gathered around the outdoor pizza oven Drew had installed and made homemade pizzas for dinner.

Connor gave in to the lure of Lexie's presence, sitting next to her on the bench seat while they were eating, close enough that he could feel the brush of her skin on his whenever either of them shifted in their seat. The salty water had caused her hair to dry with more of a curl than usual, and the sun had left a faint tinge of red on her cheekbones. Her smile and the sparkle in her eyes when she laughed was far more intoxicating than the beer he was drinking. He would have been happy to stay here forever, with his friends and Lexie, never having to return to the glare of the spotlight.

Eventually, Lexie got her camera out, joking that she would get fired for not doing her job. Being her usual laid-back and charming self, she unobtrusively took photos of them all relaxing, and quite a few of the sun as it set.

She'd told him once that photographers call the hour after sunrise and before sunset the golden hour, and he could see why. A golden, almost ethereal glow bathed the scene, and watching her slender form silhouetted against the darkening sky, the first stars shining behind her, his chest tightened.

Of all the women he could have wanted to spend more than one night with, it had to be someone who was in love with another man. Someone who through no fault of his own had left Lexie with nothing but an idealized memory that he could never compete with.

She'd obviously enjoyed being in his bed—you couldn't feign passion like that—but then she'd withdrawn completely afterward. It had been three years since Damien had died, and Lexie was still holding on to him. The thought left Connor feeling cold. He didn't want to be in the position again of being pushed away by someone who cared more about a dead person than him. He'd been through that before. He wouldn't do it again.

Chapter 27

L ater that night, after the sun had set in a blaze of reds and oranges, Drew lit a fire in the fire pit, and they all gathered around. Connor, Tex, and Zac had grabbed their guitars, and Noah had his hand drums, and now they were jamming.

Lexie sat in the darkness off to one side and took photos of the guys singing and playing around the fire. The music was incredible—Lexie couldn't believe her luck that she was getting paid to sit there and be serenaded by this amazingly talented group of men.

While she took photos of everyone, she couldn't help coming back repeatedly to Connor. He played his guitar and sang with his eyes closed, an expression of contentment on his face that she had rarely seen during the time she'd known him.

As the others got tired, they wandered away, eventually leaving just her and Connor, although she wasn't even sure he knew she was still there. She had stopped taking photos a while ago, but she couldn't bring herself to leave and go to bed. It soothed her to hear him sing, and after all the emotional turmoil she'd gone through recently, she didn't want that feeling to end.

She suddenly realized Connor had started singing a new song, one she didn't recognize. From the soft, melodic lilt of the words, it sounded like it could be Irish. The melody was so poignant and spoke so much to her own long-held pain that tears flooded her eyes. Safe in the shadows, she let the tears leak out and drip down her cheeks.

As Connor continued playing, one song seemed to flow into the next. She let herself feel all the pain and heartbreak of losing Damien, her childhood sweetheart, her first love. All the pain of their future together ripped away from them. The pain that had sometimes felt unbearable was finally let loose, and she allowed it to flow from her. The heaviness that had been weighing her down for three years finally starting to ease.

When the last guitar notes faded, Lexie looked up to see Connor watching her. He stood and walked over to her; guitar held loosely in his hand.

Placing the instrument gently on the ground, he reached for her, pulling her up to stand and wrapping his arms around her. His scent, made up of sunshine, salt, and warm male skin, enveloped her as she rested her cheek against his bare chest.

She knew he could feel the wetness from her tears, but she didn't care. He knew what she was feeling. He had his own experience with grief. Maybe that's why he'd chosen the songs he had—something to help ease her pain.

Or his.

Regardless, she didn't have words enough to thank him, so she didn't even try. Instead, she hugged him hard, and they stood there silently in the dark together. When she finally pulled back, he still said nothing, just reached down for his guitar, clasped her hand with his other one, and walked her back up to the house.

Outside her bedroom door, he kissed her softly on the cheek, murmured good night, then waited while she slipped into her room. Her heart felt bruised, but also as if it might finally be starting to heal. As she lay in bed trying to get to sleep, part of her—an ever-growing part it seemed—wished he had done much more than kiss her on the cheek.

The next morning there were a few grumbles from the guys about having to leave the beach, but after a quick swim, they all packed up and drove back to the hotel in time for soundcheck. Even though Lexie and Connor hadn't talked much since their moment the night before, she felt like the tension between them had lessened. While the lust that flooded through her whenever she was near him hadn't disappeared, maybe with time they could find their way back to the way things had been before. If only she could stop dreaming about him, it might be easier.

**

Three days later they were immersed in the bright lights and bustle of New York City. The band's PR team had scheduled in a live appearance on a late-night talk show, and they were currently running the gauntlet outside the studio.

Lexie raised her camera to take more shots of the four of them greeting their fans, signing autographs, and taking selfies with ecstatic fans. It was chaotic. She'd never experienced anything like it and wondered how anyone ever got used to that kind of attention and craziness. Screams of excitement rung in her ears as she hung back enough to get the whole band and the mass of fans in one shot.

Hearing a loud crash, Lexie turned and saw that one of the metal barricades holding the crowd back had given way. The fans rushed forward, and she saw two of the band's security detail turn back from the band to try to fend them off.

Lexie edged away from the mass of excited people and closer to the two security officers. Just as she thought she'd got clear, a hand darted out of the crowd and latched onto the strap of her camera, attempting to yank it out of her hands. Lexie clung on but was jerked almost off her feet and into the surging crowd.

Whoever had grabbed her camera strap let go, sending her stumbling to the ground where she landed heavily on her bare knees. She let out a cry of pain as the hard ground cut into her skin. Fear set in as she realized the crazed crowd of fans had closed around her completely. She tried to protect her camera by hunching her body over it, and visions of getting trampled to death started flashing through her mind.

The crowd seemed to fall back before the screams of excitement ratcheted up to even higher levels. Powerful arms encircled her waist, sweeping her up from the ground and holding her tightly against a firm chest. She knew who it was without looking up; she would recognize the feel of his arms anywhere.

Lexie didn't consider herself to be weak, but she was shaking like a leaf from the shock and adrenaline of the incident. She wrapped one arm around Connor's neck and pressed her face against his chest, taking in a deep breath to calm herself.

"It's okay, baby, I've got you," Connor said. He pushed his way through the screaming horde, his security detail holding everyone back until they got to the safety of the studio door. He didn't put her down once they were inside, and she could feel his heart beating almost as rapidly as hers. Finally, they made it to the dressing room. Connor pushed his way through the door and sat down on one of the couches, still holding Lexie against him.

Embarrassed at having to be rescued by him, Lexie pushed herself upright and attempted to extricate herself from his arms.

Instead of letting her go, Connor held on to her even more tightly. "Shit, Lexie, I saw it go down, but I couldn't get to you fast enough! I'm so sorry I let that happen to you. Are you okay? Are you hurt?" His eyes scanned her face, looking for signs of injury.

"I'm all right, Connor, just a little shaken up." Then feeling her grazed legs start to sting, she added, "I may need to clean my knees up though."

Connor finally eased his tight hold on her enough that she could sit up and extend her legs to assess the damage. She'd torn the skin on both her knees, and dribbles of blood had streaked down her shins.

"Well, that will teach me to dress more appropriately next time I go out into the field with you guys," she joked ruefully. She smiled shakily up at Connor, but he was staring at her knees, his jaw clenched.

"This was my fault, Lexie. I should have had one of the security guys sticking next to you. I thought the insanity would be focused on us, but I guess someone figured they could steal your camera and help themselves to some free photos." He finally looked back up at her eyes and gave her a strained smile. "I should've taken better care of you."

They stared at each other, and heat abruptly flared up in her as she realized she was still sitting on his lap. It seemed like he'd noticed it at the same time because she could feel him hardening beneath her. She should move, climb off his lap and put some distance between them, but he was still looking into her eyes, and she couldn't bring herself to leave.

She kept still as he cupped her cheek, not wanting to break the tension that had risen between them. Connor's eyes dropped to her mouth, and when her lips parted slightly in response to his gaze, he skimmed his hand down her face until his fingers rested under her chin, then tilted her head back.

He took his time lowering his mouth to hers, making sure she could protest or move away if she wanted. But she didn't; she couldn't. Her entire body was thrumming wildly in response to his closeness. She couldn't think of anything she wanted more at that moment than to feel his lips on hers.

The door to the dressing room flung open, and Drew came charging in with a first aid kit swinging from his hand. "I saw blood, thought you'd need this!"

Lexie jumped in shock, pulling herself out of Connor's arms and sliding onto the couch beside him. Her face burning in embarrassment, she stared down at her knees. "Uh, thanks, Drew. It's not that bad, but I probably need to clean up a bit."

Suddenly, the shock of it all, followed by the sudden surge of emotion, left her drained. She couldn't look Connor or Drew in the eye, even though she could sense Connor staring at her intently.

What had she been thinking? She'd decided already that she needed to get back to having a professional relationship with Connor. As much as her body urged her toward him, her head and her heart told her it was a terrible idea. Getting caught up in Connor, and almost certainly having her heart broken, might end up breaking her forever. She needed to stop letting herself get distracted by him and focus on the job she was here to do.

She jumped up from the couch and took the first aid kit from Drew. "Thanks, I'll get cleaned up," she said as she walked head down to the bathroom, flipped the light on, and closed the door behind her.

Chapter 28

After the incident with Lexie the night before, Connor had come to a decision. He still wanted her. Badly. And he was sick of fighting it. The thought of walking away at the end of the tour having only had her once seemed like a travesty.

There were still five weeks left—plenty of time for them to work through whatever there was between them before they parted ways. Now he just needed to get Lexie on the same page. From her reaction the night before she still wanted him, but whether she'd be interested in a short-term fling he wasn't sure. He knew it might take some convincing, but now that she'd had sex for the first time after Damien, it wouldn't do her any favors to revert to celibacy now. He could help her get over her guilt so that when they parted ways, she'd be in a good place to move on. That way they'd both get what they wanted.

During that night's concert, he spent far too much time tracking her with his eyes as she moved around the edge of the stage and through the crowd. The tension he felt at the thought of touching her again seemed to give extra energy to his performance. The excitement from the crowd ramped up the adrenaline coursing through him, and when they left the stage after the final encore, he was almost shaking with the need to release it.

"Fucking brilliant show, guys!" Drew pounded his back, then high-fived the others. "I don't know what happened out there tonight, but it was fucking awesome! The crowd is still going nuts!" Connor shook his head. The last thing he wanted Drew to know was that the extra edge to his performance that night was because of a woman.

"Anyone seen Lexie?" he asked as casually as he could, hoping no one could hear the strain in his voice.

Tex answered him. "Saw her talking to some of the techs." He gave Connor a too-knowing smirk. "Don't worry, your girl will be back with you soon."

Connor stiffened. He didn't know what Tex was playing at, but the adrenaline and tension flooding him, mixed with anger at his friend's insinuation—made worse when Drew turned narrowed eyes on him—caused him to react without thinking. "She's not my fucking girl, she's the photographer, and she should be here doing her fucking job not flirting with the crew."

Tex's grin slipped as his gaze darted over Connor's shoulder. Connor stilled; his friend's expression telling him how badly he'd just screwed up. Tex held out his hand and drew Lexie to his side, putting his arm around her waist protectively and kissing her on her head.

Connor had to take a deep breath and close his eyes before he could look at her. When he did, she had her face tipped up toward Tex, who was murmuring something in her ear while glaring in Connor's direction. For a second Lexie's eyes slid toward him, but then she averted her gaze, nodding at whatever Tex was saying.

Shit! Why the hell had he reacted so defensively to Tex's comment? Now he'd hurt her and made it sound like he didn't think she was doing her job. He looked around at the others. Zac and Noah were looking at him with furrowed brows, while Drew had his eyes fixed on Lexie, a frown on his face.

How was he going to fix this? There was no way he could explain himself in front of everyone. The only thing he could do was to get her alone later and apologize. Rubbing the back of his neck he mumbled, "I'm going to hit the shower."

He ignored the glare Tex was giving him. After all, if Tex hadn't opened his fucking mouth and tried to get a rise out of him in front of everyone, then this wouldn't have happened. He snuck a glance at Lexie before he left, but she was looking down and fiddling with her camera. Even as he turned and walked off, he knew he wasn't handling this the right way, but he didn't know what else to do.

***

The after-show party was in full swing when he finally arrived. He'd taken his time because he was still at a loss what to say to Lexie. Well, he'd just have to be honest and lay it out for her, explain why he'd said what he had. She'd understand. He was sure she didn't want all the guys knowing about their private business any more than he did. Determined to get this sorted tonight, he moved through the room looking for her.

He tried not to be abrupt with the fans that kept grabbing him as he maneuvered through the crowd, but when the third woman stopped him and lifted her shirt so he could sign her tits, he grew frustrated. What the hell was it with women wanting their bodies to be signed? It would wash away as soon as they had a shower, so what was the point?

As he started scrawling his signature with the pen she handed him, he could feel eyes on him. He knew who it would be; after all, his recent luck as far as Lexie was concerned had been terrible.

Glancing around, he found her standing in the corner of the room, watching him with an unreadable expression on her face. She was holding her camera in her hands, and as he met her eyes, she raised it and took a photo of him, the woman in front of him still with her tits on display, and then she turned and walked away.

Shit, so she was definitely pissed, then. He capped the pen and handed it distractedly back to the woman he'd just signed, blowing her off as she started gushing about how much she loved the band.

Pushing his way through the crowd and trying his best to dodge the fans with *that* look in their eyes, he tried to catch up with Lexie. When he did, she was taking a photo of a half-naked woman practically pole dancing on Zac while he casually drank a beer and chatted to Drew.

Connor leaned in close to Lexie's ear. "What are you doing?"

She must have known he was there because she didn't react to his presence. Pivoting with her camera still held up to her face, she snapped a photo of Noah sitting on one of the couches with a small giggly blonde on his lap. Seeing the lens pointed at him didn't bother Noah one bit. He raised his beer and grinned at the camera.

"Lexie." Connor spoke louder and grabbed her hand.

"Stop and talk to me. What are you doing?"

Sighing, she dropped the camera and turned to face him. He took a half step back at the expression on her face. She didn't look angry or hurt like he was expecting, but her normally clear eyes were dull, and she looked tired. Worse, she looked resigned.

"Lexie?" he tried again, and this time she answered him.

"You were right, Connor. I'm the band's photographer, and I haven't been doing the job I'm being paid for."

"That's ridiculous. If this is about what I said, you have to know I didn't mean it. I'm a fucking idiot. You've been doing a fantastic job. I love the photos you've taken. They're exactly what I wanted."

She shook her head to stop him. "Do you remember that first day; the setup for your first concert? You said you were glad that I wasn't a fan because that way I'd see you as you really are? And I tried to make a joke about the fact you didn't think I could behave professionally if I was a fan."

He nodded slowly, not sure where she was going with this.

"Well, you were right. I haven't been acting professionally. I let my attraction to you cloud my judgment." Her cheeks flared with color.

"Lexie—" He tried to interrupt, but she hadn't finished.

She stepped closer so no one could hear her. "Sleeping with you was unprofessional."

He shook his head in denial, but she surprised him.

"I said I didn't regret it, and I don't; I knew what I was doing. That's not the thing I regret. You asked me at the start of all this not to photograph what I expected to see, so instead I ended up shooting only what I wanted to see. And *that* is the most unprofessional thing I've done on this job."

There was a mix of anger and disappointment in her eyes, but she wasn't directing it at him; she was directing it at herself, which was somehow worse. He had to say something to stop this, but he had no clue what, which was ridiculous considering he wrote lyrics for a living.

Instead, he grabbed her hand. "Come with me."

When she balked, he tugged her hand more insistently, and she gave in and let him pull her along behind him. He led her out of the crowded room and pulled her into the adjacent dressing room, locking the door behind them.

Letting go of her, he ran a hand through his hair. He still wasn't sure what to say to make this right, but he had to say something.

Reaching for her camera, he took it from her and placed it carefully on a nearby table before turning back.

"Lexie. Christ. Putting aside for the moment the fact that I'm a fucking asshole for saying what I did, I love what you've done with the photos. You've caught aspects of this crazy lifestyle that others never see, and that's exactly what I wanted. Yes, some parts are less than savory—that's out of my hands. I can't control what fans ask for, and I can't control what the other guys do. But what you've seen through your lens so far is what I want to see too."

She frowned, not understanding what he was trying to say. Fuck it. When words failed him, there was only one thing left to do. Taking two steps forward, he wrapped his hands around her arms, pulled her against him, and pressed his mouth hard against hers.

She stiffened, and when she raised her hands and rested them against his chest, he thought she would push him away. But then she fisted his shirt in her hands and opened her lips underneath his. Relief washed through him, followed by a surge of lust as he got to taste her again. God, she tasted too good, and the little moan she let out as he stroked her tongue with his had him instantly hard.

He wanted to stand there with her pressed against him forever. He wanted to strip her naked and take her up against the wall. He wanted to take her back to his room and fuck her for hours. He wanted it all, and he wanted it right now, but he knew they still needed to resolve things between them before he could do any of that. For what he wanted from her, he needed her full agreement, otherwise, this would end badly, and he didn't want that on his conscience.

He eased his mouth away from hers, although he couldn't bring himself to pull too far away, keeping his lips hovering just above hers until her eyes fluttered open.

"Lexie," he murmured. She blinked, the dreamy haze clearing from her eyes. He thought she might shove him away then, but once again she surprised him by easing herself back, letting his shirt go but keeping her hands on his chest.

She tilted her head and stared at him, the slight crease between her eyebrows signaling her confusion. He took a deep breath, trying to get his thoughts together, which was difficult when she was standing so close to him.

"Lexie, baby. I hate seeing you upset, particularly when it's because of something I've done. I'm sorry about what I said to Tex—it was a stupid thing to say. But I only said it because I was trying to stop everyone seeing just how much I want you."

Her forehead wrinkled. "I don't understand. You said

you only wanted one night. We had that." She paused, then cast her eyes down as she continued. "And it didn't end very well."

He reached for her chin and tilted it back up so he could see her eyes. "Listen to me. Your reaction was completely understandable. You had a fucking nightmare about the death of your husband. Hell, I felt like shit that what we did caused you to feel one second of guilt. But I have to tell you, that night was incredible. I haven't been able to stop thinking about it— about you—since then."

"So, what does that mean? Do you want another night?" She didn't seem angry at the idea, which boded well, but she also didn't look like she was about to throw herself into his arms. Understandable considering everything that had happened tonight.

"No. I don't want another night." Was that a flash of disappointment he saw? "I want you every night, for the rest of the tour."

Her sharp intake of breath showed he'd surprised her. Then she shook her head.

"Connor, I don't know if I can do that. Don't get me wrong, being with you was amazing." She blushed but held his gaze, which he found as sexy as hell. "But I don't know if I have the emotional fortitude for what you're asking. I'm not like your groupies; I'm not used to having flings. You can have any woman you want, any time you want. What if you get bored with me before the tour is over? I don't want to have to see you every day and watch you take other women back to your room. I'm sorry, but I'm just not made that way."

He frowned. This wasn't going as well as he'd hoped. But

the way he felt about her right now, there was no way he would get bored with her anytime soon. How was he going to reassure her though?

"Lexie. You know I'm not interested in relationships. I've never even wanted to spend more than one night with any woman. Until now. I don't think it would be physically possible for me to get bored with you in the next five weeks; there are so many things I want to do to you. And have you do to me." The flare of heat in her eyes made him smile.

"I promise for the next five weeks, you'll be the only woman I touch. And if you have nightmares, we'll just work through it until that unnecessary guilt you feel is gone for good."

He raised his hand and brushed a tendril of hair back from her cheek, then stroked his fingertips down the side of her face. She sighed and angled her head toward his touch.

"Well, I can't say I haven't thought about being with you again. More than I should have." She gave him a sweetly seductive smile that sent a shot of lust straight to his cock. "I know it probably isn't what you want to hear, but can I think about it? It's kind of a lot to process. And I have to consider what it might mean for my work."

He had to laugh at himself. This was the first time a woman had ever had to think about having sex with him, and it just made him want her more. He didn't even realize that was possible. And while he was disappointed he wouldn't be able to have her tonight, he understood where she was coming from. He just hoped to God she ended up saying yes, because he was desperate for some release from the constant tension being around her caused.

"You can think about it, but just to help with your

decision…" He stepped toward her, speared his hands into her hair to hold her head still, and captured her mouth while he backed her up until she was against the wall.

Maybe it wasn't fair, but the desire he had for her was like a physical ache that nothing but having his hands on her seemed to ease. He teased her lips with his tongue until she opened for him and he could taste her again. He didn't pull any punches, pushing his hips up against hers so she could feel how hard he was and remember just how good it could be between them.

He didn't stop until she was moaning and pressing herself against him in return. It took every bit of self-restraint he had to back away from her, but he knew he had to give her the time she needed to decide she wanted this badly enough to take the risk. Otherwise, she'd end up regretting it, and he didn't want anything to ruin these last few weeks with her.

When he stepped back, he swallowed hard at her expression:

flushed and glassy-eyed, with kiss-swollen lips.

Fuck.

He'd been trying to make it hard for her to say no, but he thought he'd just made it worse for him if she didn't agree to his proposition.

"I've got an idea. How about tomorrow, we go out somewhere together, just the two of us. You still haven't taken my portrait, so maybe we could do that. No pressure, just some one-on-one time."

He gave her his best puppy dog eyes. It must've worked because she laughed. "Okay, I think we could do that.

Anywhere in particular you want to do it?"

"I'd like to do it with you everywhere." He grinned as she rolled her eyes at him, and then relented. "I'd like to go back to the beach. The other day at Drew's was the most relaxed I've felt in a while. I'd like to go to the beach again with just you this time. Would that work?"

She gave him a searching look and then nodded slowly. "I think that would be perfect."

"Great. Let's go back to the hotel. I don't want to go back to the party." He held his hands up in the air at her skeptical expression. "No funny business, I promise. I'll drop you at your room just like a real gentleman would."

She laughed. "Okay then, let's go."

When he reached out his hand to her and she took it, he didn't let himself think too hard about how good it felt.

Chapter 29

By the time Lexie got up, showered, put on a pale blue sundress, and made it down to breakfast the next morning, Connor had organized a car and let everyone know they were heading out.

Lexie just asked him to grab his guitar, and then half an hour later, the two of them were speeding out of the city heading toward the coast.

Connor was driving again, and Lexie didn't mind at all since she could relax in the passenger seat and admire the scenery—that being the sexy-as-sin man sitting in the car next to her. She let out a little sigh of appreciation at how gorgeous he was, causing him to turn his head toward her.

"Everything okay over there?" he asked with a smile.

"Just enjoying the view." She gestured out the car window, but his smile widened as if he knew what she'd actually been enjoying.

"The view is *definitely* beautiful," he replied, holding her gaze. Lexie felt the blush sweep across her cheeks, giving away her reaction to his words. Luckily, he turned back to the road, giving her body a chance to settle down.

She should think harder about the proposition he'd made her, but after tossing and turning for a few hours the night before, she hadn't been able to get any further in her thought process than wanting to throw herself at him.

"What are you thinking about?" He glanced back over at her.

She laughed. "Wouldn't you like to know?"

"I'd love to know what's going on in that gorgeous head of yours right now."

Not wanting to reveal how close she was to saying yes to him and then making him pull over so she could jump him, she tried to focus on what they were supposed to be doing.

"Right now, I'm trying to think of the right photo for you. So we're going to the beach. You said last night that you felt more relaxed at Drew's the other day than you had for a while. Why is that?"

"Are you asking why I found the beach relaxing, or why I haven't been relaxed lately?"

"Both I suppose. But you don't have to tell me if you don't want to."

"Well, the answer to both questions is partly you."

"Me?" Her eyebrows arched up. "What do you mean?"

He shook his head. "Lexie, you have no idea how hard it's been having you around all the time and to not be able to touch you. I thought after that first night with you it would get easier, but it didn't. Instead, I just knew what I was missing out on every time you went to bed on your own. I'm not used to that feeling."

"Wow. That's, um, that's incredibly flattering," she said, voice barely above a whisper.

"I'm not trying to flatter you, Lexie, I'm trying to tell you the effect you have on me. That's one reason I haven't been relaxed lately. Then that day and night at Drew's, getting to hang with you and my friends, no expectations, no one wanting anything from me, that was amazing. I just wish I had time to do that sort of thing more often. Seeing you in a bikini, also a big plus point."

He surprised a laugh out of her. "Seeing you wandering around without a shirt on wasn't too bad either."

"I'll strip for you anytime you want, baby."

Just like that, they were back to flirting.

Lexie knew by the feel of her heart tripping in her chest that she was 99 percent sure she would be saying yes to him before the day was over.

They sat in a not-uncomfortable silence for another few minutes before Connor indicated and turned left.

"Where are we going?" she asked.

"One of the crew who's from around here told me about this little beach which for some reason is usually dead this time of the year. Apparently, it's perfect if you want some privacy." When he glanced over at her, the look in his eyes was scorching.

Oh my God. Lexie had to clasp her hands together in her lap to stop them trembling.

A few minutes later they pulled up to a small deserted parking area, from which led a sand-covered path disappearing over the top of a dune.

When Lexie opened her door and stepped out, the fresh salty air rushed through her, dissipating some of the tension from her body. She closed her eyes and breathed it in. A light breeze fluttered the tendrils of hair that had fallen out of her ponytail around her face, and the sun warmed her skin.

Smiling, she turned toward Connor, only to see him leaning against the bonnet of the car watching her. The glitter in his green eyes made her breath catch.

Standing up straight, he walked toward her, clasped her hand in his large warm one, and stepped backward toward the path, his eyes never leaving hers as she followed him. When they got to the path, he turned and led her over the top so she could see the pretty little cove laid out in front of them.

"Wow, this is gorgeous!" she exclaimed, shading her eyes from the brightness of the sun. A small half-circle of white sand fringed the deep cobalt blue of the water. A rocky headland closed off one end of the beach. "I can't believe there's no one else here."

"I'm going to have thank my man Doug when we get back. This is perfect. Just you, me, the sun, sand, and sea."

He tugged her closer and ran his hands down the bare skin of her arms, leaving goosebumps trailing in their wake. She watched him follow their progress across her skin, his expression serious. She should feel embarrassed about her body's reaction to him, but at that moment she was beyond caring.

He closed his eyes and took a deep breath, then stepped back from her. When he opened them again, their normal clear green had turned stormy, and he ran his hands through his hair before saying, with slightly forced humor, "Okay, so let me guess, you want me to strip off for this portrait, then? Maybe a photo of me frolicking naked in the sand?"

Grateful that he'd broken the highly charged moment and reminded her why they were here, Lexie looked around. It was all gorgeous, but something about the stark beauty of the rocky headland made her think of Connor.

She ran back to the car to get her camera and his guitar

and then got him set up against the cliffs. He laughed when she asked him to take his top off.

"I knew this was just an excuse to get me shirtless."

Rolling her eyes and trying unsuccessfully to suppress her smile, she got him to lean his back against the cliffs. He held the head of his guitar in his left hand and rested the base in the sand by his bare feet, then tipped his head down slightly so that his hair fell forward and shaded his eyes.

The result was beautiful—both the man and his instrument surrounded by the darkness of the rock behind them but lit up by the shimmering sun that seemed to caress both the curves of the guitar and the hard angles and planes of his body. With his eyes shadowed, you couldn't tell his expression, but he had an air of pensiveness about him, even with all the surrounding sunlight.

She snapped photos from multiple angles until she was satisfied she had what she wanted. When she was done, she let the camera drop on its strap and just stared at him for a few seconds. When he raised his eyes and met her gaze, time seemed to almost stand still as a breath shuddered out of her.

"All done?" he asked.

"Yep. I've got plenty to work with. The camera loves you, just like everyone else." She was joking but then blushed when she heard what it sounded like. "Um, you know, all your fans."

Okay, now she was just making it worse.

He laughed. "So you're trying to tell me you don't love me? Way to break my heart, Lexie."

She couldn't help but laugh back at him. "Oh yes, I'm sure you're devastated."

He held out his hand to her. "Come on, let's go sit in the

sun for a bit. We've still got a while before we have to be back."

She took his hand, the guitar string callouses slightly rough against her skin, and walked with him over to one of the dunes. He sat and then pulled her down next to him. Letting go of her and leaning back on his hands, which, considering he was still shirtless, nearly rendered her speechless. He closed his eyes and turned his face up to the sun, which meant she had time to study him without embarrassing herself by having him catch her.

Her eyes lingered on his face, the long dark lashes brushing his high cheekbones, the seductive curve of his lips, the strong jawline. She drifted her gaze down the column of his throat to his wide shoulders and muscular pecs, down along his sculpted six-pack, to the waistband of his jeans.

The man was utterly, breathtakingly gorgeous, and her mouth went dry as she realized she'd already made her decision.

There hadn't really ever been any doubt about what she wanted, just fear of how much it would end up hurting. But the fact of the matter was, it would hurt regardless. She was already in too deep, so she might as well get her fill of him while they were together. Once the tour ended, she'd never see him again except for on the cover of a magazine.

She didn't know if sleeping with someone to get them out of your system ever actually worked, but surely having the next few weeks with him would be better than trying to force herself not to touch him the way she wanted to.

As she was trying to figure out how you go about telling a rock star you want to have a fling with him, he opened his vivid green eyes and glanced over at her. "So, I've been meaning to ask, what's next for you? After the tour I mean. Do you have another project lined up?"

Taken off guard, she tried to refocus her thoughts. "Uh, yes I do. A couple of weeks after I'm finished up with you guys, I'm contracted for a shoot in Canada. It's for a travel magazine, so I'll be taking lots of landscapes and some street photography, which will be nice. I'll spend the couple of weeks between jobs putting together a mock-up of your book so you can look at it while I'm out of the country."

Something flickered in his eyes. "You love your work, don't you?" He sounded almost wistful.

She nodded, surprised. "I do. It keeps me out of my own head and lets me explore the world. I think it's what stopped me becoming bitter after Damien's death."

Even now the words were hard to say. But she had a question she wanted to ask him. "So how about you? What's it like to be living the dream?"

He paused for a beat before responding. "For a long time, it was amazing. We were on top of the world. Fame, fortune, me and my friends getting to play music together and being paid obscene amounts for it. But now..."

He turned his head to face her. "I haven't told anyone else this, but I'm starting to get tired of it all. The constant touring, the pressure of expectation from the fans and the label, the push to write the next hit song. I feel fucking ungrateful because we just keep getting bigger and bigger, and I should feel on top of the world. But I don't. Now it just feels like everyone wants a piece of me. Who I am as a person has been completely subsumed by this persona of a rock star." He paused. "I don't feel that way with you though. I feel like maybe you can see me for who I am." He turned to look back at the ocean.

"What are you going to do about it?" she asked quietly.

He shrugged. "I haven't figured it out yet. Probably nothing. I'm thinking this is just a phase I'm going through, and soon I'll go back to feeling like king of the fucking world."

Lexie wasn't sure what to say to that. Before she could get her thoughts together, he turned to her, a massive smile on his face, and said, "Let's go for a swim."

Lexie laughed in surprise at the abrupt change of topic. "It'll be cold, and I don't have a swimsuit on me."

"Who needs a swimsuit," he said, and standing up, he unbuttoned and dropped his jeans, leaving him in only a tight pair of black briefs. Lexie couldn't stop her gaze drinking him in. Good God, it should be illegal for a man to be as sexy as Connor.

He held out his hand to her and gave the kind of smile that just dared her to throw caution to the wind. Laughing, she grabbed it and he pulled her to her feet.

"Do you need me to help you out of your clothes?" he asked with a devilish smile.

"I've got it."

She started unbuttoning her sundress, extremely aware of his eyes on her fingers as the material parted over her breasts. She was wearing a bra, but still, it was impossible not to notice the hard peaks of her nipples jutting through the thin material. She quickly finished shimmying out of the dress.

Connor made an inarticulate noise, and she met his eyes, noting his expression was almost pained. Dropping her eyes, she saw the very prominent evidence of his reaction to her innocent striptease.

"Sorry, can't be helped." He smirked, before grabbing her hand and pulling her toward the water.

Reaching the shoreline, he dropped her hand, then ran and dove into the dark blue depths. Lexie watched in appreciation as he surfaced a few seconds later, flicking his wet hair out of his eyes and then turning to her and smiling in invitation.

Even though her toes felt cold where the small waves lapped at her feet, there was no way Lexie could resist the invitation in that smile. He seemed so happy and carefree, as if the weight of the world had been lifted off him, and she wanted to bask in his undivided attention.

With a slightly embarrassing girly squeal, she splashed through the waves and launched herself into the water, surfacing next to him. He laughed at her when she did, so she splashed him in the face with her hand. Realizing her mistake when she saw the promise of retribution on his face, she turned to swim away. She only got a few strokes in before she felt his warm hand close around her ankle and drag her back toward him.

Running his other hand up her body, he grabbed her by the waist and pulled her up against him. The contrast of the hard heat of him against her breasts and stomach and the cool water everywhere else had her skin overstimulated. When he dropped his head down and pressed his mouth against hers, she didn't hesitate to open to him. It would end up hurting her, but there was no conceivable way she could say no to this.

She ran her hands up his arms and linked them around the back of his neck to give herself more leverage to press against him. Both of them were breathing unevenly when he pulled away. He slid his hands down to the back of her thighs and lifted her up.

"Wrap your legs around me," he said, voice rough.

She did and felt him hard and ready against her. She rubbed against him and he groaned, dropping his forehead down and pressing it to hers. "Fuck, Lexie. Please tell me you've decided. I can't take much more of this." The restrained need in his voice had her body vibrating.

"I'm saying yes," she whispered.

He lifted his head and studied her eyes. "Say it again," he demanded.

She licked suddenly dry lips and said, "Yes," louder this time.

In the next second his mouth was on hers, and he was kissing her deeply as he pulled her harder against him. He shifted his grip, and the fingers of his right hand slid underneath the bottom of her panties, moving over her skin to where she was crying out for him to touch her.

Just before he got there, a piercing whistle sounded. Lexie jumped and Connor pulled his hand away. Looking at the beach, Lexie couldn't believe it when she saw a couple walking down the path, a Labrador running backward and forward on the sand in front of them.

Connor cursed. "Worst timing ever," he groaned.

Lexie dropped her forehead against his chest, letting out a shuddering breath. Turning her head toward the beach, she saw the couple lay down towels, before walking down the sand and throwing a ball for the eager dog. "It looks like they're planning to stay for a while. You should probably let me down."

Reluctantly he let her slide down his body, giving her an excruciating vision of what might have happened if they hadn't been interrupted.

They walked out of the water hand in hand. Connor scrubbed his free hand over his face. "It's getting late anyway. We should dry off, then head back. The guys won't appreciate it if I miss soundcheck."

Tugging her toward him, he crushed his mouth against hers, his tongue thrusting between her lips, filling her with the dark, masculine taste of him. The slow, deep kiss was so intoxicating and full of promise she lost her breath.

Finally, he pulled away saying, "We'll pick this back up tonight, after the show."

She nodded shakily, and he tugged her down onto the sand so they could dry off since they hadn't thought to bring any towels with them. The sun was hot as it approached midday, so they sat close enough for their arms and legs to touch and watched the Labrador chase a ball around the beach. When they'd dried enough, Connor passed her sundress to her and pulled on his jeans, leaving his shirt off.

While she got dressed, he picked up his guitar, walked down toward the water, and stood looking out at the ocean, guitar slung casually over his shoulder. Her heart skipped a beat at the sight, and she grabbed her camera, uncapped the lens, and snapped a couple of photos. Those ones would be just for her; to help her get through the pain when they went their separate ways.

She blinked back tears. They hadn't even started, and she was already sad about it ending.

Still, when he turned and walked back toward her, a relaxed smile on his gorgeous face, Lexie knew she was all in. At least for the next five weeks.

Chapter 30

L exie could barely concentrate during the concert. The anticipation for the night ahead had her completely worked up. Wherever she was shooting, either in the crowd or backstage, her eyes were drawn to Connor. Her camera was full of photos of him because she couldn't think of anything else.

As he prowled around the stage in black jeans and a tight white V-neck t-shirt that emphasized his muscular arms and chest, her eyes tracked his movements. Her breath became erratic as she imagined having all night with him, to touch and taste as much as she wanted.

When she was in the pit in front of the stage, her camera focused on him, he stalked toward her and stared straight into the lens as he sang. After snapping a couple of shots, she had to drop the camera from her face to stare up at him, mesmerized as he shot her a smile so hot it stole her breath.

She shivered, her nipples hardening beneath the thin material of her dress as excitement swept through her. God, she was so on edge she would explode the moment he touched her.

When the band finished their last set, Lexie moved quickly to the side of the stage. She found the guys huddled together, catching their breath and rehydrating with water after their intense performance.

As she walked up, trying to appear casual and not like she was about to jump out of her skin, Noah reached out and hooked an arm around her shoulders, hauling her into his sweaty side.

She glanced over at Connor and gave him a slight smile when she saw that he'd tensed at the display of affection by Noah. He released a breath, then seemed to shake the tension off, giving her a seductive smile that had her pulse skyrocketing.

She wished they could skip the after-party, but there was no way for both of them to miss making an appearance without arousing suspicion. Hopefully, it would be a short one tonight, because Lexie didn't think she would survive the sexual tension for much longer. The way Connor was watching her, all stormy-eyed intensity, made her think she wasn't the only one being driven crazy by the wait.

Lexie was a nervous wreck during the party, so much so she had to stop pretending there was any chance she'd take a decent photo. In fact, by the time the party wrapped up and everyone prepared to head home, she was starting to have second thoughts. Was she actually going to do this? Have Connor come to her room intending to sleep with him again?

Sitting next to him in the limo on the way home, his denim-clad leg pressed against hers, she fiddled with her camera, popping the lens on and off until he put his hand on hers and squeezed it gently.

Glancing up at him, she noticed his dilated pupils and the tic in his tense jaw. Knowing he was feeling the anticipation just as much as she was calmed her down a bit. Thinking she was all tied up in knots while he was completely unfazed had made her slightly queasy.

The elevator ride up to their floor seemed to last forever. At least no one seemed to have noticed that Lexie and Connor were equally tense and silent.

Connor and Tex both had their rooms further down the hall than Lexie, so she had to make a show of saying good night to everyone and going into her room. Rushing to the bathroom, she stared at herself in the mirror, noting how wide her eyes were and the slight flush that highlighted her cheekbones. She took a quick shower, then changed into some lacy lingerie and slipped back into her dress. She then paced nervously until she heard a soft knock.

Her heart was in her mouth when she unlatched the door and swung it open. Connor was standing there, looking deceptively casual in his jeans and t-shirt, but her mouth went dry at the sight of all the coiled energy contained in his large frame. Smoothing her hands nervously over the skirt of her dress, she stepped back in invitation.

He walked in, his hand brushing hers as he passed. She closed the door and turned, but before she could take a breath, he was on her. Crowding her against the wall, his tall body pressed against her, his hands cupping her face as he crashed his lips against hers.

Gasping, she arched up, opening her mouth to him and moaning as his tongue thrust into her mouth. Her nipples hardened, and she clutched his shirt, trying to get closer to him, all nerves forgotten in the surge of lust that rocketed through her.

Pulling away, Connor lowered his forehead against hers, his breathing harsh. She could feel his already hard length against her stomach, and she couldn't stop herself rubbing against him.

He groaned. "Lexie, you're killing me. I haven't been able to think of anything today but this moment, when I get to taste you again. I want to take my time with you tonight, but you're not making it easy for me."

"We've got all night." The huskiness of her own voice shocked her.

He raised his head, and his lips curled up, his eyes glittering. "Yes, we do. And I don't want to waste a second."

Without giving her a chance to react, Connor's mouth was hard on hers again, urging her to open for him. He kept one hand cupped around the back of her head, holding her to him, while his other hand slid slowly down her neck, across her collarbone to the row of buttons that ran down the front of her dress.

He flicked the first one open, his finger brushing the now-exposed upper curve of her breast, causing her skin to erupt in goosebumps. As he flicked the second button open, the dress gaped further, revealing the sheer lace of her bra.

Connor broke the kiss and looked down.

Lexie followed his gaze, seeing his long fingers undo the third button, revealing her lace-covered breasts completely. Her nipples jutted out, and they both watched as his fingers tugged the cups of her bra down, exposing her to his hungry gaze. Lexie's breath was rasping in and out of her now, the anticipation of his touch a sweet ache that made her breasts feel heavy and swollen.

After what seemed like forever, he finally cupped her breast, his thumb stroking over her hard nipple, the roughness of his skin rasping exquisitely over the sensitive peak. Lexie couldn't watch anymore; she threw her head back, feeling like she couldn't get enough air.

When he dropped his head and sucked her nipple into his mouth, she thought she might come then and there. The suction of his mouth was like a direct line to between her thighs, and she grew slick with need. When his teeth grazed her, she moaned low in her throat, a sound she didn't recognize as having come from her.

He moved to her other breast, giving it the same attention. By now she was squirming against him, desperate for some kind of relief. "Connor, please," she panted.

She felt his lips curve up as he smiled against her skin, but then he lifted his head and took her mouth again in a deep, drugging kiss. As he did, he ran his hand along the curve of her waist and down her thigh until he reached the hem of her dress, then stroked up along the soft skin of her inner thigh until he reached her panties. Slipping his fingers underneath, he brushed his knuckle along her center.

"So wet," he groaned.

She couldn't even feel embarrassed, his voice was so strained with desire.

He pulled his hand out, gathered up her skirt, and lifted it above her hips, dropping to his knees so his face was in front of the scrap of lace between her legs.

"Beautiful," he murmured and pressed a kiss on the lace directly over her clit. Lexie whimpered, and he must have taken pity on her because he hooked the fingers of one hand into the waistband of her panties and dragged them down her legs, helping her step out of them before tossing them to the side.

Now she was fully exposed to his gaze, and she didn't

think she'd ever been so close to coming without having even been properly touched. The feel of his breath fanning against her sensitive skin had her squirming, but he held her hips still with his hands. Just as she thought she would have to beg, he leaned forward and ran his tongue along the oversensitive skin between her legs, before stroking it against her clit, causing her to shiver.

As he continued to lick and suck, she looked down at him. The sight of his dark head between her legs, the skirt of her dress hiked up to her hips and her breasts overflowing from the front of her dress, was one of the most erotic things she'd ever seen.

When he slid two fingers inside her, stroking in and out just the way she needed, the tension radiating from her core overwhelmed her. She clutched at his hair as she ground herself against his mouth, gasping and shuddering as she came.

He pressed a soft kiss to her inner thigh, then stood back up. The pupils of his eyes were so dilated, only a thin ring of green was visible around the black. Brushing his lips against hers he murmured, "You taste so sweet, I think I could do that all night long."

Still coming down from her intense orgasm, Lexie shivered again and then pushed up on her tiptoes so she could whisper in his ear, "But I want to taste you too."

"Fuck, Lexie," he growled.

He lifted her up, hands under her thighs, and she wrapped her legs around his hips as he made his way toward the bedroom, his lips fused with hers.

Chapter 31

Connor didn't think he'd seen anything sexier than Lexie as she sat on the bed looking up at him with those big gray eyes; her hair disheveled, cheeks flushed, and breasts still on display where he'd pulled her bra down.

He was excruciatingly hard, but he needed to give himself a moment otherwise he'd probably come the minute she put her mouth on him. So instead of stripping, he dropped to his knees in front of her and kissed her again. The soft little sounds she made and the way her arms curled around his neck, fingers teasing the hair at the nape of his neck, drove him crazy. Then her hands dropped to the hem of his shirt and she pulled it up, trying to drag it over his head, and he was forced to stop kissing her so she could.

Once his shirt was off, she leaned back to take him in, her eyes seeming to stroke over every inch of his bare chest. Then she reached out and ran her fingers lightly across his tattoo, from his shoulder to his heart, then leaned forward and pressed her lips where her fingers had just been, her tongue darting out to taste him.

He groaned, his head dropping forward and his hand cupping the back of her head, cradling her against him as she teased. Her hands smoothed down his abdomen, over the waistband of his jeans, and rubbed lightly over his cock. He hissed between his teeth at the feel of her hand on him, even through his jeans, and he couldn't stop his hips jerking forward to try to increase the contact.

"Lexie," he growled, and he didn't know if it was a warning or a plea. She tipped her head back to look him in the eye, a slight smile tipping the corners of her mouth, though her eyes were dark with arousal. Standing up, he took a step back from her. The smile dropped from her lips as her eyes drifted to where his hands were undoing his fly.

He stripped out of his jeans and underwear and then had to give himself a couple of quick strokes to get some relief after seeing the expression on her face as she took all of him in. He stepped forward again, stopping just in front of her, and then reached for her nipple, rolling it between his fingers, while his right hand still gripped his cock.

She moaned at the feel of his fingers on her, then leaned forward, placed her hand over his where he held himself, and wrapped her lips around him. He made a feral sound at the back of his throat as she took him into the wet heat of her mouth, then slid her lips down as far as she could. He couldn't help himself, fisting both hands in her hair but refraining from trying to control her movements.

She fluttered her tongue against him, then pulled back so that her mouth was just wrapped around the tip. Sliding back down, she sucked hard, and this time he couldn't quite stop himself holding her head and thrusting.

Looking down and seeing her with her lips around him, her bare breasts jutting out of her dress, had him right on the edge. If he didn't want to blow his load, he'd need to stop her right now, but he fully intended to enjoy her mouth on him again before the night was over.

Using his hands in her hair to tug her gently back, she glanced up at him with questioning eyes. "That's too good, baby, but the first time I come tonight won't be in your mouth, so you need to stop there."

She nodded, her eyes looking slightly dazed and unfocused as she gave him one last lick, which was so hot it almost had him pushing back between her lips. Instead, he reached out and slipped first one strap and then the other off her shoulders, so that the already half-undone dress dropped to her waist.

"Lean back, baby," he told her, and when she did, he had to stop and stare again because it was so fucking sexy. She was leaning back on her hands with her breasts pushed up by her bra, her dress pooled over her hips, and since he'd already stripped her panties off, he knew she was bare underneath the thin strip of fabric.

"Lift your hips," he demanded. She complied immediately, and he dragged her dress off, discarding it to the side. "Take your bra off." This time it came out like a demand, and he waited with bated breath as she complied.

He suddenly realized she hadn't said a word since she'd told him she wanted to taste him. Concerned he might be pushing her, he dropped to his knees in front of her again so he could see her eye to eye. He reached out and cupped her chin. "Are you still with me, baby?"

She blinked at him and then nodded jerkily. "God yes. I'm sorry, I'm just so turned on I don't think my brain is working properly."

Heat rushed through him. "Well, in that case, move up

the bed and lie down. Let me take care of you." The look she gave him as she did was pure lust. Reaching down to his jeans, he fished out a handful of condoms and threw them onto the side table, then climbed onto the bed. Without him telling her to, she opened her legs, and he crawled in between them, sliding his erection across her damp folds as he slid himself up her body and claimed her mouth. They both groaned in unison at the feel of his hard muscles pressing against her soft curves.

Breathing heavily, he broke the kiss, and she panted, "Connor, I need you inside me right now."

"Not yet, baby. I don't want to rush this; I've been waiting too long."

Then he dropped his head to her chest and sucked her nipple into his mouth, causing her to clutch at his hair and squirm against him. He nipped her in warning, and she stilled under him, the only sound in the room their heavy breaths. As he turned his attention to her other breast, he slid one hand down the soft skin of her stomach and over her hip, until he reached the wetness between her legs. He used his thumb to slide over and around her clit, and she gasped, her hips jolting up against him in response. "Feel good, baby?"

"So good." She pushed her hips up again, trying to get more pressure, more friction, so he gave it to her until she was writhing under him.

"Connor, I need more," she whimpered, and he slid one, then two fingers into her slick heat. This time he groaned; she was so goddamn tight.

Fuck it, he was done waiting.

He rolled over onto his back, pulling her with him until she was straddling his hips. "I want you to ride me."

She looked down at the hard length of him jutting up in front of her. "I want that too," she said, reaching out and stroking him until his hips were thrusting up helplessly.

Fuuucckk, she was going to kill him. Gritting his teeth, he reached down and put one of his hands over hers to stop her, while the other reached for a condom. After he sheathed himself, she lifted up and positioned herself above him. His breaths were coming in pants as she gripped his cock, slid the tip through her wetness a couple of times, and then sunk down. They both groaned in unison as she took him in a couple of inches, before rising back up and sinking down again.

Connor couldn't drag his eyes away from the sight of Lexie taking him into her body one inch at a time. By the time her hips were pressed flush against his, he was so close to coming he had to grip her hips to stop her from moving until he had himself under control.

He stared up at her, her long dark hair hanging down in waves over her shoulders, her cheeks flushed, eyes wide, and lips pink and swollen from his kisses. He felt something shift in his chest at the sight of her, but he pushed it out of his mind, instead using his hands on her hips to encourage her to move. She lifted herself again, pausing for an excruciating second before driving down on him, causing all his muscles to tighten in an effort not to piston up into her. She rolled her hips against his over and over again, gradually increasing her pace and pausing now and then to grind herself against him.

When she threw her head back, he used the opportunity to reach up and palm her breasts, playing with both of her nipples, rolling them between his fingers, then pinching and tugging on them. She whimpered, and he could feel her tightening around him, close to coming. As incredible as it felt having her ride him, for some reason he suddenly wanted to be pounding into her when she came, taking her, making sure she came harder than she ever had before.

Sitting up, he put his arms around her, then rolled them both so he was resting between her legs. She gasped in surprise but then wrapped her legs around his waist and arched into him. "Connor, I need to come."

His mouth crashed against hers as he started pumping into her. He knew he wouldn't last—he'd been waiting for this too long, but he'd make it up to her next time. Now he just wanted to feel her come around him and then lose himself inside her.

Bracing himself on one arm, he reached down and stroked his thumb over her clit. Once, twice, and just like that she came, throwing her head back, gasping and shuddering around him, clenching him so tight he could barely move inside her. Not that it mattered; he was right there with her.

With one last, almost violent thrust, he held himself still as his release blasted through him, feeling like it went on forever, while at the same time ending far too soon. Coming down, he pressed his lips against hers over and over, wanting to prolong the moment before he had to pull out of her.

He could still feel residual shivers running through her body, and when she finally opened her eyes, they were wide and liquid as she gazed up at him, and he felt that shift in his chest again. The one he didn't want to think too hard about. He brushed a few strands of hair away from her face. "Worth waiting for?" He smiled down at her.

"Definitely," she laughed.

That laugh, while he was still inside her, did all kinds of interesting things to him. Already semi-hard again, he gave a few lazy pumps, which made her gasp and shift against him. He leaned down and whispered in her ear, "We're just getting started." Then he had to pull out to take care of the condom, tying it off and throwing it in the wastebasket in the bathroom.

When he came back, she'd rolled over onto her stomach and was looking at him coyly over her shoulder. He ran his eyes down her perfect curves and felt himself harden fully. They wouldn't be getting much sleep tonight.

***

As the door closed behind Connor, Lexie sighed, then pressed her flushed face into the cool pillow. Last night had been amazing. Beyond amazing. She'd lost track of the number of times and ways he'd made her come. And in between, they'd talked. Not about anything serious, just getting to know each other better. Finding out things like favorite countries they'd visited, favorite foods, favorite songs. They'd fallen asleep after Connor set his alarm so he could leave before anyone was wandering the halls.

She'd been the first to raise whether to say anything to the other band members or Drew. They'd agreed to keep their fling quiet. Neither of them wanted to answer the myriad of questions that were bound to be asked or risk Lexie's professional reputation. She knew they would face some difficulty trying to ensure no one found out, but since they were both in uncharted territory, it made sense to keep it quiet.

Rolling over, she stared up at the ceiling. Like probing a sore tooth, she thought of Damien, testing her feelings about what she was doing. While the ever-present sadness was there, the guilt she'd felt last time didn't overwhelm her. She hadn't had the dream either, which made her think maybe she had passed a turning point in her grief. Part of it was what Connor had said last time. Damien wouldn't want her to be alone forever. Just like if she'd been the one to die, she would have wanted him to move on and find happiness with someone else. She would always love Damien; nothing or no one could ever change that. But without him here, that love couldn't sustain her for the rest of her life. She wanted to give her heart to someone and have someone give their heart to her. She wanted to meet someone she could fall for as hard as she'd fallen for Damien.

What if you've already met him?

She pushed the thought away. The physical connection she had with Connor was undeniable. He'd brought her body back to life, blown her mind with the intensity of feeling he could draw from her, and shown her she could move past her grief. But there was no future for them after the end of the tour. He was a rock god, with thousands of willing women at his beck and call. It would be hard enough while they were sleeping together to watch all those women throw themselves at him. She couldn't imagine what it would be like if they were actually together.

The temporary desire he felt for her was just that—temporary. So instead of wishing things were different—that he wasn't what he was—she would grab the next few weeks with both hands and then deal with the inevitable pain when it ended. Sighing, she got out of bed and headed to the shower.

She ended up being the first one down to breakfast. Putting some fruit and toast on her plate, she settled into a booth by the window, losing herself in thoughts of the night before until someone slid in next to her. Turning her head, she saw Noah's blue eyes sparkling at her and couldn't stop the small spike of disappointment that it wasn't Connor. Hoping it hadn't shown on her face, she gave him a warm smile.

"You looked deep in thought?" He raised his eyebrows at her in question.

"Oh, you know, just thinking about the book." She hoped her flushed cheeks didn't give away the lie.

"How's that all going, anyway?"

Before she had a chance to answer, the others arrived in a group. She caught Connor's eye and flashed him a slight smile. When Drew tried to slide into the seat opposite her, Connor casually grabbed his shoulder and said something to him Lexie couldn't hear. Drew nodded and then strode off, while Connor slid into the spot across from her. Lexie couldn't help the warmth that flooded through her at the evidence that he wanted to be near her, even outside the bedroom.

Smiling at him, she asked, "Where's Drew going?"

He cleared his throat and looked slightly embarrassed. "I told him my throat was sore and asked him to get me some orange juice."

Noah raised his eyebrows. "You couldn't get it yourself? You know he's our manager, right, not part of the crew? Don't tell me the fame's finally gone to your head and now you expect to be waited on hand and foot."

Connor scowled at his friend. "You didn't see him complaining, did you? I think the money we make him will compensate for any inconvenience."

"Wow, someone got out on the wrong side of the bed this morning. Didn't you sleep well or something?"

The slow burn of a blush spread over Lexie's cheeks, and she lowered her eyes so she wasn't looking at Connor as he replied.

"Actually, I had an amazing night... of sleep. I wish I could have stayed in bed longer."

Glancing up finally, she met Connor's dark gaze and couldn't stop the corners of her mouth tugging up at the sight of his smirk.

"Well, glad you enjoyed it because we're back on the bus tonight," Noah grumbled.

Connor frowned. She wondered if he was as disappointed as she was that there wouldn't be a repeat of last night. Not until they reached the next hotel stop, which wasn't for another couple of days.

Drew returned with a pitcher of ice-cold orange juice for the table, and conversation halted as everyone dug into their food. After a few minutes, Noah sat back and then turned to her. "You never answered my question about how everything was going with the book."

"Oh, right. I think it's going well. Probably too well. Since I've got so many good photos, it's going to take some tough decisions to narrow it down for the final draft. I've started some mock-ups just to get my thoughts down. I've still got to do Zac's portrait though, when we get a chance." She looked down at the end of the table where Zac was sitting.

He stopped eating and glanced over at the mention of his name, his dark eyes questioning.

She raised her voice slightly. "I was saying I still have to get your portrait. Everyone else's is done."

He nodded. "Sure, just let me know when you need me."

She smiled at the serious bassist in acknowledgment. She probably knew the least about him out of all the guys, which was making it hard to figure out his portrait. There were a couple of vague ideas bouncing around in her head, but nothing definite. She made a mental note to spend some time chatting to him over the next few days to see if she could come up with a firm idea.

Noah put his arm around her and pulled her against him, something he'd done regularly since she'd been with them. This time she noticed something flash in Connor's eyes, and he turned a narrowed gaze on his friend.

"You know, not everyone is as touchy-feely as you are, Noah. Did you ever stop to ask Lexie if she likes being manhandled all the time?"

She gaped at him. Where the hell had that come from? Apparently, she wasn't the only one surprised at his words.

"Lexie's never had a problem with me being affectionate." Noah turned to her. "Have you?"

Her eyes darted toward Connor, who was now looking down at his plate, jaw tense. Uncertain what to say, she looked up at Noah. "Um, I don't have a problem. We're friends. I know you don't mean anything by it."

Noah grinned and winked at her. Then she turned her eyes to Connor, who was staring at her, brows drawn together. She wasn't quite sure what was going on here, but if he wasn't careful, everyone would catch on to what was going on between them. He'd never struck her as the possessive type before, so she couldn't understand why he was reacting this way.

She frowned at him and tried to tell him with her eyes that they would talk later, but he turned and stared resolutely out the window. She didn't know what to do about his reaction, and as much as she hated to admit it, a far too big a part of her was thrilled that he might be feeling possessive.

That part of her would end up getting her heart broken.

After a few minutes, she felt a pressure against her leg under the table, and she looked at him from under her lashes. He seemed to have shaken off whatever had been bothering him, and now his green eyes were warm as he pressed his leg against hers. His expression made her flutter. *She was in so much trouble.*

Chapter 32

Just over a week later, the convoy was rolling into New Orleans. Lexie had spent the last few days hanging out with Zac, trying to find out more about him. It hadn't been easy drawing the enigmatic bassist out, but they'd fallen into a rhythm of asking and answering questions. He'd turned out to have an amateur interest in photography, so they'd had some enjoyable conversations where he'd picked her brain about that, and she'd given him some pointers.

This morning he was trying to explain to her what the difference was between a bass and a six-string guitar, which was something she'd never thought about before.

"The simplest difference is the pitch range. Bass guitar plays notes an octave lower than a six-string guitar. But the fundamental difference is the role of the bass. Along with the drums, it provides the foundation of a song, so that the other instruments and vocals have a solid base to work from."

"So, pretty important, then?" She smiled over at him, enjoying the way his hazel eyes lit up as he talked about the instrument.

"Yep. There aren't many bands that don't have a bass player, though there are quite a few without guitarists. But you also have to make sure not to upstage anyone else, because the bass can end up being too loud and overwhelming. The role of the bass is about improving the whole tune and blending in so that the music itself stands out."

"So, you don't get to do many solos?"

"Not really. I mean, you can solo on the bass, it's just not what it's meant for. But if you listen to a song and lock in on the bass, you can hear the rhythm driving the song and feel the music as much as hear it. Here, let me show you."

He grabbed his phone and set it on a speaker dock, then touched the screen a few times, until Queen's "Another One Bites the Dust" started playing.

"The first notes you hear are the bass, and the song is instantly recognizable just from those few notes on their own."

She nodded, frowning as she concentrated on tuning out the other instruments and the vocals so she could focus on the bass. When she did, she could easily pick out the low, driving notes, and a smile spread across her face as she felt the bass kick in her chest.

"I hear it. It keeps the rhythm going the entire way through."

He stopped it and started another song playing. "This is a good one."

She smiled as she heard "Come Together" from The Beatles. Now that she was listening out for it, the bass was so obvious.

"Last one." He grinned as he searched for a song, then started it playing.

She laughed as she heard the distinctive notes of the Red Hot Chili Peppers' "Give it Away."

"It's so clear when you listen out for it." She was unreasonably delighted, as if she'd discovered something new and amazing. Well, it was new to her, anyway; she'd always been more into photography than music. "I feel like I want to go and listen to all my favorite songs now just to try to pick out the bass."

He laughed. "Don't do that. Remember, the bass isn't supposed to stand out—it's all about joining with the drums to provide the song's rhythm. It's not about being in the spotlight." He glanced over as Tex wandered through the living area on his way to the coffee machine. "I leave the flashy showing off to Tex, while I'm the one that gets everybody moving."

Tex rolled his eyes at Zac. "You just keep telling yourself you don't want to be in the spotlight. Don't forget, I've been with you at karaoke enough times to know you love getting out in front."

Lexie turned back to Zac, who was looking down at his guitar with a slight smile on his face. "You like karaoke?"

"He's there every chance he gets," Tex butted in, then grinned when Zac narrowed his eyes at him.

"So what? I like to sing. You realize I do backing vocals on all our songs, right?"

When he saw Lexie looking at him and smiling, he gave her a suspicious look. "What?"

"I've got an idea."

**

Which was how they came to be sitting at the bar of a karaoke club at eight o'clock in the morning. They were the only ones there except for some college-aged kids sitting at the front that were drawing out the end of a big night.

Zac had a cap pulled down over his face, but that was it as far as a disguise went. She'd been worried about taking him to a public place like this, even at this time of the morning when it was dead. It wouldn't take more than one of the kids at the front to recognize him and call their friends, and they could end up mobbed before the end of the photo shoot. Still, when she'd mentioned it to him, he hadn't been concerned, just shrugging and saying something about being able to blend in easily.

Looking at him now, she couldn't understand what he was talking about. He was a very attractive man, tall and broad-shouldered, with gorgeous hazel eyes. Today, his long legs were clad in black jeans, and he was wearing a worn black leather jacket over a fitted gray t-shirt. As far as she was concerned, heads would definitely turn whenever he walked into a room. He had plenty of fans, so she wasn't sure why he thought no one would recognize him. Maybe it had something to do with the fact that he wasn't in the spotlight as much as Tex and Connor, so he thought he was less recognizable. She didn't agree, but still, at this time of day they were about as safe as they could get.

She'd put a fake name for him down on the list, and he would be on in a few minutes. Her camera was set up on a tripod, and she'd adjusted for the dim light conditions. The darkness of the club and the stage, highlighted by smoky lights, provided a great atmosphere for the background. She'd got a couple of strange looks from the group at the front, but she'd already spoken to the bartender and got his okay to photograph Zac.

When the guy currently singing finished his off-key rendition of "Sweet Home Alabama," he jumped down, stumbling drunkenly to the laughter of his friends. Lexie smiled at Zac. "You're up."

He gave her a nod and flashed her an unexpectedly nervous smile. Lexie positioned herself behind her camera, focusing on him when he walked out on to the stage. It was strange seeing him up there without his bass hanging off him, but he seemed confident enough now as he strode up to the microphone.

When the music started, she was surprised to hear him start singing Calum Scott's "Dancing on My Own." Her jaw dropped. Zac's voice was fantastic! Deep, smoky, with just enough of a rasp to make you feel it in your gut. She'd heard him sing backing vocals before, but it was nothing compared to what he was doing now.

The college kids in the front row had stopped goofing around and were staring at the stage, nudging each other and whispering. She wondered if they'd recognized him or were as stunned as she was by his vocals. Realizing she was just standing there staring at him, mouth agape, she bent down to her camera and started shooting.

She'd decided to go for a black-and-white portrait because it created the type of moodiness that emphasized facial expressions and emotions. That's exactly what she wanted to focus on for Zac's photo, since his face and eyes were so expressive. The monochrome enhanced the glow of the lights on the stage behind him, forming a smoky halo around his face as he sang. With his eyes closed, lashes long against his cheeks, mouth almost touching the microphone as he crooned huskily into it, there was so much contained emotion in his expression it made her heart ache.

When he finished, she enthusiastically joined in the applause the kids and the bartender were giving him. When he jogged back to her, his face lit up with a massive smile. She couldn't help throwing her arms around him. "Oh my God, that was incredible, Zac! I had no idea you had such an amazing voice! Why on earth don't you sing more on your albums? I mean, you're a brilliant bass player, but that was fantastic."

His grin grew even bigger at her exuberant response. "Thanks, Lexie. I love singing, but the band doesn't need another singer when we've got Connor's voice. I don't really compare with him." His smile dimmed a little.

Her brow creased. "I don't understand. You've got a different voice than Connor, but it's still great. The others must know how good you are. Have you ever said anything to them about doing your own songs?"

He shook his head. "When we first started, we decided Connor would be our lead singer, since he has a better range than I do. At the time, I was happy playing the bass and doing backing vocals. Then when we got discovered, the label didn't want us messing with a successful formula." He shrugged. "It's fine, I can't complain. What we have works well."

She raised her brows. His expression made her think he wasn't as happy about it as he was letting on. Still, it wasn't her business what the band did or didn't do. She was just a temporary interloper in their lives and didn't have any right to make any judgments. They'd got where they were today without her input, and they'd keep doing just as well once she'd gone. She tried not to think too much about how sad the thought made her.

Chapter 33

The music thumped loudly, the techno beats grating on Connor's nerves. They were out at a club in Austin, for a PR event organized by the label. Connor would have been happier staying behind on the tour bus with Lexie but knew there was no way he could get out of an appearance.

That he was on edge probably had less to do with the music and more to do with the fact that Lexie was out on the dance floor with Zac.

When the bass player had asked her to dance, she'd flicked a tiny questioning glance his way. But since he didn't want anyone to know what was going on between them, he couldn't justify staking his claim and warning Zac off, as much as he might want to. So he forced himself to keep his expression neutral, and she'd turned away from him and smiled up at Zac as he'd grabbed her hand and pulled her out onto the dance floor.

Now he was suffering by having to keep up a conversation with Tex while he watched Zac put his hands on her, albeit only an innocent touch on her waist. But it was killing him when all he wanted to do was walk over there, pull her away from Zac, and claim her in front of everyone.

Annoyed at the unfamiliar possessive emotions, he forced his gaze away from the two of them, glancing over to the other side of the VIP area where Noah was uncharacteristically sitting by himself in a dark corner.

Connor frowned. Noah was normally the life of the party when he was out. Actually, he'd been a bit off all day, but when Tex had asked him what was wrong, he'd shrugged it off.

Tex nodded over at Noah. "What do you think's wrong with him?"

Connor watched Noah rub his forehead. He looked sick, and Connor's concern sharpened. Noah being that quiet was out of the ordinary. "I'll see if I can get it out of him," he offered, standing up. Before he left, he leaned down to Tex. "Keep an eye on Lexie."

Tex's brows rose in amusement. "What, you don't trust Zac to keep his hands off her?"

"It's not Zac I'm worried about." It came out as a growl as he glared at all the other men standing around, looking on admiringly as she shimmied her hips.

"Are you sure you trust me? She looks mighty fine tonight." Tex grinned and gave Lexie an appreciative look.

Connor glanced over at her again. She was always gorgeous, but now, wearing a figure-hugging short black dress that exposed almost all of her back, she was stunning.

He turned back to Tex. "Not really. But if you want me to find out what's eating Noah, then you'll fucking do it."

Tex smirked. "You got it, man. I won't take my eyes off her." He made a show of adjusting himself as he looked over at her.

Connor narrowed his eyes at his friend. But knowing Tex would look out for her, he wandered over to Noah, now with a barely dressed woman sitting pressed up against him. He appeared to be ignoring her.

"Give us a minute, will you, love," Connor said to the woman, who gave him a flirtatious smile before sashaying over to the bar. Noah barely seemed to notice her leaving, so Connor sat down next to him. "Are you okay? You've gone white."

Noah looked sideways at Connor, squinting against the light as he tried to focus.

"It's my head. It's been coming on all day."

Shit. Noah occasionally got nasty headaches, verging on migraines. He hadn't had one for such a long time it hadn't even occurred to Connor that's what it might be.

"Why the fuck didn't you say something sooner? You shouldn't even be here. Come on, it's time to head back to the bus, anyway. We'll have to leave in a couple of hours if we're going to make tomorrow's venue in time."

Connor thought Noah would argue with him, but after blinking blearily a couple of times, he just nodded and got to his feet, staggering slightly. If Connor didn't know Noah had barely touched his drink tonight, he'd think he was drunk. He got his arm underneath Noah's, and then one of the security guys had his other side. Next thing Tex was striding next to them, looking at Noah with concern. "One of his headaches," he muttered to Tex.

"I'll get them to call a car to the back entrance so we can try to avoid the paparazzi. People will assume he's wasted if they see photos of him like this."

"Good idea." He looked around but couldn't see Lexie

247

and Zac, which bothered him more than it should. "Can you round up Lexie and Zac too?"

Tex nodded and headed off, while Connor and the security guy got Noah out the back and then into the car that pulled up for them. A few minutes later, Lexie, Zac, and Tex came out of the same door. Lexie's expression was concerned, while Tex and Zac had their heads close together, probably trying to figure out the best way to help Noah. When they slid into the limo, Lexie sat opposite him and gave him a worried smile.

By the time they got back to the tour bus, Noah was groaning, his head in his hands. Connor asked Lexie to tell Maggie what was going on since she'd know where they kept the painkillers. Once they got Noah inside the bus, Maggie handed him a glass of water and two pills, which he downed immediately.

Lexie spoke up. "I think he should stay in my bedroom tonight. It'll be too difficult trying to get him into his bunk, and he'll be close to a bathroom if he needs it. I can take his bunk." Connor paused, thinking. As much as he didn't want to kick Lexie out of her bedroom, she was right—it would be better for Noah to be in a bed rather than a bunk tonight.

He nodded at her. "Thanks, Lexie. After we've got him in the bed, we'll get the linen in his bunk changed out for you."

She smiled at him, her gray eyes flashing silver as they reflected the overhead light, and it suddenly hit him that Noah's bunk was below his, so she'd be sleeping underneath him tonight. The thought gave him a ridiculous thrill considering he was a twenty-eight-year-old rock star that had fucked his way through most states of America when he was younger. Shaking his head at himself, he and Tex half-carried Noah into the bedroom.

Maggie went with them to help, shaking her head and looking concerned. While he and Tex got Noah's shoes and socks off, Maggie got a bottle of water and put it by his bed, then went to help Lexie change the sheets in Noah's bunk.

After Connor and Tex got Noah into bed, they left the room, closing the door quietly behind them. Lexie stood next to the bunks, her eyes worried. "Will he be all right?"

Connor rubbed the back of his neck. "He hasn't had one of these for a while, but with the painkillers and a good night's sleep, he should be better tomorrow morning."

By the time everything had been sorted, they were all ready to crash. Lexie got changed in their tiny bathroom while Connor, Tex, and Zac just stripped and changed in the aisle as they normally did when there weren't any women around.

When Lexie came out of the bathroom, Connor's heart rate went through the roof. She was wearing a thin white tank top that didn't in any way hide the fact that she wasn't wearing a bra and a pair of tiny pajama shorts that only just covered her ass. Lexie's eyes widened and she froze, clearly not expecting them all to still be lingering in the aisle. She quickly raised her bundle of clothes to cover her breasts, but the stunned silence from the three men caused her face to flush bright red.

Connor cleared his throat and looked pointedly at Tex and Zac until they stopped staring, mumbled good night, climbed into their bunks, and pulled their curtains shut.

As soon as they did, Connor took two steps until he was standing in front of her. He said nothing, just wrapped his arms around her, grabbed her ass, and pulled her up against him so she could feel what she did to him. She let out a small gasp that he silenced by covering her mouth with his, unable to resist the temptation of tasting her.

It was difficult, but he broke the kiss quickly, not wanting either Zac or Tex to look out and see them. When he did, she was staring at him, eyes flaring with desire. He ran his hand through his hair and blew a breath out, then leaned close and whispered in her ear, "Get into bed, Lexie, before I take you right here."

She shivered but nodded and then raised herself on her tiptoes and pressed a feverish kiss to his mouth before ducking down and disappearing into the bunk.

Connor groaned and scrubbed his face with hands. Now he had the hard-on from hell, and considering the situation, not much he could do about it right now. Grumbling, he pulled himself up into the top bunk and closed the curtain, hoping sleep would come quickly. Two days from now they had another hotel stay, and he couldn't wait to get Lexie in his bed again.

***

Later that night, Connor lay in his bunk, acutely aware that Lexie was sleeping below him. He tossed and turned for what seemed like hours before he finally heard familiar soft snores from both Tex and Zac. Lying there in the dark, looking up at the ceiling of the bus, he felt like a teenager again, constantly horny. Hearing restless shifting from the bunk below him, he stilled, wondering if Lexie was also having trouble sleeping.

After a few more minutes of rustling from the bunk

below, and then a quiet frustrated sigh, Connor smiled to himself. He climbed out of his bunk and quietly lowered himself to the floor next to Lexie's curtained alcove. Squatting down, he whispered her name, not wanting to startle her into making a noise and waking the others. When he heard her quiet questioning reply, he pulled the curtain back and slipped in next to her.

Lexie seemed surprised but didn't protest when he shimmied in next to her and pulled the blankets up over both of them.

"Hey," he whispered. "Couldn't sleep."

She laughed quietly. "I know the feeling."

Lying on their sides facing each other, he pulled her flush up against him, lowered his mouth and pressed his lips against hers until she opened for him. She moaned as he swept his tongue into her mouth, and he broke away to whisper in her ear. "Not too loud, baby. Zac and Tex both sleep like the dead, but I don't want to take any chances."

He slid his hand up under her shirt, stroking the warm soft skin of her side, before moving up further, his fingers grazing the soft skin of her breast. He palmed her and then rolled the hard point of her nipple between his fingers. Lexie's breathing became uneven, but she stayed quiet, running her hand up over his shoulders and smoothing it down his back.

Connor didn't want to push his luck any further than he already had and pulled his hand away, prepared to leave and let her get some sleep. But when Lexie started shimmying out of her shorts, he couldn't resist helping her take them off, then pulling her hips tight against his so she could feel the hard ridge of him pressing against her. She was already so wet, his heart thudded almost painfully in his chest.

Still in complete silence, Lexie ground against him, and Connor reached around behind her to pull her even closer. He felt almost out of his mind with lust, just from having her rub up against him.

He should stop this now. When he'd come down here, he'd only been intending to make out with her a bit, never expecting she'd want to take it further while they were in the bunks. He put his mouth close to her ear and whispered, "Lexie, baby, we don't have to do anything tonight. I know this isn't the best place for it. We can wait until we get to a hotel."

But Lexie didn't seem like she wanted to stop and just pressed her lips against his while staying determinedly silent. Her hand slipped down to the small of his back and then around to his front, her fingers hooking into the top of his briefs and pulling them down to expose his erection, and he couldn't have stopped if he tried.

Now both of them were naked apart from Lexie's shirt, he slid his hard length against her slick core, the feeling so exquisite he shuddered against her. Lexie finally let out a slight whimper, then so quietly he could barely hear her, she whispered. "I want to feel you inside me."

Fuck. He wanted it so fucking badly, but he didn't have a condom. Hadn't expected things to go this far, which considering the sexual chemistry between them, had been sheer stupidity on his part.

"I don't have a condom, baby," he whispered back to her, just as quietly, while he continued grinding himself against her softness. He'd already told her he'd never gone bareback with any of the women he'd slept with and got tested every six months just to be safe, but there was no way he wanted to knock her up. She felt so good against him though; he could easily get both of them off, just doing this.

He heard Lexie's breathing shallow, and then she tipped her head forward so that her lips were right by his ear and whispered so quietly he almost didn't catch what she said. "I'm on birth control. I can't wait until the hotel; I need you now."

Connor's fingers tightened on her hip to stop her rubbing up against him, as the thought of sinking into her with nothing between them almost making him come then and there. If the whiplash of lust that surged through him had been anything but funny, he'd have almost laughed at himself. The playboy rock star almost blowing his load just at the thought of having her without a condom.

His breathing was ragged as he pressed his forehead against hers. "Are you sure?" It almost killed him to say it, but he didn't want her to have any regrets.

"I'm sure," she breathed and then reached down to guide his cock to her entrance. He drew a deep breath in through his nose as he began a long, slow glide into her tight, wet heat. Fuck, the feel of her stretching around him was incredible, and by the time he was fully seated in her, they were both holding themselves almost rigid with the restraint needed to stay quiet.

Lexie had her top leg hooked over his hip and her face against his chest. He could feel her hot shuddering breaths wash over his skin as he held himself still, trying to grapple back some level of control.

When he felt the tension in her body relax slightly, he

pulled almost all the way out of her in another long, slow glide before pushing back in. In order not to make too much noise, he was forced to slide slowly in and out of her, which was both frustrating and incredibly erotic. A long, slow build toward something incredible.

Keeping quiet in the dark, the primary senses in play were touch and taste, and he wanted to touch and taste her all over. Raising his hand, he gripped her hair and tugged her head gently back so that her body arched slightly away from him. He pushed her shirt up over her breasts and dropped his head down to take her nipple and suck it deep into his mouth, which had her squirming against him.

With nothing between them, he could feel Lexie's body, getting slicker, hotter, and tighter with every long, deliberate stroke, and his orgasm built with shocking intensity. Sweat broke out on his skin at the control he was exerting to not just give in and thrust hard into her so he could feel her explode around him.

Lexie's breathing was becoming more and more rapid, and suddenly she tightened even more, then begin to flutter around his cock as her climax neared. With one last long, slow, almost agonizing thrust into her, she arched her back and came hard. He covered her mouth with his, muffling the low cry she unsuccessfully tried to restrain. The feel of her contracting around him had him erupting, and he had to suppress his own deep groan at a release that seemed to go on and on.

When it finally eased, he could feel Lexie quivering against him, the strength of her orgasm having obviously matched his. He bent his head and feathered soft kisses over her face and lips as he tried to compose himself.

"Lexie..." he whispered, but didn't finish, not knowing what it was he wanted to say.

She didn't reply, just pressed herself against him and tipped her head back to place a long, slow kiss against his lips.

Christ, she killed him. Sex with her was beyond amazing. Every fucking time. As his heartbeat slowly returned to normal, he pulled out of her. He reluctantly smoothed her shirt back down and felt around for her pajama shorts, helping her pull them back on. He did the same for himself.

Still not having said anything, he turned her so her back was against his chest. While he could feel sleep tugging at him, he waited until her breathing slowed and evened out before kissing her gently on the head and rolling out of the bunk. He wouldn't embarrass Lexie by being seen by the others climbing out of her bed in the morning. Returning to his bunk, he lay in the dark with one arm thrown over his eyes, his mind working overtime.

What the hell was he doing? He kept waiting for his attraction to Lexie to wane, both expecting it to happen and dreading when it did. But instead of lessening, it seemed to keep growing stronger. She was becoming an addiction, and for the first time, he realized that while he'd spent so long worrying if she'd be hurt when this was over, he'd never considered he might be the one that ended up hurt.

Chapter 34

The next morning when Connor got out of his bunk, he saw the curtain across Lexie's had been drawn back and the bed was empty. The sight of the rumpled sheets brought flashbacks of the night before, and he needed to adjust himself before wandering out to the living area. As soon as he got out there, his gaze zeroed in on Lexie having breakfast with Noah sitting next to her. He looked slightly the worse for wear with bloodshot eyes but nowhere near as bad as he had the night before.

Lexie glanced up at him as he approached the table, her gaze dropping to his bare chest before meeting his eyes with a slight smile. The red tinge that spread across her cheekbones told him she was having the same flashbacks he'd had. The thought of her reliving the memory of what they'd done the night before made him start to harden again, so he quickly turned away and casually stood looking out the window while he got himself under control. This girl could do things to him just with the look in her eyes.

When he'd recovered, he wandered back over to the table and slid into the seat opposite Noah. "How are you feeling?"

"Yeah, mostly better. Thanks for looking after me last night."

"Of course. Though I don't know why the hell you didn't say you were feeling shit. You didn't need to come out with us."

Noah shrugged. "I didn't want to let you guys down, and you know the label doesn't like it when we skip PR events. I hoped a few drinks might sort me out."

Connor shook his head. "The only way you could let us down is by not looking after yourself. And fuck the label. We'd have to do a lot more than missing a few PR events for them to drop us."

He sighed and rubbed his temples. "Yeah, you're right, it was stupid. Anyway, I should be good for tonight, but I might lie back down for a bit."

"No problem. Just rest up and see how you feel later. We can always get a substitute drummer for tonight if we need to."

That got a reaction. "Over my dead body," Noah growled.

Connor smirked at that. He *was* feeling better.

As Noah got up to leave, he turned to Lexie. "Thanks for swapping out with me last night. Were you all right in my bunk?"

Lexie flushed slightly at Noah's innocent question, but she kept her eyes fixed on him as she answered. "Um, the bunk was surprisingly enjoyable. If you need to keep using the bed for a while, that's fine."

Connor's heart rate sped up at the thought of a repeat of last night, and he was disappointed when Noah replied, "If you don't mind me just using the bedroom again this morning, I'll be good to be back in the bunk tonight."

"That's no problem." She hid her disappointment well

enough to not let on to Noah, but Connor could hear it in her voice.

Noah nodded, then headed back to bed. Connor slid over so he was sitting opposite Lexie. Since none of the others were around, he let himself reach over and pick up her hand where it rested on the table. She looked up at him through her lashes, a smile flickering over her lips at his touch.

"Nice try." He grinned at her.

She rolled her eyes at him and laughed softly. "It makes me crazy not being able to touch you when you're only a few feet away from me all night."

He knew how she felt. It was infuriating having her so close but not be able to do anything about it. Part of him wanted to say to hell with it and just tell the others. Tex already seemed to have his suspicions. Not having to sneak around anymore would have its advantages. The thought of sharing the bedroom with her every night caused him to shift in his seat.

The downside was that everyone would assume it was some kind of relationship. And if he made it clear that it wasn't, the others would probably kick his ass for taking advantage of Lexie.

Not that he was. Well, he didn't think he was, anyway.

Looking at her now, with a soft smile on her face as he stroked his thumb over the back of her hand, confusion overtook him. She'd said nothing to him about wanting more and had seemed happy enough with the plan to go their separate ways at the end of the tour. Was there a chance she did want more from him? Did *he* want that? He had to admit that he didn't feel anywhere near done with her yet. In fact, he spent most of his time these days just looking forward to when he could be alone with her.

Fuck.

Anger, sudden and heated, coursed through him. What the hell was he thinking? This was supposed to be a short-term thing, just to get him through the tour, nothing more. He didn't want it to be anything more. He pulled his hand away and rubbed the back of his neck. When Lexie looked at him curiously, he gave her a stiff smile.

"What's wrong?" A crease appeared between her brows as she searched his face. Now he felt even worse. It was himself he was angry at. He didn't want to take it out on her.

"Nothing, just tired. Didn't get a lot of sleep last night." He'd meant it as a joke, but the tension in his voice made it ring with accusation.

He gritted his teeth when she flinched. Shit, he was an asshole. But the concern that he'd got too involved with her, too reliant on her being around, made his skin prickle as if he was about to break out in a cold sweat. This kind of shit was why he avoided getting attached. Who needed this kind of emotional roller-coaster ride? The confusion he was feeling now meant he'd already gotten too invested in whatever this was between them.

He met Lexie's gaze again, his chest tightening at her wounded expression. Pissed at himself for overthinking everything and hurting her, he reached across the table again and took her hand.

"I'm sorry, Lexie. I was kidding. Terrible joke I know. I'm an asshole. I was the one that started it last night, and it was fucking amazing."

She smiled, but it didn't quite erase the guarded look in her eyes. "Well, just over a week left before the end of the tour, so you won't have to worry about me keeping you awake much longer."

He hated the reminder that he only had a few more nights with her. And here he was wasting this time being a dick. He was in the middle of trying to figure out how to make it up to her when footsteps sounded from behind him. Releasing her hand, he turned to see Tex wandering into the room wearing jeans and nothing else. When he saw them sitting at the table, he ran his hand through his shoulder-length hair and gave Lexie a warm smile.

Connor gritted his teeth. It still galled him knowing Tex had kissed Lexie before he had. Hell, that he'd kissed her at all pissed him off. He turned back to Lexie to see her returning Tex's smile, and that annoyed him too. Deep down he knew there was nothing but friendliness in her smile—it wasn't anything like the smiles she gave him in private—but it still made him crazy. Because in just over a week she would be gone, he'd never see her again, and some other man would be on the receiving end of all her smiles.

It shouldn't fucking bother him, but it did.

He slid out of the seat, giving Lexie as close to a normal smile as he could, before turning and leaving the room. He needed to get himself under control and soon. He only had a short amount of time left with her, and he didn't want to ruin it now.

Chapter 35

The weeks had gone past so quickly. Too quickly—it was less than a week before the tour ended. Lexie's camera felt heavy in her hands as she held it up to take photos of the packed stadium. The music and the screams of the crowd reverberated through her chest, but that wasn't what was making it feel so tight.

She knew she'd gotten in too deep with Connor, but she hadn't known how to stop herself. Had known from the start anyway that this would happen. She was so conflicted. Still drawn to him like a moth to a flame, all the while knowing she'd end up burned.

Over the last few days, she'd noticed a change in his behavior too. It was subtle, and at first, she thought she was imagining it. In private he acted as if he still couldn't get enough of her. But in public, he seemed to be slowly but surely drawing away. Everything was just a little bit less. Less talking, less flirting, less just being near her for the sake of it. It was obvious to her that he was preparing to walk away in a few days.

It wasn't like she didn't know it was coming. He'd been clear about his expectations from the start and had been nothing other than open and honest about what he wanted from her. He'd laid it all out, and like every other woman in the world would have, she'd rushed to sign on the dotted line.

As painful as it was, she knew it was for the best. Knew there was no future where the two of them would end up together. Knew it, even as her heart cracked a little more every time he looked away from her. So, she would keep her head held high, keep a smile on her face, and never let him know how much it hurt.

Tonight, she was photographing the concert from the pit, the area in front of the stage behind the security barrier. She was shooting the crowd, focusing on the reaching hands, the combination of ecstasy and desperation on the faces of the fans.

Knowing the song list off by heart by now, she knew the song coming up next. It was her favorite, almost guaranteed to make her eyes well up with tears whenever she heard it. It was one of only a couple of acoustic songs during the concert, where Connor sat on a stool and played his guitar, just him alone in the spotlight.

The song, "What Could Have Been," was about a missed chance at love, and the soulful words, sung in Connor's velvety, dark tones, were like an emotional sucker punch. When she'd first heard it, her thoughts had been of Damien. Now she couldn't help but think of Connor, and how it would feel to walk away in a few days when the tour finished.

As she heard the familiar chords from behind her and saw the emotions on the fans' faces, she couldn't stop herself from turning around to watch. If she only had a few days left, she wanted to make as many memories as she could.

Sighing in appreciation, she took in the scene. The rest of the stage was dark, and Connor was sitting on a stool lit up by the spotlight. His muscular arms cradled his acoustic guitar as his fingers strummed the chords of the song intro. He tipped his head back slightly so he could sing into the microphone, but kept his eyes closed. As the song approached the chorus, Lexie felt the stinging at the back of her eyes heralding the tears she couldn't seem to hold back whenever she heard this song.

When the chorus kicked in, he finally opened his eyes, but rather than looking out over the crowd as he normally did, his eyes found her. They stayed on her for the whole song. Even though the two of them were in a stadium filled to bursting with tens of thousands of fans, the moment felt intimate, as if they were alone and he was singing just to her.

She tried to hold back the tears, but they were already so close to the surface that despite her best efforts, they overflowed, trickling down her cheeks. She wanted to turn away, to compose herself, but she felt pinned to the ground by the intensity of his gaze. Instead, she subtly tried to wipe the tears away and saw him narrow his eyes as she did. When the last notes of the song faded, the crowd went berserk. And so did her heart. Damn it. Walking away in a few days was going to kill her.

Later, during the after-party, she felt Connor's presence behind her while she was taking a photo of Tex talking animatedly to a fan. Turning slightly toward him to acknowledge his presence, she shivered as his fingers skated up the bare skin of her arm. Leaning down, he murmured in her ear. "Let's go."

She turned to him surprised, since the band had only

arrived about twenty minutes before. He usually liked to stay for a while since people had paid money or even won competitions to meet the band. By the determined look on his face, he wasn't asking.

When she didn't respond straight away, he grabbed her hand and started pulling her along behind him. That was even more surprising since they usually tried not to do anything too suspicious in public. But his urgency was thrilling, and she could feel her body react to the thought of what was to come.

By the time they got back to her hotel room, her body was practically vibrating with need. As soon as she opened her door, he pushed inside slamming it behind them. Then his mouth was on hers, and it was unlike any kiss they'd shared before, a desperate clash of lips, teeth, and tongue. She moaned and arched up against him, and he reached behind her, lifting her until she could wrap her legs around his waist. He ground his erection against her, and she shuddered at the feeling against her sensitive core.

His lips were hard against hers—almost bruising—his tongue thrusting into her mouth, claiming it, claiming *her*. The masculine taste of him overwhelmed her, every one of her nerve endings coming alive with the promise of what was to come.

He kissed her like that until she was breathless and then dropped his head to her neck, licking and kissing down the column of her throat while he braced her back against the wall and trailed his hand down her thigh. She was so needy by then she thought she'd come as soon as he touched her between her legs. Suddenly, he released her and when her feet touched the floor, he turned her so his large, hard body was pressed up against her back.

As he teased the sensitive skin of her neck with his lips and tongue, his hand reached around and unbuttoned her cutoffs before pulling them and her panties down her legs so she could step out of them. He still hadn't said a word to her, and she was in such a lust-filled haze she couldn't find any words of her own. She wondered if he was feeling half as desperate as she was.

He grasped the bottom of her tank top and pulled it up and over her head, then undid her bra and let it fall off her shoulders. Now she was naked, her overheated body and sensitive breasts pressed against the coolness of the wall. He was still completely clothed as he reached around to her front and slid his hand down to the apex of her thighs, groaning as his fingers slid into her slick heat.

"Always so wet for me," he murmured against her skin, almost too quietly for her to hear. In response, she widened her stance to grant him more access and then shuddered as he pushed one finger and then two into her. She was so close, it didn't take more than that and a couple of swipes of his thumb over her clit before she was moaning and quivering against the wall, her legs trembling.

Only then did he move back from her, and she heard him stripping. She turned to watch, but he ground out, "Don't move." His voice was so deep and strained, he sounded almost feral.

Lexie turned back and rested her forehead against the wall, her hands braced on either side. Her heart pounded so hard in her chest she could feel its throb everywhere in her body. She wasn't quite sure what was happening; all she knew was that she didn't think she'd ever been more turned on.

Suddenly, hot skin and hard muscles pressed up against her, and she lost her breath in an instant. He wrapped his arms around her, one hand rising to cup her breast, while the other trailed down her stomach until it reached her core. He dipped his fingers back into her, making sure she was ready for him. The whimper she gave must have told him everything he needed to know, because he pulled his hand away, and she felt the hot, hard length of him slide between her folds, then push up into her.

She arched her back to give him better access, and when he slid deep in one smooth thrust, she couldn't help calling out his name. She was already on the verge of coming again, her internal muscles fluttering in preparation.

At the sound of his name, he stilled and all she could hear was the rasp of his breath behind her. Reaching back, she grasped his hip, trying to get him to move, but the tension in his muscles let her know he was hanging on by a thread too. She didn't care. She was so close, she wanted him moving inside her and she wanted it now.

"Don't stop," she said breathlessly, trying to arch her back more, to take more of him, although she didn't think he could possibly be any deeper than he already was. It was like her body was telling her what her heart already knew; she'd never get enough of him.

"God, Lexie, you're perfect," he said, before slowly withdrawing almost all the way. Her body cried out at the emptiness so that when he slammed back into her, the pleasure was almost overwhelming.

"Oh my God," she gasped and then cried out again when he pulled out and thrust back in. Both of his hands were on her breasts now, rolling her nipples between his fingers and pinching, holding her on the edge until she was desperate for release.

She realized she was begging him over and over, "Please, please, please." She would have been embarrassed except she didn't care if he knew what he did to her. All that mattered was the man behind her. The man inside her body; inside her heart. His breathing was getting ragged too, and he dropped his mouth to that sensitive spot on her neck that made her crazy and pressed hot, wet kisses against it. She squirmed back against him. "Connor, I'm so close. Please make me come." She knew all it would take was one touch of his finger against her clit and she'd be gone. Instead, he pulled out of her, leaving her disoriented and panting.

She didn't have long to wonder what was wrong, because he spun her around to face him, reached behind her to grasp the backs of her thighs, and lifted her up. Instinctively she wrapped her legs around him as he backed her against the wall again and slid home in one hard thrust. She cried out and tried to arch against him as best she could when he had her pinned between the steel of his body and the wall.

The new position gave her the friction against her clit she needed, and after just two thrusts, she was coming As her body clenched around him, he dropped his mouth to her neck, his lips moving against her as he whispered something. She couldn't hear what he said over her own harsh breaths and whimpers, but the next moment she felt his open mouth on her skin, the heat and suction telling her it would leave a mark. It was the first time he'd ever done something like that, and the thought of him branding her that way was like throwing fuel on the fire of her orgasm.

She writhed in his arms at the intensity of the pleasure exploding through her, ricocheting from where he was pumping into her to the furthest reaches of her body and back again. Two strokes later and he joined her, thrusting to the hilt and then holding himself rigid as he pulsed inside her.

They stood like that for several long moments, the only sound in the room the harsh panting of their breaths. She had her head buried against his neck, and when she finally pulled back and looked up at him, her heart stuttered at the intensity in his green eyes as they blazed down into hers.

Feeling suddenly exposed, sure that everything she felt for him was clear on her face at that moment, she let out a shaky breath.

Instead of saying what her heart wanted to say, she forced herself to pull it together enough to smile up at him. "That was amazing."

For a second his eyes searched hers. As if he was looking for something more. She kept the now slightly tremulous smile on her lips—not wanting him to know how affected she was—until his mouth curled up in return.

"Every time with you is amazing, Lexie," he said as he let her slide down until her feet touched the ground. She closed her eyes at the pain his words caused because he was right—what they had between them physically was incredible. She knew now he had ruined her for any other man, and in a few days, he would cut her loose, and she'd be left trying to find someone who could make her feel the way he did. She sighed and pressed herself against him, brushing a soft kiss over his heart.

He put his hand under her chin and tilted her head back,

looking searchingly into her eyes again, then bent down and skimmed his lips over hers. Pulling back, he smiled again. "Come on, let's have a shower. The night's still young, and I've got plans for you."

She forced a laugh. She would make sure she imprinted every second of tonight in her memory, something to hold on to in the long, empty nights to come.

Chapter 36

A few hours later, Connor was lying in the dark, Lexie's head on his chest. Her fingers stroked softly over his skin as she talked about her family.

"Things with Mom have been difficult. I love her like crazy, but it's like she doesn't know how to talk to me anymore, or that she wants to fix me. Every time she calls, she ends up just encouraging me to date, or sometimes she even tries to set me up with single men she knows. She doesn't seem to understand that I haven't been ready to move on. And Mom and Dad, they never mention Damien's name anymore, even though I know how much they loved him when he was alive. It's as if they're afraid hearing his name will send me into a spiral of depression." She exhaled.

Tension tightened Connor's muscles at the thought of how much she still loved her late husband. It was clear in her voice, suppressed emotion making it huskier than normal. He felt her let out a small gasp before she looked up at him, eyes wide and sorrowful. "I'm so sorry, Connor, that was insensitive of me."

He looked down at her, confused. Had she sensed what he was thinking? Did she realize he'd somehow, ridiculously, found himself jealous of Damien's place in her heart?

He was relieved when she went on. "It's so selfish of me, complaining about my parents when you've lost both of yours." She seemed so ashamed, and he was so relieved that the actual reason he'd tensed wasn't clear, that he smiled and brushed his thumb over her full lower lip.

"There's not a selfish bone in your body, Lexie." She gave a slight shake of her head in denial, but he kept going. "I don't resent the fact you have parents that care about you, even if they don't know the best way to show it right now."

No, he was the selfish one. Because while he didn't resent her having loving parents, he did resent the fact she loved someone else. "I'm glad you have a family to support you. I wouldn't wish my screwed-up situation on anyone else."

Her crystal-clear eyes flicked backward and forward between his as if trying to read him. Seeing his sincerity, she laid her head back down on his chest and sighed. "It's just, I hate that it happened to you. It makes my heart hurt for the little boy that you were." The tremor in her voice let him know that she meant it, and her compassion was just one more thing about her that killed him.

Just like the last time he'd spoken to her about his parents, being alone with her in the dark let him talk about things he normally couldn't. He stared into the darkness of the room as he spoke.

"When Mom died, it was long and brutal. My dad had already started pushing me away as she went downhill. Every molecule of care he had was focused on her. When she died, it was like a light was snuffed out in him. There was nothing left for me, or even for himself. I was eleven, I was devastated, and I needed my father, but he didn't give a fuck.

Too wrapped up in his grief, and then the bottle.

"Luckily, he wasn't a violent drunk, just a miserable one. He kept me alive, and that was it. I was basically left to fend for myself. I made some friends, older than me, and they took me under their wing. Most of them had shitty family lives just like me. They became more my family than my dad. The only reason I kept turning up to school was because of the music lessons. Every time I picked up an instrument, or opened my mouth and sang, I felt like my mom was there with me. I couldn't let that go, so I stayed in school, thank God. My dad didn't care about what I was doing or who I was doing it with, as long as I wasn't bothering him with my presence."

He stroked his hand down her back, the feel of her warm body nestled up against his side relaxing him as he spoke. "It was only a matter of time until my friends got into drugs, so I started to dabble too. I was fourteen when we started shoplifting to pay for drugs, then boosting cars. Things weren't looking good for me. But then my friend Callum, he overdosed in front of me. He didn't end up dying, but I thought he was going to."

He paused, the memory still affecting him all these years later. "It shook me up badly, even for the hard little bastard I was turning into, and I went screaming home to my dad in tears. For the first time since my mom died, he did something to help me, or maybe it was to help himself, fucked if I know. He called my Aunt Maureen, my mom's sister. She'd moved to Ohio years before, and he asked her to take me. The wonderful thing about the Irish is that they don't say no to family. He sent me kicking and screaming over to live with her, and I haven't seen him since." He felt himself getting tense again; as much as he hated it, thoughts of his dad's rejection still had the power to hurt him.

Lexie wrapped her arms tight around his chest and squeezed. "I'm so sorry, Connor. It makes me so angry that he did that to you." He smiled at the fierceness in her tone.

"Well, I suppose if he hadn't, I wouldn't be where I am today."

She raised her head and looked at him, her eyes glimmering in the moonlight coming in through the window. Unable to help himself, he reached up and traced the side of her face with his finger. Her eyes drifted shut, and she sighed in pleasure at his touch, and he fucking loved that he could do that to her.

He had to restrain himself from flipping her over and losing himself in her again, because he liked talking to her too, liked being able to share things with her that he'd never even talked to his friends about. He ignored the warning bells going off in his mind that told him he was playing with fire when it came to her. He'd already pushed so far past his comfort zone; he couldn't afford to start wanting more.

"Are you in contact with him?"

"No. At the start, I thought he was calling me but turns out my aunt had called him and forced him to talk to me. She just let me believe he was calling me. Those conversations were hard, and I think my aunt realized she was doing more harm than good when I'd fly into a rage after every conversation. Eventually, she stopped calling him, and he never bothered to call me. I've got no interest in having anything to do with him, and he's made it clear he wants nothing to do with me. Which is fine. My aunt's been a better parent to me than he ever was."

"I'm glad you had her. She must be an amazing woman for you to have turned out as well as you have." She smiled to let him know she was teasing him.

He laughed. "She is. But it was a rough start. I was a real shit to begin with, and she didn't take it easy on me. She laid down the rules, and she enforced them. I hated her for that. But the day I realized that she cared about me, that she saw the hurt little boy through the wall I'd put up, was the day she bought me my first guitar and paid for me to get lessons. I broke down and cried because I knew then that she saw me, saw who I was inside, not the person I was pretending to be.

"It wasn't all happy families from that moment on, but it got better every day. I decided then what I wanted to do with my life, and I put everything I had into it. I started doing better at school, made an effort to make friends, particularly those that loved music like I did. I put my head down, and I focused on that goal and forced my life in the direction I wanted it to go."

She frowned at the tone of his voice. "Isn't that a good thing? You should be so proud of yourself, Connor. How many people could turn their lives around the way you have?"

He said nothing for a few moments as he slowly drifted his fingers up and down the smooth skin of her back.

"The problem is, now that I've done it, I'm not sure it's what I wanted it to be. My mom is still dead, my dad still wants nothing to do with me, and apart from my aunt, my friends are my only family, the only people I love." He paused, enjoying the feel of her smooth skin. "So what do I do if this isn't enough? Where do I go from here? Who am I if not the lead singer of Fractured? The guys are my family as much as my aunt, so how could I ever abandon them? I don't know if I can walk away from them, from this, even if I could think of something else I want to do. Someone else I want to be."

"And you haven't told any of the others about the way you're feeling?"

Just the thought made his chest feel tight. "Once I tell someone, I'm going to have to deal with it, have people trying to convince me of what I feel, what I should do. I need to figure it out myself. After all, if this is just a phase brought on by tour fatigue, I might wake up in a month wondering what the hell I was worried about."

She nodded slowly, considering what he'd said, but not judging him. "Still, part of having a family to support you is to help you work things through. Yours might not be a traditional family, but they're still your family. Sometimes having someone to talk to is what we need to see things clearly."

He shut his mouth just in time before he blurted out what he was going to say. *I've got you to talk to.* Because in a few more days, she'd be gone, and he wouldn't have her to talk to anymore. His chest tightened more than it had when he'd thought about telling his friends how he was feeling. He didn't want to think too hard about why that same panicky feeling filled him at the thought of Lexie leaving. He also didn't want to think about why he'd whispered "mine" against her skin while he was making love to her earlier. His feelings about that were too complicated to think about now. Pushing it out of his mind, he had a sudden thought. "Where's your camera?"

She shifted to look at him curiously. "It's in the living

275

room. Why?"

He climbed out of bed, smiling at her suspicious expression. "Come on."

He had to stifle a groan as she got out and walked toward her suitcase, the moonlight coming in the window skimming her silky skin the way his fingers suddenly itched to do again. Well, it wasn't morning yet—there'd be time for more of that later, but now he had something he wanted to do. She went to her suitcase and pulled out some underwear, a lacy bra and panty set. Watching her put on her underwear was just as much of a turn-on as seeing her stripping them off, and he was already getting hard again.

When she turned back toward him, her eyes automatically drifted down his body before coming to rest on his growing erection. When her eyes widened, he had to force himself not to stalk over there and rip those skimpy pieces of lace right off her gorgeous body. Instead, he shook his head to clear his mind, then reached for her hand and led her out to the front room. Locating their discarded clothes, he pulled on his briefs.

"So, what's the big mystery?" she asked.

He turned toward her and saw she'd pulled her camera out of its bag.

"I'm assuming you can put that thing on a timer?"

She looked down at the camera. "Yeah, I can set it up for a delay of up to twenty seconds. Or I've got a remote to trigger it to shoot if you think you'll need longer than that."

"Oh, I'll definitely need longer than that for what I want to do." He smiled at the blush that stole over her cheeks. He loved that she reacted that way, even when she was standing in front of him practically naked after he'd made her come multiple times over the last few hours.

"So you'll need to tell me what you're planning so I can set the camera up. Though I can probably take a good guess." She slanted a look at him out of the corner of her eye, a smile playing over her lips.

"I'm going to teach you how to play the guitar." He grinned at her surprised expression.

"We don't have a guitar here!"

"We don't need one."

"I'm so confused," she said, then laughed.

God, he loved her laugh—the sound always made him feel lighter. Again, he pushed away the thought about how he would feel when she left. He'd deal with that later; this was about remembering this moment and this woman. Something he'd never felt the need to do before.

He pulled a chair out of the corner of the room and placed it in the middle. "We're going to sit here, and I'm going to teach you how to play the guitar."

"Without a guitar?" she butted in, skepticism clear in her voice.

"Without a guitar," he agreed. "And I want you to take a photo."

She looked at him, a curious expression on her face. "But this isn't for the photo book, right?"

"No, this is just for me… for us, I mean. A memento."

An emotion flashed across her face, too quick for him to see what it was. But then a smile tipped up the corners of her mouth, and she turned to look at where he'd placed the chair, studying it, and he could see her picturing it in her mind, figuring out what she needed to do to make it work. It was a total turn-on seeing her concentrating on her craft. As soon as they did this, he was taking her right back to the bedroom.

"Okay," she said. "I'll need my tripod."

She got it from her case and set it up, angled slightly so it was side on to the chair. Then she set her camera up on it, checked the screen, pressed a few buttons, and then checked again. "Can you sit in the chair so I can check the focus?"

He went over and sat down, leaning back in the chair and looking over at her where she was bent down, looking through the viewfinder. "I think I'm going to shoot it as a black-and-white photo." He saw her finger press the capture button, and then she peeked over the top of the camera at him, a smile on her face. "You look incredible. I could sell that photo for an awful lot of money."

"Are you going to?" Not that he really thought she would.

Her smile dimmed slightly, and then she repeated his words back to him quietly. "That one's just for me."

She straightened and looked at him.

"All set?" he asked.

"All set. So now what?"

"Come over here." He heard the rasp in his voice at the thought of having her in his arms again, and she must have heard it too because he saw her eyes darken and her nipples harden through the lace of her bra.

She picked up a small remote and came over to stand between his legs, looking down at him with big gray eyes. She looked like a dream, with her dark hair tumbling over her shoulders and the smooth expanse of her creamy skin just begging to be stroked.

He closed his eyes and took a deep breath, concentrating on what he wanted to do.

"Okay, sit on my lap with your back to my chest."

She raised an eyebrow at him but turned around and sat down, nestling her gorgeous ass against him, making him instantly hard. He was sure she wriggled around a little more than was strictly necessary to get in place.

"Put your legs over mine." His voice was husky.

She moved her slim legs so they were draped over his. Then he ran the fingers of his left hand down her left arm, his lips curving up at the trail of goosebumps that followed his touch. He caught her hand in his, then repeated the movement on the other side, with his right hand holding hers. He bent forward so that his back was flush against her and his chin rested on her shoulder, then moved her arms and hands to replicate the position they would be in if she were holding a guitar.

The feel of her smooth warm skin pressed against him had his breathing becoming shallow, but he tried not to let himself get distracted.

He moved the fingers of her left hand to make a basic chord, then ran his thumb along the back of her right hand. "C," he whispered and brushed his lips against her neck, hearing her breath hitch as he did so. He moved her fingers again and strummed the back of her right hand. "G." He trailed his lips down her neck and kissed another spot. "E minor." Another chord, another kiss, and now her breathing was as shallow as his.

He kept it up, his hands on hers, his lips on her neck, as both of them got hotter and hotter. He was as hard as a rock underneath her, and he could feel the heat of her core through both layers of their underwear. He wouldn't be able to keep this up much longer. "C." This time instead of kissing her neck, he brushed his mouth against the shell of her ear. "Lexie?"

"Y-yes," came her breathless reply.

"Take the photo."

He felt her start as she remembered what he'd been intending. She'd placed the remote on a nearby table that wasn't in view of the camera, and she dropped her right hand down and pressed the button before placing her hand back in his. "It'll shoot in twenty seconds, then twice more over the next minute."

He kept going, teaching her the chords to the song he'd sung to her that night at the concert, the one that had made her cry. Probably because it reminded her of her husband, but a selfish part of him hoped that some of it might have been because of him.

Another chord, another kiss, and then she dropped her head backward, turning it to give him better access to her neck. As he pressed his lips to her throat, he heard the shutter click. He kept going, but he knew they were both done with this lesson. He ran his hands back up her arms, using one to tilt her head back as he claimed her mouth in a deep kiss that had her twisting and arching up toward him. The shutter clicked again. He ran his other hand down over her chest and cupped her breast, before moving down further to stroke over the lace of her panties. He heard the shutter go a third time, but he was beyond caring. All he wanted at that moment was to be deep inside her again, imprinting himself on her so she'd never forget him, would never be with another man without thinking of him. He should feel guilty about wanting to ruin her for anyone else when he couldn't be the man to give her what she needed, but he couldn't bring himself to feel it.

She pulled away from him, then turned so she was straddling him. She ran her hands through his hair as she slanted her mouth over his and ground herself against him. He could feel how wet she was, how her body pressed against him like she couldn't get close enough. This entire thing had basically been extended foreplay, and they were both on the knife's edge.

He ran his palms down her back and pressed her hips more firmly against him, thrusting up against her heat. She threw her head back and moaned, and he couldn't take it anymore. Lifting her hips so he could reach under her, he pulled his briefs down and kicked them off. Then he put his fingers into the side of her panties and dragged them off her. He felt her hands move down to his shoulders so she could raise herself enough that the head of his cock slid through her slick folds.

"Fuck, Lexie," he groaned. Her left hand dropped away from his shoulder for a second, and then she was pressing down onto him, engulfing him in her tight, wet heat. He struggled to get enough air in his lungs as she took him in, rocking her hips as she slowly worked her way down his length. Just as she bottomed out, he reached up and brought her lips down to his, his tongue thrusting into the sweetness of her mouth. As he did, he heard the click of the camera shutter again and realized she must have triggered the remote with her left hand. The thought that he couldn't wait to see those photos percolated through his lust-filled brain, but then was lost as Lexie slowly lifted off him and then dropped back down, just as the shutter clicked a second time. He knew he wasn't going to last long—the pressure building was too much, too intense, he just needed her to get there before he could. He reached down between them and circled her clit, once, twice, three times and she came. Her head dropped back, breasts arched up, and body clenching hard around him. That's all he'd needed. He gripped her hips and thrust up, groaning her name as he came harder than he ever had before. The shutter clicked a third time.

Chapter 37

When Connor's alarm had gone off that morning, he almost said screw it and stayed right where he was, curled around Lexie's warm, soft body. At this stage, did he care if the others learned they'd been sleeping together? He ended up forcing himself out of the bed though, because he wasn't sure how Lexie would feel about being outed, and he didn't want to upset her. After getting dressed, he stood looking down at her for a long minute, frustrated by the push and pull of his emotions when it came to her. His eyes swept over her sleeping form: her dark hair fanned out over the pillow, long lashes brushing her cheekbones, and lips slightly parted. She was beautiful, inside and out, and that unfamiliar emotion rose in his chest again. The one he'd been trying not to think too hard about over the last few weeks. Part of him wanted to bend down, kiss her, stroke her awake, and hold her close, to lose himself in her. The other part of him wanted to walk away and never look back. The way he'd always been able to before.

He scrubbed his hands over his face, then sighed and left her sleeping. It was still early morning, but there was no way he could get back to sleep, so when he returned to his room, he took a shower to try to clear his mind. In a few days, the turmoil he was feeling about Lexie would no longer be an issue. She'd leave, he'd deal with whatever fallout there might be, and then things would go back to normal. Well, as normal as his life ever got, anyway.

He was just turning the water off in the shower when he heard his cell phone ring. He checked the clock, brow furrowed, wondering who was calling him that early in the morning. Wrapping his towel around his waist, he walked over to where his phone sat on the bedside table. His aunt's name was on the screen, and he frowned, answering and putting it on speaker while he dressed.

"Connor, my boy, I'm sorry to call you so early. I hope I didn't wake you." His aunt's voice, with its still-strong Irish accent, was normally soothing, but the unusual timing of the call had him on edge. She sounded tense rather than distraught though, which meant there probably wasn't anything seriously wrong.

"No, it's fine, I was just having a shower. What's the matter?"

She sighed heavily. "I had a phone call from Ireland this morning." He tensed as she paused, knowing a call from there couldn't mean anything good. "I'm sorry, Connor. I hate to tell you this over the phone, but your da is dead."

Connor went still as he tried to absorb her words. "Dad's dead? He was only in his early fifties. What happened?"

"Apparently it was a heart attack, so it was quick. Not like... well, not like it could have been."

Connor knew she was talking about his mom's long and painful death. He clenched his jaw at the thought his mom had to go through all that pain, while his dad had gone quickly. Not that he wished anyone a painful death, but still, it didn't seem fair somehow.

He wondered if his aunt was expecting him to go to the bastard's funeral. Any love or concern he'd had for his dad had died a long time ago. He didn't owe the man anything, and he certainly wouldn't cut short the tour to fly back to Ireland for it. Considering the miserable bastard his dad had been, there probably wouldn't be anyone at his funeral, anyway.

"I'm not going to the funeral," he stated bluntly, just in case his aunt was preparing to convince him it was the right thing to do.

There was a pregnant pause on his aunt's side before she responded quietly. "They've already had the funeral, lad. I only just found out this morning, but they buried him a few days ago."

Connor was stunned. Not that he'd wanted to go, but to not even be given the option to attend his own father's funeral was fucked up.

"Well, who buried him since we're his only family? Can they even do that without contacting next of kin?"

Another heavy pause, and his muscles tensed in anticipation of what she was going to say next. When she spoke, the sympathy was clear in her voice. "His wife and stepson buried him. He remarried a few years back. I'm sorry that I didn't tell you when it happened, but he didn't want to talk to you about it, and I didn't want him to hurt you any more than he already had."

Connor sat down on the bed and dropped his head into his hands. That bloody bastard. His father had thrown him away without a second thought and then gone and got himself a whole new family. He hadn't even bothered to contact Connor to let him know.

"Who called you to tell you he was dead?" It was the only thing he could think of to ask.

"His wife. She was going through his address book and found my contact details."

He didn't want to ask but couldn't help himself. "She didn't think to try to call me?"

Another pause had him bracing for another blow. "She didn't know about you, love. I don't think your da ever told her. She thought I was his only family, and I figured I'd keep it that way. No point opening a can of worms and having your name getting out in the press."

"Thanks," Connor responded mechanically, but numbness had taken over. What had he ever done to make his dad hate him? Hate him so much that he'd cut him out of his life and not even acknowledge his existence? What sort of man can turn his back on his child just because of the pain of losing his wife? This was a fucking joke.

His aunt was still talking, trying to make it better somehow, but Connor didn't want to think about it anymore. He was done with this conversation, he was done with thinking about his dad, and he was done with being hurt over someone who'd stopped loving him a long time ago, if he'd ever loved him at all.

He interrupted his aunt. "Well, thanks for letting me know. I've got to head out now, but I'll call you when the tour is over. I'll come for a visit."

He barely waited for her to finish apologizing again and telling him she'd love to see him before he hung up.

He paced his room, his jaw clenched as anger burned

through him, barely stopping himself from punching the wall. For a second, he considered knocking on Lexie's door and talking to her about this shitstorm, but then realized what a mistake that would be. She wasn't a permanent part of his life; she was just passing through on her way to somewhere else. To *someone* else. Which was fine with him, because he sure as hell didn't want to get emotionally involved with someone who was still in love with another man. Even if that man was dead. Especially if that man was dead. Because he'd already learned the hard way that you can't compete with a ghost for someone's affections. You'd always end up coming up short.

He never again wanted to allow someone to be in a position where they could hurt him. Now he'd screwed up by spending time with Lexie, by letting her play with his emotions, by starting to rely on her to be there for him. Because relying on Lexie to be there for him was a mistake. One he couldn't afford to make when he knew she'd walk away and not look back when this was done. When it came down to it, the only people that truly cared about him, as a person, were his bandmates and his aunt. That's what he had to remember. He was furious at himself for almost falling into the trap of getting too close to Lexie, and furious at her for coming into his life and making him feel things he didn't want to.

He closed his eyes and tried taking calming breaths. But the fury whipping through him didn't subside. He needed to get out of his room before he did something stupid. Like trash it. He picked up the phone and called down to the band's security detail to have someone meet him so he could get the hell out of there.

Chapter 38

When Lexie woke the next morning, Connor had gone, leaving her satisfied but slightly sore in both body and heart. She lay in bed for a few minutes staring sightlessly at the ceiling, wondering how she would ever meet someone else who could make her feel the things Connor did.

She sighed and threw the covers off, climbing out of bed. She considered looking at the photos they'd taken the night before, but she was too emotionally raw to do it just yet. Better to wait until she was less likely to cry when she saw them.

Biting her lip, she wondered how they had turned out. She'd never been naked in front of the camera before and certainly never taken photos while she was having sex. After the first three she'd taken for Connor, she'd had an overwhelming urge to capture the way they fit together, the way he made her feel when he was inside her. She was afraid that after they parted ways, her memory of their time together would fade, just like her memories of Damien had started to.

Lexie fought back the tears that were always too close to the surface these days and headed to the bathroom to have a shower. Glimpsing herself in the mirror, she stopped in front of it and ran a finger lightly over the mark Connor had left on her neck. She wondered what she should do about it since it would be visible in most of her clothes. While he'd deliberately marked her skin, she was sure Connor didn't want everyone to see it and start asking questions. The last thing he'd want is for everyone to find out what they were doing together.

Sighing, she turned the shower on and stood under the hot water until the slight ache in her muscles eased. After drying off, she rummaged through her suitcase until she found a high-collared, short-sleeved blouse to wear that mostly covered the mark. Just to be sure, she also applied some makeup over it. Happy that it wouldn't be easily visible, she headed downstairs to breakfast.

When she got down there, everyone was at the table except for Connor. She smiled at all the guys, said good morning, then slid in next to Tex, who gave her a little shoulder bump. "Not long to go now before you can escape from us. Can you believe it's been three months already?"

"Not really." The smile she gave him wavered. "I'll miss you guys."

His eyes softened. "We'll miss you too. It's been great having you around. But hey, we'll keep in touch, right? You can always come visit us in LA. Or when we're in the San Francisco area, we can drop in for a visit. And I'm sure we can swing some free tickets to any of our concerts you want to come to." He winked at her.

She reached over and squeezed his hand. "Thanks, Tex. That means a lot." But she knew she wouldn't do any of those things. It would be way too hard to cut ties with

Connor without tormenting herself by trying to push her way back into his life. Or even worse, watch him from the audience at one of his concerts, just another fan. She needed a clean break and time to get over her feelings for him.

She was halfway through her breakfast when she realized Connor wasn't just running slightly late. Concerned, she turned to Tex. "Where's Connor?"

"Uh, apparently he wanted to have some time on his own this morning, so he headed out with Will in tow." The look he gave her was suspiciously sympathetic.

"Oh, right." It was all Lexie could think to say. She felt deflated at not getting to see him, even though they'd only parted ways a couple of hours before. She wanted to make the most of every moment they had left together, as if she could make a lifetime of memories with him in the next few days. But she had no claim on his time, and if he needed some space, then he should be able to take it without worrying about her.

***

Connor still hadn't returned by the time she packed, loaded her stuff on the tour bus, and headed to the venue with the others. It turned out he'd already stashed his bags on the bus before heading out that morning. Noah assured her Connor was probably planning to meet them at the stadium, but when they got to the venue, he wasn't there. Lexie's concern grew when she saw Noah's frown. "Is he going to miss soundcheck?" she asked him.

He shrugged. "We've still got a little time. I'm sure he'll turn up. Since we played here last night, we might get away without him at soundcheck, though it's not ideal."

Lexie found herself checking the clock more frequently as Connor's absence continued. She tried to keep her mind occupied by going about her business, taking shots of the crew testing and checking the equipment to make sure it was still in working order after the last concert.

She was taking a shot of the lighting techs working when Joe, the man who had asked her out at the start of the tour, wandered over, hands stuffed in the pockets of his jeans. They had chatted a few times over the last couple of months, once they'd got over the awkwardness of her turning him down. So, when he came and stood next to her, she gave him a friendly smile.

"Are you going to miss all this craziness?" he asked.

Lexie suppressed a frown. She hated being reminded of the ticking clock. As much as she knew her time with Connor was almost up, she was doing her best not to think about it. She wanted to drag out every minute of the next few days. Not that she could tell Joe that, so she thought of something else which was true in its own right. "I'm looking forward to getting back out in the field. I enjoy being in nature, traveling, seeing the beauty in people just living their lives. This has been an amazing experience, but it's been intense. It's not something I could keep doing. I need to get home and start figuring out what's next for me."

Joe nodded. "I can understand that. It takes a certain kind of person to be on the road all the time." He paused, rubbing the back of his neck before blurting out, "Hey, I know your answer will probably be the same, but I was wondering if I could get your number and when I'm next in San Francisco we could catch up, get a drink?" His dark eyes looked at her hopefully.

Lexie's smile froze. She liked Joe but had no interest in starting anything romantic with him. Now she had to think of a way to let him down gently. Again. "Oh Joe, you're very sweet…" She stopped midsentence when she saw Joe's eyes flick over her shoulder and his smile drop.

A low voice, dripping with ice, came from behind her. "We don't pay you to stand around trying to get into Lexie's pants, Joe. How about you get back to work."

Lexie looked over her shoulder and stared at Connor in shock. She'd never heard him sound or look so angry. Joe, looking suitably chastised, nodded a quick goodbye at her and walked quickly away.

She turned to face Connor. His severe expression made her stomach drop. She glanced around to see if anyone was nearby before putting her hand on his arm and lowering her voice. "What's wrong, Connor?" She didn't think she'd ever seen his face look as hard as it did then. His jaw was clenched so tightly she could see a muscle tic in his cheek.

"Was it what Joe said? I wasn't going to say yes."

He shook her hand off and hurt stabbed through her. Why was he angry at her?

"Connor, I don't know what I said to upset you. Please tell me what's wrong." She didn't want their last few days together to be ruined by what might be a silly misunderstanding. He looked at her, his expression cold. There was something else in his eyes too, but for the life of her she couldn't figure out what it was.

"If you're ready to go home, then don't feel you have to hang around. After all, I think we're pretty much done here."

Lexie's heart stopped, before kicking back in at double

time. The sudden rush of blood through her veins made her dizzy. He couldn't be saying what she thought he was, could he? Not after last night?

"We've still got three days left." She was still hopeful she'd misunderstood him.

His icy expression didn't change. "I imagine you've got all the photos you need by now; you even got some bonus exclusive content."

"Don't do this, Connor," she whispered, hating the coldness in his eyes.

But he kept going, sticking the knife in and twisting it. "And I got everything I needed from you."

She inhaled sharply as shock and pain flooded through her. So, this was how he was going to do it. As tender as he'd been with her, she'd thought he'd at least be kind about it. But it seemed like he wasn't going to even wait until the end of the tour to throw her out of his bed. It was so out of the blue. There'd been no sign that this was coming when they'd been together last night. As intense as that entire experience had been, she'd even started to believe he might have developed some feelings for her.

She blinked back tears and reached out to him. "Connor, please—"

He turned and walked away.

Lexie stared after him in shock, then looked down at the camera she was holding in her trembling hands. She wasn't going to be able to hold back the tears any longer. She needed to get out of here. Right now.

She composed herself long enough to rush from the building, before hitting the pavement outside and bolting as scalding tears poured from her eyes. Her heart felt like it had been ripped from her chest. She had known the end was going to hurt. How could it not, once she realized she'd fallen in love with him.

She had tried to tell herself that she was prepared, as if being prepared for it to end would leave her heart in one piece. But then she also hadn't been expecting him to be so cruel about ending it. She'd hoped that they'd have one last amazing night together before going their separate ways.

But that's not what had happened, and now she was paying the price for her stupidity. She had thought she'd got to know the man behind the rock star persona, but she'd been wrong. Turns out she didn't know him at all. She wasn't sure where to go, she just needed to get out, get away, and spend the rest of the day on her own while she figured out what she needed to do to get home. Then she'd come back for the rest of her stuff. She'd miss the last few concerts, but there was nothing in her contract that said she had to be at every one.

Her laugh was bitter. Connor had as much as ordered her to leave anyway. He'd been right when he said she had more than enough photos for the book. She rubbed her forehead. She'd still have to spend time editing the photos and putting it all together, then sending a mock-up for approval. She wasn't going to be able to cut ties with the band just yet. But hopefully she could get it done before she left for Canada, and then she could take the time to grieve for what she'd lost here.

She didn't take any notice of where she was going, she just kept moving away from the man who had come to mean so much to her. Today, it was going to be just her and her camera, the way it had been ever since Damien had died.

Chapter 39

Connor checked everywhere for Lexie, as well as calling her phone.

No answer. *Fuck.*

He'd checked with Maggie and Lexie's stuff was still on the bus, so she had to come back at some stage. His stomach twisted at the thought of her leaving, and he cursed his stupidity. Why the hell had he said those things to her? He'd been an absolute bastard, and he'd regretted his words about ten minutes after walking away from her. That was just enough time for the painful pressure in his heart and mind to ease after he'd heard her say she wanted to get back to her life and figure out what was next for her. And then Joe had asked her out, just like any number of men would ask her in the future. One of who would end up being the perfect man for her, one she'd probably end up marrying, having a family with. The thought of her leaving him to be with someone else had been too much to handle so soon after finding out about his dad. He'd lashed out, wanting only to hurt her before she had the chance to do it to him. By the time he came to his senses, it was too late—she'd disappeared.

Connor sat down heavily on one of the couches on the bus and slumped forward, elbows on knees and head in hands, wondering how he'd screwed everything up so badly. He'd taken his hurt and anger at his dad's actions and focused it on Lexie, the last person in the world who deserved it. The only thing he could do now was give her the space she needed, and then as soon as he saw her again, he'd apologize, then take her in his arms and show her just how sorry he was. If they only had a few days left, he wanted every minute of those days with her.

Lexie still hadn't returned by the time Connor had to go onstage. When the others asked him where she was, he just shook his head, not knowing how to answer. When Drew pressed him, worried, and wanting to know what had happened, he had to tell him they'd had an argument. Drew gave him a sharp, too-knowing look at that and sent one of their security detail back to the hotel in case Lexie had headed back there. Connor had never felt so little desire to get out on stage and perform. The fact he'd ended up drinking far more than he normally would before a show hadn't helped.

His performance that night was one of his worst. The crowd seemed happy enough, but he could see Tex, Zac, and Noah giving each other concerned looks when his distraction became obvious. He kept searching the crowd and the side stage, hoping to see her standing there, camera in hand. But she never appeared. At one point it got so bad Tex had to pull him aside for a second between songs to tell him to get it together.

By the time they finished their last song, he'd had enough and walked offstage while the others were still thanking the crowd. He didn't care, he just wanted to find her. But she wasn't anywhere backstage. He cornered Drew to ask if he'd heard anything, but Drew shook his head. "Her stuff is still on the bus though, so she has to come back. I just hope it's soon because we have to head out in a couple of hours."

Connor showered in the green room, then headed for the after-party, hoping against hope she'd be there. He searched the room but couldn't see her. He had no patience for his fans that night, practically ignoring them when they approached him.

One little blonde didn't get the hint and kept following him around as he bided his time before he could head back to the bus. She just wouldn't leave him alone, when all he wanted was to be by himself, drowning his sorrows in a bottle of whiskey. God, here she came again, pressing herself up against him, trying to get him to engage in her attempts at seduction. Eventually, he had enough. He didn't like being rude to his fans, but she was not getting the hint. He grabbed her shoulders and pulled her toward him, putting his face so close to hers that her eyes almost crossed trying to focus on him, and hissed at her to *leave him the fuck alone*.

Which was when he heard Tex calling out Lexie's name. She'd come back! By the time he released the blonde woman and turned, all he saw was the door swinging shut behind a fast-moving Lexie. He cursed and pushed his way through the crowd, but Tex grabbed his arm and growled in his ear. "Don't you think you've done enough damage?"

Connor jerked his arm out of Tex's grip, "Fuck off, you don't know what you're talking about." He tried to push his way past Tex, but his friend grabbed him again.

"You need to calm down and let her go. I saw the expression on that girl's face, and she's not going to listen to anything you have to say right now."

"Let me go or I'll fucking kick your ass." He stared Tex down, breathing heavily.

Tex searched his face, then released his arm, shaking his head. "You fucked up, man."

Connor barely glanced at him before forcing his way through the crowd to the door, swinging it open and rushing out. He looked around but couldn't see Lexie anywhere, so he ran down the hall and out the exit, looking around desperately. She wasn't there, but seeing the tour bus, he had a sudden hope he'd find her in her bedroom. He sprinted over to the security officer watching the bus.

"Is Lexie in there?"

The guy shook his head. "She was, but she left."

"What do you mean? She left just now?"

He looked worried, obviously concerned he was going to get in trouble for something. "She just left in a cab."

Still hopeful, he asked, "Did she have her suitcase?"

The guy nodded. "She grabbed it off the bus and loaded it into the cab before she went inside the venue."

Connor pulled out his cell phone and dialed Lexie's number. It rang twice and then went to voicemail, meaning she'd rejected his call. He dialed again with the same result. The third time he called it went straight to voicemail. She'd turned her phone off. He left a quick message urging her to call him back.

She didn't have much of a head start; if she was going to the airport, he could still catch her. He ran back inside and found Tex and Drew standing and talking in hushed tones just inside the door. Tex had his phone out, and Connor wondered briefly if he'd tried to call Lexie too, and whether he'd had more luck.

"Drew, I need a car." He scowled when Drew glanced at Tex, and then slowly shook his head.

"I'll call a fucking cab, then." He went to pull his phone out of his pocket again, but Tex put a hand on his shoulder before he could get it out. "Before you end up doing something even more stupid, we need to talk."

"I have to catch her!" He was almost yelling now.

"Where do you think she's going?" Tex asked.

"I don't know—probably to the airport."

"Or to a hotel for the night?"

"Maybe, but I can't search every hotel. I can go to the airport though."

"And buy a ticket just in the hope she'll be there waiting for you?"

"Why the hell not!"

"Because this is not a fucking romance movie, and things like that don't work in real life!"

"Not to mention, we have to leave and get on the road in the next half an hour to make Phoenix tomorrow, which is in the opposite direction to the airport." Drew spoke calmly, but Connor could see the restrained anger in his face.

Connor shook his head, ready to tell him he didn't give a fuck, but Tex's next words stopped him in his tracks.

"You can't confront her in a public place like that. Not when she's going to be as upset as she looked when she ran out of here. You'll back her into a corner, and you'd better be prepared for a fight."

"I just need to explain to her why I said the things I did. I need to apologize. I screwed up, but I can fix it if I can just talk to her."

Tex raised his eyebrows. "How exactly are you going to

299

explain to her why you were kissing that woman back there?"

Connor's head jerked up. "What are you talking about? I didn't kiss anyone."

Tex narrowed his eyes at him. "I saw Lexie when she came in. She told me you'd had a falling-out and she was leaving, but she wanted to say goodbye to everyone first. I tried to talk her out of going, but she was determined. That's when we both saw you across the room with your tongue down some blonde's throat. Lexie turned white and bolted. So, you tell me what the hell was going on if you weren't kissing her. Since there was obviously something going on between you and Lexie, you'd better make it a good explanation, otherwise, I'm going to make you regret hurting her." Tex's anger and disappointment in him was palpable.

Connor rubbed his temples, frustration surging through him. "I wasn't kissing her. I was telling her to leave me the hell alone. She'd been following me around all night. I grabbed her and told her to piss off."

Tex's gaze became slightly more sympathetic. "I'm sorry, man, it really looked like you were kissing her."

"So, I just need to explain that to Lexie."

Tex shook his head. "I already told you. You don't know if she's going to the airport tonight, and even if she is, you can't make a scene. Can you imagine if you go storming in there? You'll get mobbed. And I think that's the last thing she'll want to see while you're trying to apologize to her. And if you find her, manage to not get noticed, and apologize, make her believe you weren't kissing that girl, and convince her not to leave, what then? Have you even thought that far ahead?"

Connor hesitated. "I'll bring her back here."

"And then what? You'll bring her back just so you can screw her and then take her back to the airport and wave her goodbye again in a couple of days? What is your actual long-term goal here? You can't keep messing around with her. You need to figure out what you want, or you should just let her go."

Shit. He didn't have a plan; hadn't been thinking past finding her and begging for forgiveness.

Tex's voice softened. "She cares about you. And you obviously care about her. As much as you can, anyway." Connor gave him a sharp look. "But if you were planning to say goodbye at the end of the tour and never see her again, then please do not go chasing after her just so you can appease your guilt. It might even be easier for her if it ends this way. It might be easier for her to move on if she thinks you're a bastard."

Connor closed his eyes and took several deep breaths. He hated that what Tex was saying made sense. He'd been refusing to think past the end of the tour. His emotions were so tangled up, he didn't know what he wanted. Particularly in the aftermath of finding out about his dad's death. How could he drag Lexie back and then just let her go again?

All the fight went out of him, and he sagged against the wall. "I don't know what I want," he admitted quietly.

"Then you need to figure it out before you talk to her again. Because if you keep screwing her around, all of us will kick your ass."

Connor scrubbed his face with his hands.

And he'd deserve it.

Chapter 40

The door swung open before Lexie could knock, and Piper rushed out, gathering her into a comforting hug. She pulled back to scan Lexie's face, worry evident in her blue eyes and furrowed brow. Her look of concern broke through Lexie's hard-fought control, and hot tears overflowed and trickled down her cheeks.

"Oh my God, honey, what happened?" Piper asked as she guided Lexie into the house. "I wish you'd let me come and pick you up. You shouldn't have had to get a taxi."

"I didn't want to create a scene in the airport, and I would have broken down seeing you there. Plus, I didn't even call you until I was already here, so it was quicker just to get a cab. I'm sorry for the late notice."

"Don't worry about that; I'm just glad you came to me. Come on inside. I'll make you a cup of tea, and you can tell me about it." She grabbed Lexie's suitcase out of her hand and led her further into the house.

Lexie followed her sister-in-law into the warm, cozy kitchen. She sat down at the wooden farmhouse-style table while Piper busied herself boiling water.

"It's so good to see you, Piper. I should have visited earlier. It shouldn't have taken something like this for me to get my butt down here."

Piper placed a steaming cup of tea in front of Lexie, then sat down across from her. She reached out and squeezed Lexie's hand. "I'll take you any way I can get you, honey, but you need to tell me what happened."

Lexie sighed, picked up her tea, and breathed in the soothing chamomile scent before taking a small sip. Where to start? Along with the pain, the familiar surge of guilt overwhelmed her. How could she tell Damien's sister what she'd done? What would Piper think of her? True, she had encouraged Lexie to have a fling, but she would never have believed Lexie would be stupid enough to fall for someone like Connor. She'd even warned Lexie against it before the tour.

"So, which one was it?" Piper asked, after the silence had stretched on for too long.

She should have known Piper would guess straight away. After all, what else would have had Lexie turning up on her doorstep in tears?

"Connor." More tears slipped out and dripped down her cheeks. She wiped them away angrily. He didn't deserve her tears. She'd already given him too much of herself.

"Tell me what happened."

The sympathy in Piper's voice caused Lexie's throat to tighten. She took another sip of tea, taking a few seconds to compose herself before letting it all spill out. She left out some details—after all, there were things she couldn't share with her late husband's sister, like exactly how amazing the sex had been. How he'd made her feel things she'd never felt before. How she'd let herself fall so hard for someone so completely wrong for her.

When she finished, Piper looked at her, head cocked to the side and eyes searching, as if she knew Lexie was leaving things out. "So obviously he's a major jerk to treat you like that. I may be a pacifist, but that doesn't mean I won't get violent on his ass if you need me to."

Lexie managed a smile for her friend, then frowned when Piper paused and chewed on her lip. She obviously had something else she wanted to say, and it wouldn't be Piper if she didn't have some words of wisdom to share—welcome or not. Lexie sighed. "What do you want to say Piper?"

Piper scrunched her face up apologetically. "Well, this is going to sound bad, but Lexie, it might not be such a terrible thing it happened." She put her hand up as Lexie opened her mouth to protest. "Wait, hear me out."

Lexie closed her mouth and leaned back in her seat, frowning as Piper continued. "I know it hurts now, honey, and that sucks, no doubt about it. But you've taken the first step, and that's a good thing. You've faced your fear, had your heart broken, and yes, it's painful. But you're still here, you're still standing. It hasn't broken you. *He* didn't break you."

She reached out and grabbed Lexie's hand, squeezing gently as she continued.

"So, my advice to you is, thank that douchebag for the orgasms and move on to bigger and better things." She waggled her eyebrows. "If you know what I mean."

That shocked a laugh out of Lexie. It was a nice sentiment, but hard to imagine it being possible.

Her laughter died, and she sighed. "Maybe you're right. I

just feel so stupid. I mean, I knew it wasn't going to last—he was clear about that. But I trusted him, you know? I thought he at least cared enough to be kind." Her voice started to waver. "I guess that's what I get for letting myself fall for someone I knew from the start was wrong for me."

"Don't feel stupid, honey. How could you have known he was wrong for you unless you tried? He obviously had some good traits, otherwise you would never have even slept with him, let alone developed feelings."

"I should have known because he's so different from Damien! I'm angry because I let myself fall in love with him anyway, even knowing he wasn't right for me." Lexie's emotions spilled out again, and she burst into tears.

Piper got up and grabbed a box of tissues off the counter. She passed the whole thing to Lexie before sitting back down and reaching across the table to clasp Lexie's hand again.

"Lexie, Connor being different from Damien has nothing to do with whether he's wrong or right for you. I don't know how you got that idea in that head of yours. I think it's good you chose someone different. I'd be far more concerned if you picked someone too much like my brother."

Lexie wiped her nose and looked at Piper in confusion. "Damien and I were perfect together. Why would finding someone similar to him be wrong? I mean, obviously not someone exactly the same, that would just be weird—"

"No kidding," Piper smirked.

"—but someone with the same traits, the same values. Someone I know will fit me, who'll love me the way I want to be loved. The way Damien did." Tears trickled down her cheeks, a seeming never ending stream that mourned the loss of Damien as well as the man she'd thought Connor was.

"Listen to me Lexie, you and Damien *became* perfect for each other. You were just kids when you met, and you grew to fit each other. But you're a different person now. His death forced you to be different—more independent, more adventurous—so you need to be with someone different. Have you ever thought maybe the reason you turned down all those sweet men that asked you out wasn't because you weren't ready, but because they were too much like Damien? Maybe deep down you know you need someone different now. And to be honest, if you and Damien met for the first time today, I don't know if you'd end up together."

Lexie started shaking her head, but Piper plowed on. "You need to find someone who fits the new you, and that means keeping your mind and heart open, Lexie, because you don't know who might end up being the next love of your life. And if Connor hadn't been such an asshat, there's no reason it couldn't have been him. You took a chance, and I'm proud of you for that. You just have to make sure you keep taking chances, because one day, the chance you take will be worth it."

Lexie brushed more tears from her cheeks, taken aback by Piper's words. While it was hard to listen to, what she was saying rang true. She knew she had a lot of thinking to do, but right now was not the time. Everything felt too raw. First, she needed to get over Connor.

She squeezed Piper's hand. "Thank you. I don't know what I'd do without you."

"No problem, honey. You know you're like a sister to me. I just want the best for you. Now, I know you left out all the juicy details before. Connor was a jackass, but that doesn't mean I don't want to hear about how he was in bed."

Lexie felt a fiery blush suffuse her at the memories that flooded through her. "Um, yeah. He was good."

Piper narrowed her eyes. "Just good?"

Lexie sighed and rolled her eyes at her friend. "Fine, he was really, really good. Mind-blowingly good."

"Multiple orgasm good?"

A laugh escaped her. "Yes, definitely."

Then the laugh died as the pain hit her again. "I just wish it hadn't been so good. I let our physical connection fool me into thinking there was more to it. I let myself believe he might have felt something for me. But that's on me. He told me up front that he doesn't have relationships. It was just physical for him."

Piper scowled. "Well, that's bullshit."

Lexie's brow furrowed. "What do you mean?"

"I'm sorry, but having sex with you exclusively, living with you on the bus, spending all his spare time with you. That *was* a relationship, even if it wasn't meant to be permanent. If that prick was too chickenshit to admit it to himself, then that's his loss."

Once again Piper had made her smile. Lexie stretched across the table and hugged her sister-in-law. "This is why I love you so much. I think you've managed to call him enough names now to make me feel better."

Piper lifted her cup in salute and winked. "What's family for if not for insulting loser exes."

The smile slipped from Lexie's face. "I just need to get back to work and take my mind off everything."

"When's your next job?"

"I'm heading to Canada in just over two weeks."

"Great, you can stay with me until you have to go home

and pack. We can sunbathe, drink wine, and indulge in all-important retail therapy. What do you think?"

Lexie mustered a watery smile. "It sounds perfect."

Chapter 41

The last concert was done, and Connor couldn't be more relieved to finish a tour. He hadn't seen or heard from Lexie since she'd left three days ago. He'd ended up confessing everything that had been going on between them to the others, as well as what he'd found out about his father and the things he'd said to Lexie afterward.

Drew had been angry to find out what he and Lexie had been up to, primarily because he hated being in the dark about anything that could impact the band. The others had been more understanding; they'd noticed the change in him when she was around.

Everyone was sympathetic, but they needed to finish the tour. He did what he could to bring the same energy to the last few shows as he had when Lexie had been in the crowd smiling up at him, but it was all an act. He just wanted it to be over so he could figure everything out.

Now Connor was sitting on the stage next to Tex after the last concert, looking out at the empty stadium as the crew tore everything down. His best friend had listened to him patiently as he spoke about Lexie. And after that, Connor finally opened up about his unhappiness with where the band was heading. His concern about his future, his fears about what his decision might mean for his friends.

When he finished, Tex stared at him with his brow furrowed. "Why the hell am I just hearing about this now? I can't believe you didn't think you could talk to me—any of us—about this. We're friends for fuck's sake. We've been through thick and thin together; you don't think we could have a mature conversation about our future?"

Connor scrubbed his hand over his face. Now that he'd finally said it out loud, it did seem ridiculous that he hadn't thought he could talk to his friends about it. He looked at Tex ruefully. "Sorry, man. I don't know what I was thinking."

Tex shook his head. "You weren't thinking at all. You've always been wary of sharing too much of yourself with anyone, Connor, too worried about being rejected. And you take too much responsibility for other people's happiness. We've been doing this thing for a long time; we're all fucking tired of the touring. What keeps us going is making music together. But don't think we haven't all thought about other things we might like to do. So why don't we all sit down and discuss it like adults."

Connor let out a strained laugh. "Yeah, we should probably do that."

"So, have you spoken to Drew about this, or am I the only one you've told?"

"I haven't mentioned anything to Drew. The only other person I told was Lexie."

Tex raised his eyebrows. "So, you've told Lexie things you haven't told anyone else? Not even your best friends you've known since you were a kid?"

Connor nodded, the pain of her absence hitting him anew. He still didn't know what he was going to do about her. The times he'd broken down and tried calling, she hadn't answered. He knew Drew had her address, but before he did something stupid like turn up at her door unannounced, he needed to figure out what would be best for both of them, not just for him.

Tex was looking at him, his expression inscrutable.

"What's that look for?" Connor asked.

Tex shook his head and sighed, before saying quietly, "You're an idiot, Connor. Lexie is one in a million. When are you finally going to admit you're in love with her? Head over heels, crazy in love. She's smart, and kind, and funny, and one of the most naturally sexy women I've ever met. You would have to be the biggest fool in the world to not be in love with her."

"You sound like you're the one who's in love with her." Even Connor could hear the accusation in his voice.

Tex shrugged but didn't deny it. "If you hadn't made it obvious from the minute she came on board the bus that you wanted her bad, I would've made a move for sure."

"You did make a move. You kissed her," Connor growled.

Tex shrugged again. "Only because you were taking your sweet time to do anything about it. And I didn't know if you would ever pull your head out of your ass, so yeah, I took a shot. It was clear there was nothing there on her side. She was just as torn up about you as you were about her."

Shit, he'd screwed things up so badly. Hurt her when that was the last thing in the world he ever wanted to do. He still felt ill knowing she thought he'd been kissing another woman. "I don't know what to say to her, how to get her to believe me that I wasn't screwing around."

There was a tense silence from Tex, and then he said quietly, "She knows." His expression was sympathetic.

"What the fuck do you mean she knows?"

Tex sighed. "I got through to her on the phone once, the day after she left. I explained to her what happened."

Connor glared at him. "Why the hell are you only telling me this now?"

"Because she needs time, and so do you. You need to get your shit together before you go after her."

"Do you think that was your decision to make?"

Tex shrugged and stared at him impassively.

Connor ground his teeth, then asked, "So she believed you?"

Tex nodded.

"Just like that?"

Now Tex was angry. "Yes, just like that! She loves you, which means she believes you. And she knows I wouldn't excuse your sorry ass if I didn't believe it."

"If she loves me, why the fuck didn't she come back. Why hasn't she contacted me, answered my calls?"

"Because, you moron, she loves you!"

"You are making no fucking sense right now. What the hell are you talking about? If she loves me and she believes me, why didn't she come back?" He was standing and yelling now, uncaring who heard.

Now Tex wasn't just angry, he was furious. His eyes narrowed, but rather than yelling, his voice got low and icy cold. "Because she also believed you when you said you didn't want a relationship. She believed you when you told her you didn't need her anymore. And she believed you every time you *never fucking told her you loved her*!"

Connor stared at him in shock, then sunk back down, his heart thundering in his chest. Shit. He felt sick, hollow, gutted. He *did* love her. He couldn't deny the truth anymore. He loved her, and according to Tex, she loved him back. And he'd pushed her away at every turn. From the first moment he'd realized he was attracted to her, he'd tried to keep her at arm's length. Even when he'd given in to his desire and touched her, he'd made sure to let her know it was just a fling. Even when he'd been inside her, he'd never let himself think about what exactly he was feeling. Pretending it wasn't there. Pretending he'd be able to walk away at the end. Pretending he could watch her walk away and not care that she'd end up belonging to someone else.

He had been so stupid. Was it too late to make up for it? He didn't want to think so, couldn't think so. He had to make this right. He wanted Lexie in his life—that was the only thing he felt clear about at the moment. But Tex was right. He needed to sort things out before he spoke to her. He stood up. "Let's go."

"Where are we going?"

"I'm going to get my shit together, and then I'm going after her."

Tex grinned. "Finally."

Chapter 42

It had been five weeks since Lexie had left the tour, and she was still waiting for the pain to ease. She'd got back from Canada a week ago. It had been good to escape from everything, to go somewhere she couldn't be found, to have time to think and process her feelings. But then again, all that time on her own had given her plenty of opportunity to feel all the pain and regret.

She didn't know if she'd done the right thing by ignoring Connor's phone calls those first few days after she'd left. Talking to Tex and finding out the truth about what happened on that last night had blunted some of her anger but hadn't lessened the pain. Talking to Connor wouldn't help. She loved him, but he didn't love her. He hadn't wanted anything more from her than her body—he'd made that clear. And even if he did care about her, he wasn't someone she could have a future with. She needed to focus on that and do her best to forget him. Talking to him would have just meant ripping her heart to shreds again, and she wasn't strong enough for that.

Before she'd headed to Canada, she'd finalized the mock-up of the photo book and sent it off to Drew. Doing it had been heartbreaking, but it also ended up making her smile.

There were so many amazing photos, so many incredible memories. She'd never forget her time with those four amazing, talented men, regardless of how it had ended. Eventually, the pain would ease, and she'd remember only the good times. And as much as he'd ended up hurting her, Connor had first started healing her, had shown her that love after Damien was possible. She rubbed her chest, over her heart, hoping to ease the ache as she thought of him.

She had ended up swapping out Connor's portrait, replacing the one he'd posed for with the candid she'd taken at the end of their morning at the beach. Just looking at the photo made the love and pain surge up in her. The play of light and shadow over his back emphasized every toned muscle, highlighting the beauty of his body. But that wasn't what captivated her. It was the way he stood, holding his guitar and looking out at the ocean as if searching for answers in the endless blue. She hoped eventually he would find whatever it was he was looking for.

She had also forced herself to look at the photos they'd taken on their last night together. They were amazing, beautiful, heart-wrenching, brutal. You could see every emotion on her face, and she'd cried far too many tears at the memory. Then she'd dried her eyes and saved them onto her personal hard drive. A bittersweet memory she'd keep for the rest of her life. No matter what else happened.

This morning, she was updating her online portfolio with examples of her most recent work when a knock sounded at her door. She frowned, curious as to who it could be, pushing aside the little voice in her mind wondering if it could be Connor. She knew it wouldn't be, and she hated the part of her heart that clung to the hope he might come for her. So, when she opened the door and saw him standing on her doorstep, looking sexy and disheveled as if he'd just run his hands through his hair, she just stared at him with wide eyes.

"Hi, Lexie." Two words said in that oh so sexy deep voice had her heart threatening to beat out of her chest.

"C-Connor? W-What are you doing here?" Great, now she was stammering.

He smiled, but his expression was guarded. "I'm here to see you. Can I come in?"

She started, realizing she'd been staring at him and blocking the doorway.

"Of course." She stepped back and he brushed past her, his clean, crisp smell bringing with it a rush of memories.

He walked over to the dining table, looking down at some prints from her Canada job she'd laid out. She had to shake her head to make sure she wasn't dreaming. Seeing him in her house was surreal.

She took a few steps closer, but not too close. She was already fighting the urge to touch him.

He was still looking at the photos—landscapes, some candids. "These are beautiful," he said quietly.

"Thank you." She wasn't sure what else to say.

Finally, he turned and looked at her. His green eyes burned into hers, but she couldn't read his expression. They stared at each other for what seemed like forever before he finally spoke.

"I wanted to apologize," he started, and she felt the small balloon of unwelcome hope that had begun inflating in her chest deflate. He was just doing the decent thing and coming to apologize to her in person, nothing more. She blinked back the tears that were always so close to the surface these days. "What I said to you was unforgivable. I lashed out at you, and you didn't deserve that. I can't tell you how sorry I am that things ended that way between us."

She nodded, her chin trembling with the effort to hold back the tears. She just needed to get through this, and then she could fall apart when he'd gone.

He sighed. "And then having to see what you did that night. Tex told me he let you know what happened. I promise you, Lexie, I would never have done that to you."

"I know," she whispered. Wanting him to go and never leave at the same time.

When he just looked at her, she continued. "When I saw you and her, I thought it was exactly what it looked like. But as soon as Tex told me, I knew it was true."

"Why did you talk to Tex and not me?" He sounded upset now, which made her a little mad.

"Because I didn't want to talk to you! By the time I spoke to Tex I'd already been too hurt. Even though I knew then that you weren't screwing around, it was still over between us. I was already gone—why put us both through that? We both needed to move on."

His eyes narrowed, the green glittering with anger. "I said some terrible things that I didn't mean, Lexie, but you should have given me the chance to apologize. You didn't think I might be hurting too?"

Taken aback, she paused before responding. Had she thought he'd be hurting? Not really—she had honestly thought he'd want a clean break. But looking at him now, with his tense jaw and narrowed gaze, she realized that maybe she'd been blind to what was actually going on with him. Too absorbed in her own pain to see what he might have been feeling.

"I-I'm sorry, I just assumed this would be easier for both of
us to, you know, move on..." She trailed off as his jaw clenched tighter.

"I may not have said the words, Lexie, but I was showing you how I felt. Even when I didn't know it. Yes, I said some stupid things because I was upset and I handled it badly, but then you pushed me away when I tried to make it right. I'm sorry, sorrier than you can ever know, that I hurt you. But you hurt me too."

Lexie felt her chin trembling harder than ever, and then her entire body started to shake, because she could see from his expression that she *had* hurt him. And she realized that maybe a small, mean part of her had wanted to hurt him. She should have known, after what he'd told her about his father, that ignoring him and pushing him away would hurt. So, what did that say about her? Shakily, she managed to get out, "I'm sorry, that was wrong of me. I should have spoken to you, cleared the air."

He ran both hands through his hair in frustration. "You don't get it. I don't want to just clear the air so we can move on. I don't want to move on, Lexie. I want you to stay with me, to be with me properly. I want to try to make this work between us."

She sucked in a shocked breath. She'd never expected that from him. He'd told her over and over that he didn't do relationships. Could it be true? And if it was, what did that mean? She knew she loved him, but she couldn't figure out how they could be together. He was a hugely successful rock star, and she was just a normal person. How could it ever work between them?

This time she couldn't stop the tears spilling over. "Connor, being with you was beyond incredible. I lo… like you so much, but that's your life, not mine. You're a rock star, and I'm not cut out to be a rock star's girlfriend. You must know that as well as I do."

His brows drew together, and he frowned. "What does that even mean, Lexie? What sort of person do you think you need to be, to be a rock star's girlfriend? Surely all it takes is wanting to be with me?"

"I do want to be with you. So much. But I also don't want to be on the sidelines of your life, waving goodbye every time you head out on tour, watching women throw themselves at your feet, spending long nights wondering if you might be lonely enough to…" She paused and gave a slight shake of her head. "Wondering if I'll be enough for you. It might sound selfish, but I want to be someone's priority. I want love, marriage, a family. You have your own priorities, Connor, and they're important because they're yours. Tex, Noah, Zac, they're your family. The band is your life right now, even if you're not sure what the future holds. I can't lose myself in you, then have my heart broken all over again. It's going to hurt like hell to walk away, but it's the best thing for me, for both of us."

He shook his head in frustration. "We'll talk about the future of the band later. What I need to know right now is how you feel about me. Do you love me, Lexie? Because I love you. Nothing else matters."

Her heart stopped, then kicked back in at double time. He *loved* her?

He stepped closer and reached for her, cupping her chin and tilting her face up to his. "Stop seeing the truth only through your camera. I need you to see me, who I really am."

He took her hand in his and pressed it against his chest, just over his heart. "This belongs to you. I've never given it to anyone else. You're the only one I ever want to give it to." His green eyes searched hers. "I'm asking you to give me a chance. To give us a chance."

She could feel his heart beating under her palm, fast, but strong and sure, and as she looked up into his beautiful eyes, it was like she could finally see past what he was to who he was. For a second, she could see the possibility of a future with him unfold in front of her, if she was just willing to give them that chance. Love, laughter, passion. Maybe one day dark-haired children that would nestle in their father's arms as he sang lullabies to them, while their mother took a thousand photos. Different to the future she used to imagine, but just as real.

Lexie felt the tears well up in her eyes and overflow. She'd been so stupid to walk away from him. No, not stupid—frightened by the intensity of her feelings for him and the potential for more heartbreak. But there can only be heartbreak when there is love, and she didn't want to spend her life frightened of love in case she got hurt again. She was stronger than that. And he was here, standing in front of her, offering her his heart. It might be hard, but she realized she would forever regret not giving them a chance.

So, as he reached up to brush away her tears, his pain and hope clear in his eyes, the words spilled from her. "I love you so much Connor. I'm so sorry for walking away from you. I was so scared of letting myself love you in case I lost you.

After Damien, I was scared I could never love anyone again. And then I met you, and I was scared of loving the wrong person and having my heart torn out again. I didn't think I could bear the pain, but I was wrong. Being with you is worth the risk. It's worth everything."

He closed his eyes in relief, before opening them and giving her the most heart-rending smile. "Thank God. I don't know what I would have done if you'd said you didn't love me."

She smiled at him, even as she felt more tears fall. "Was there ever any doubt? I still can't believe no one saw it written on my face whenever I looked at you."

"Tex saw it. He saw through both of us right from the start."

She nodded slowly. "Yes, I think he did."

He leaned closer and smirked as he whispered, "I can't believe you kissed him."

Lexie's eyes rounded, and she blushed. "He told you?"

"Yeah. I would've punched him if he hadn't been holding my guitar." She laughed at that. "But he told me you weren't interested, so I let him off with a warning."

She started to say something else, but before she could his mouth was on hers. She moaned and stood on her tiptoes so she could press herself closer to him. Her nipples hardened, and she pushed her sensitive breasts against the hard planes of his chest. He groaned and she could feel him, hot and hard against her stomach.

He broke the kiss. "Bedroom?" His voice was tight and urgent.

She pointed down the short hallway running off the living room. "Last door on the right," she panted. Then his mouth was back on hers, and he grabbed her under her thighs, lifting her up against him. She wrapped her legs around his back, and he carried her down the hall and into her bedroom, never taking his lips from hers.

Chapter 43

Connor collapsed back on the bed. He didn't know how long they'd been making love, but regardless of how long it had been, he knew he would never get enough of her. Now she was draped over him, her head resting on his chest and her fingers stroking circles over his skin. He still couldn't quite believe that he'd managed to get her back. He smiled in satisfaction. Whatever it took, he was going to make sure Lexie never regretted taking this chance with him.

He'd also found the time to tell her what had happened with his dad, the morning it had all gone bad. Her anger on his behalf made him realize how little his dad's actions could hurt him anymore. Somehow loving her, and having her love him, had lessened the pain of that last betrayal. His dad had moved on; he owed it to himself to do the same.

She finally broke the contented silence. "You said something before about the band's future. What did you mean?"

He smiled more broadly. "I should have listened to you and spoken to the others earlier. After you left, I knew I needed to get my shit together before I talked to you again. That's why it's taken me this long to come for you. We had a few decisions to make and meetings with the label. But now it's all sorted."

Lexie propped herself up on one elbow, brows raised and a small smile playing on her lips as she waited for him to elaborate.

"So, the band has made a unanimous decision to take a hiatus. Everyone was kind of over the intense touring schedule. Tour fatigue and all that shit. Anyway, Tex and I have decided we want to try writing songs for a kind of stripped-back acoustic album, as well as focusing on more actively supporting the music therapy charities we're involved in."

"That's fantastic! I'm so excited for you, Connor." Lexie's eyes were shining, and he had to stop to kiss her thoroughly before continuing.

"Zac and Noah are starting their own band as a side project. Zac will be the lead singer, and we're all going to collaborate on writing an album for them. We'll be spending a lot of time writing songs, but I can do that from home initially, or on the road with you if you want me to come with you when you travel. We've got a few gigs we've signed up for that Fractured will still need to do. Some of those are overseas, but if you don't have any projects on then, I'd love you to come with us. After we release the new album, we'll probably have to do a tour, but it won't be stadiums. It'll be just a few small, intimate venues to suit the stripped-back style of the album. We're all looking forward to toning it back and just enjoying playing music with each other again. I can't promise we won't have to do a stadium tour at some stage; you never know what the future holds. But Lexie, I want you with me always. We'll deal with it together if it happens."

Lexie pushed herself up and pressed her mouth softly against his. Pulling back, she smiled at him. "You look so happy."

"I am happy. The happiest I've been in a long time. I've got my friends, my music the way I like it, and best of all I've got my woman. Add in the ability to use my fame and money to help kids. What else is there?"

She gazed up at him, so much love shining in her eyes, his heart surged in his chest. "Nothing. There *is* nothing else." Her lips met his in a long, searing kiss, and he'd never felt more sure of his future.

Epilogue

He'd known he was going to marry her almost as soon as they'd started officially dating. She'd shown him the photos they'd taken that last night they were together on tour. Apart from being incredibly erotic, he'd been struck by the love he'd seen shining from her face, and his, even though he hadn't known at the time that he loved her. The knowledge that he was going to make her his forever had hit him like a sledgehammer. He wanted them bound together in every way possible, in body, soul, and marriage, something he once thought he would never want.

He knew it was far too early to say anything to her then, since she was still nervous about whether their different lives would mesh. He wanted to give her time to see how well they could work together. And he knew they would because he was prepared to do everything he could to make sure that they did, even if that meant leaving the band altogether.

But he hadn't needed to since their lives had slotted together almost perfectly. With him at home, concentrating on writing songs, doing a few gigs here and there with the others, mostly charity events, and figuring out how their new sound would work, Lexie had relaxed and eventually thrown herself into it all. As well as doing her freelance photography, she also continued taking photos of Fractured, as well as Zac and Noah's new band which had already started to take off in a big way.

She now had a huge social media following for her photos of the four of them, and even though the band was on hiatus, pending the release of their new album sometime in the future, their popularity hadn't dimmed. The label was busy promoting the new direction they were taking and figuring out how to get their money's worth without relying on huge stadium tours.

That was their problem to deal with though. Connor had made his decision, and now all he cared about was doing the things that made him, Lexie, and his friends the happiest. And hopefully, the fans would enjoy the results.

But now it was time for the moment he'd been planning for almost a year. He was hoping he'd given her enough time to overcome her fears because he wasn't sure what he'd do if she said no.

Now, he was saying goodbye to Tex, Zac, and Noah at the front door of the house he and Lexie had moved into a couple of months earlier. The guys had been over to have a practice session for some of the new songs he and Tex had written, and it had gone incredibly well. They were all feeling positive about where things were heading. They also knew what Connor had planned for today, so Zac and Noah both wished him luck and slapped him on the back as they left, but Tex lingered for a minute to talk.

"How are you feeling?" he asked.

"I feel like I'm going to be sick," Connor grumbled.

Tex laughed. "You've got nothing to worry about, man.

There's not a chance in hell she'll say no. You two are meant for each other."

"What if it's too soon? What if she's still not sure?"

"I've seen the way she looks at you, and I've seen the way you look at her. Lexie knows what's in your heart, and that's the only thing she'll be thinking about when you ask her." Tex sounded a little wistful as he spoke.

Connor hoped like hell Tex was right. But if he was wrong, and she said no, then he'd just have to give her more time and ask again, because he wasn't ever letting her go. Even if they never got married, he was planning on being beside her for the rest of her life.

"You good?" Tex asked.

He took a deep breath and nodded.

"Go get your girl, then!"

Connor nodded and said goodbye. Moment of truth time.

He headed back into the house and returned to the room they'd been practicing in. Lexie had been with them during the session, taking photos as always, and had stayed behind to finish up while he'd walked the others out. Now he stopped in the doorway and just watched her, his heart beating painfully fast. When he'd gone up to say goodbye to the guys, he'd left his guitar propped on one of the chairs near the large picture window that looked out over the garden. Lexie, wearing one of the sexy little sundresses he loved, was down on her knees, camera in hand, taking a photo of the instrument. The late-afternoon sun streamed in the window, lighting up the honey-toned patina of the guitar and glimmering in the dark silk of Lexie's hair. Golden hour. The hour after the sun rose and before it set, when everything took on a soft, magical glow perfect for photos.

Hopefully also perfect for what he was planning.

He put his hand in his pocket and touched the ring he'd bought months ago, then waited patiently for Lexie to finish and get to her feet before he walked over and wrapped his arms around her from behind. She angled her head to the side to meet his lips in a soft kiss.

"So, I was thinking I could give you another guitar lesson."

She turned in his arms so she was facing him and gave him a coy smile. "With or without the guitar?" Her voice was husky.

Lust surged through him at the memory of that night, but he couldn't get distracted now. "Let's start with the guitar this time."

He picked up the instrument and then sat down on the chair, pulling her down on his lap and encircling her in his arms so that she held the guitar and his hands were over hers. He got her fingers positioned just right for the first chord, then let her strum the strings. "G." He whispered it in her ear, then changed chords. "C." Then twice more. "C. C."

They kept going, but as recognizable as it was, it only took her seconds to pick up on the melody. She looked over her shoulder, eyebrows raised. "You're teaching me the bridal chorus?"

"I thought you should get familiar with it. You know, before you walk down the aisle." He smiled and waited, even though his heart was beating hard.

Lexie's eyes went round, and her mouth parted, but no sound came out.

His smile deepened.

"I-Is that a proposal?" she asked shakily.

He took the guitar out of her hands and placed it on the floor next to the chair, then helped her turn around so she was facing him, straddling his hips. She watched his every move with wide eyes as he reached into his pocket and pulled out the ring. When she saw the sparkling diamond, she covered her mouth with her hand and her eyes filled with tears.

"Lexie, you've filled a hole in my heart and my life that I didn't even know was there, and I never want to let you go. I love you, and I'll continue to love you with every beat of my heart for the rest of my life. I want you by my side forever, so please, will you marry me?"

Her gaze flickered backward and forward between his eyes and the ring he was holding up between them, and the few seconds before she answered him were the longest of his life.

"There's nothing I want more," she said in a trembling voice, before throwing her arms around his neck and pressing her lips against his.

Relief flooded through him. When she pulled away, and before she could change her mind, he grabbed her left hand and slipped the ring on her finger. He looked back up into her eyes, and his heart clenched as the tears overflowed and trickled down her cheeks.

"I hope those are happy tears," he murmured, using his thumb to wipe them away.

She nodded, a tremulous smile on her lips. "I love you so much, Connor. I don't know what I did to deserve you. To deserve all the love I've been blessed with in this life."

He knew she wasn't just talking about his love, but the love she'd shared with Damien too. Not so long ago, it would have killed him to think of the love she'd had — still had — for someone other than him. But now he was just grateful that he was the one that had been there to make her heart whole again and give her the happy ever after she deserved.

"I love you too, Lexie, more than anyone or anything in the world. I can't wait to spend the rest of my life proving that to you." He cupped her cheek and tilted her head so he could brush his lips against hers in a tender kiss that soon deepened, heat flaring between them.

Reluctantly, he pulled away just far enough to whisper, "How about you get your camera set up and we'll have ourselves a private engagement photo shoot."

Her gray eyes darkened, and the sexy smile that curved her mouth almost did him in. As she climbed off his lap to get the camera ready, he smiled to himself as he realized he finally had everything he'd ever wanted.

Note from the Author

Thank you for choosing to read my debut novel! I know you could have picked from any number of great books, so it means a lot that you chose mine.

I hope you enjoyed reading Lexie and Connor's story as much as I enjoyed writing it. If you did, please consider taking the time to share your thoughts by posting a review. Your feedback and support will help me to keep improving my storytelling skills.

If you would like to get in contact, please feel free to email me at author@lmdalgleish.com.

More From L.M. Dalgleish

Join my mailing list at www.lmdalgleish.com/newsletter for news and updates, as well as to be the first to hear about new releases, sales, and giveaways.

Or if you'd prefer not to receive any newsletters, you can keep in touch via one of the methods below.

Keep in Touch:
Website: www.lmdalgleish.com
Facebook: www.facebook.com/DalgleishAuthor
Instagram: www.instagram.com/lmdalgleishauthor
BookBub: www.bookbub.com/profile/l-m-dalgleish

My Books
Fractured Hearts
Fractured Dreams
Fractured Trust
Fractured Kiss

About the Author

L. M. Dalgleish is a lifelong book lover whose passion for romance novels began in the long sleepless nights following the birth of her first baby. Two more babies later and she's still in love with strong, sassy heroines and sexy, but emotionally unavailable (at least to begin with) heroes.

She lives in Canberra, Australia, with her husband, three kids, and a very large, very fluffy cat. In her spare time, she enjoys hanging with her family, reading, eating too much pasta, and watching horror movies.

Made in the USA
Monee, IL
02 August 2023